ALSO BY LIZ ALDEN

The Love and Wanderlust Series

The Night in Lover's Bay (free prequel short story)

The Fling in Panama

The Slow Burn in Polynesia

The Second Chance in the Mediterranean

The Rival in South Africa (novella)

The Player in New Zealand

The Best Friend in Indonesia (free standalone short story)

Wanderlust Resort Series

Beach Boss (free standalone short story)

Beach Resolution

Put it in Beach Mode

Holiday Retellings Series

Nutcracker with Benefits

Aged Like Fine Wine Series

Rosé with My Fake Fiancé

Riesling with My Roommate

Prosecco with My Professor

RIESLING WITH MY ROOMMATE

AN OVER 40 STEAMY ROMANCE

AGED LIKE FINE WINE
BOOK 2

LIZ ALDEN

RIESLING WITH MY ROOMMATE

Copyright © 2023 by Liz Alden

All rights reserved.

ISBN-13: 978-1-954705-35-7

No part of this book may be reproduced in any form or by any electronic or mechanical means, including information storage and retrieval systems, without written permission from the author, except for the use of brief quotations in a book review.

This is a work of fiction. Any similarity between the characters and situations within its pages and places or persons, living or dead, is unintentional and co-incidental.

First Edition

Library of Congress Control Number: 2023909148

League City, Texas, United States of America

Cover Design by Kate Mahon

Proofread by Lisa Matsumura

To that guy in the coffeehouse in Amsterdam who told me eating half a bonbon would be fine.

It was not.

At least I got a good story out of it.

TO CONCERNED READERS

This book includes a widowed female main character. There are discussions about the death of her husband and the death of the male main character's mother, both from cancer, prior to the start of the book. There are drug (marijuana) and alcohol use on page, and off-page use of various hard drugs. The male main character smokes cigarettes (until he gives it up, because it's gross, of course). There are multiple explicit, on-page sex scenes (because that's how I roll).

1

Sara

I WILL NOT PANIC. I AM HEALTHY AND SAFE AND COMFORTABLE.

For now.

I sip my steaming tea and close my eyes, taking an enormous inhale, holding it, and then slowly and steadily releasing it. It's not working super well because there's still a moderate buzz of anxiety in my head.

I pick up my phone and open the screen to the photos of my new apartment I had taken less than half an hour ago. With each swipe, I lose my cool even more.

Mushrooms growing out of the drywall. Swipe. A bathroom that's not sparkling white like the listing photo but is, instead, grimy and old. Swipe. The inside of the filthy refrigerator.

I can't swipe anymore. I think a good, solid panicking is in order.

SARA

I HAVE A FUNGUS EMERGENCY.

> Actually, it's an entire apartment emergency!!!! HELP!

My messages shoot off via WhatsApp to my three best friends: Tessa, Emma, and Jade. The four of us moved to Europe for a year of chasing our dreams and, in my case, staying close to my daughter while she studies abroad.

Unfortunately, that year is not starting well. I helped my daughter, Zoe, move into her apartment in Munich, which was even worse than when I dropped her off at college at the start of her freshman year. She's the one who suggested we both follow my best friends to Europe, and I'm so proud of her for taking a huge leap. While Zoe was excited, she was also nervous and clingy, which made it hard to say goodbye.

Thank god I flew to Paris for a weekend with my best friends after that. It was two days full of French pastries, dancing in nightclubs, and walking past amazing landmarks like the Eiffel Tower and the Seine River. We're going to meet up every month for a weekend in a new city.

Then I went back to Munich, checked in on Zoe one more time, and was relieved to find her happy and settled in.

Things aren't looking so great now. The cute little house that I rented in Baden-Baden, a German spa town, is not living up to its promises.

TESSA

I'm here! What's your emergency?

Relief washes over me, and I'm so glad I have someone to talk to. Jade is at work in her new office in Madrid, and Emma, who's living with Jade for a month, is out sightseeing. Tessa, on the other hand, is in Tavira, a coastal town in The Algarve of Portugal that's popular with tourists and expats. She's just moved into her new apartment too, but she works remotely, so I had hoped that she would be free to talk.

I respond with pictures that are worth a million words.

When the three dots pop up, telling me Tessa is typing a response, I click the video icon and put my headphones on.

She answers right away, her face filling the screen as she puts her earbuds in. Tessa's forty-two, one year younger than me, but it's hard to tell because her golden hair hides her gray ones, and her heart-shaped face and fair skin are smooth and perfectly made up. She's pulled her hair back to reveal simple diamond earrings and her earbuds in place.

"Hey," Tessa says and then frowns at me. "Where are you?"

"I'm at a café," I say and sniff. Just the sight of Tessa's familiar face is making me well up. I know I'm having a crappy day when even seeing a friend digitally is emotionally triggering. I focus on the real problem: where am I going to live? "My apartment is horrible. Horrible, Tessa! There's a huge water stain on the ceiling, and the bedrooms are much smaller than I thought. And the mushrooms! Tessa! I can't live with mushrooms in my bathroom. I like to eat them, not live with them!"

"What happened to the apartment you were going to rent?"

"That *was* the apartment. Or, at least, I'm pretty sure it is. It's definitely the same outside picture on the listing, and I spent a good fifteen minutes trying to compare the interior photos to reality and then another ten minutes arguing with the landlord, who conveniently doesn't speak English. It's much harder to argue in German when you don't know German." I highly suspect that my landlord does speak English, and he's just being horrible.

Behind Tessa, I can see the trappings of her new apartment, which we got a video tour of a couple nights ago. I hear something in the background, and Tessa moves. A door opens, and another voice joins her.

"Hey, Sara, Luc's here," Tessa says. She turns to Luc, and I can see the edge of his face and his ruffled brown hair. To Luc, she says, "Sara's having a crisis."

Luc and Tessa met last weekend in Paris and hit it off. Technically, he's her fake fiancé, but they're so cute together, and now he's visiting her in Portugal, so we have our suspicions that things aren't as fake as Tessa claims. He's white, French, and too charming for his own good.

While Tessa and Luc move around her apartment—it looks like Luc brought groceries—I discreetly blow my nose with the tissue I stuffed in my pocket earlier. "Am I interrupting your date?" I ask.

Tessa looks at him, and then Luc looks back at me sympathetically. "Put her on speaker phone," he suggests.

Tessa does, and I catch Luc up, and Tessa shows him the photos. Luc grimaces. "That does not look good."

"Right?" His sympathy encourages me to keep the rant going. "The Wi-Fi is supposed to be good, but I tried to video chat with Zoe, and it was laggy. That's why I'm at this café. That and I had to get out of there. It smells. I'm pretty sure there's meat juice coagulated into the grooves of the refrigerator. I can't sleep there, much less do yoga or eat. How am I supposed to film my video for Wednesday?" I hear a strangled cough that doesn't come from Tessa or Luc, and I glance up.

The lone patron of the café darts his eyes away from me and tries to cover his laughter with another cough.

Seriously? I'm having a terrible day, and this guy thinks it's funny that my new apartment is a HazMat zone? My eyes well up, and I'm horrified and humiliated all at once. "Oh, you think this is funny?" I snap at the man.

"What? No! I'm not laughing," Tessa says in my ear.

The guy's face falls. "No, no, I'm sorry," he says, waving his hands and coming to his feet. His blonde hair is pulled back into a bun at the nape of his neck. He's got a thick accent, too, definitely German. "It's just . . . I might have a place for you to stay."

"Sara, who is that?" Tessa's voice in my ear pulls me back to my phone. Luc and Tessa both crowd the screen, staring at me in concern.

My gaze flicks back up to the man now standing in front of me. "He's another patron of the café, and he might have a place for me to stay. Tessa, can I call you back?"

"I want a call or text within the next ten minutes," she says sternly, and I quickly agree and blow her a kiss before hanging up. Removing my headphones from my ears, I tuck them away and give the guy my full attention.

"If your apartment is terrible," he says, "Germany has a lot of protections for tenant rights. You should be able to file a complaint and get your money back."

That's only one part of the problem. I'd booked this apartment months ago, and finding another two-month lease at the last minute was going to be expensive. Plus, I also needed a place to stay *right now*.

"Well, that's good to know," I respond. At least this guy is being helpful. "But I don't have a lawyer. Or a grasp of legalese in German. Or a place to live." Each point makes me slump a bit more. I knew I was biting off more than I could chew. What was I thinking, deciding to take a risk—financially and personally—to up my life and move halfway around the world?

"I can help you with that."

Oh, right. I search his face for signs that he's teasing me or joking, but I don't see any. In fact, he's dead serious, almost frowning, which does nothing to dampen how attractive he is.

"I have a house," he continues. "I can let you stay in it at the same rate you'd pay for that other place."

I look this guy up and down. I wear very casual clothes— I'm a yoga instructor, so my life is mostly yoga pants and sports bras and tank tops. This guy has a similar dress ethos of comfort over appearance because he's wearing thin cotton pants and a long-sleeve T-shirt of a band I've never heard of.

"I'm Chris," he says, offering me his hand. He doesn't smile, and neither do I while I shake it. He looms over me, with wide shoulders and at least a few inches on my height.

"You have a house?" I prompt.

He crosses his arms on his chest and steps back to lean on the table next to me instead of towering over me. "You'd have your own space, but it's out of town—"

"Wait, wait, I'm sorry. You said you have a house. You mean *your* house? Where I would live? With you?"

"I'm a good roommate. I work from the house, but I have a room for my office, and I'd keep to myself. I'm a nice guy, I promise." His voice is kind, but his frown says that while he may be nice, he's also not overly friendly.

"They all say that," I say faintly. "Especially the murderers."

"Well, I'm not a murderer," he continues. "But seriously, it's better than mushrooms, right?"

Is this a German thing? Are people that nice here? I feel like back in the US, if someone heard a grown woman crying over toilet mushrooms and shitty Wi-Fi, people would roll their eyes and think that it's not their problem.

Hell, I would do that.

So how do I politely tell a stranger—maybe a murderer, maybe not—that I don't want to live with them?

"You might be a good roommate, but what makes you think I am?" The words spill out, and I tick off my fingers with each point. "I'm vegan. I do yoga. My friends are coming to visit next month. And my daughter is living in Munich and is going to visit me. A lot."

"That's okay," he says, a flicker of bemusement in his eyes.

"I don't speak German. I have a lot of hair products. And clothes."

"I'm pretty sure you're trying to make up reasons to say no. But I will admit I'm intrigued by the hair products."

With a glance at his bun, I'm not surprised.

"I can't afford to pay rent since . . . well, since I've already paid rent, and I don't know when and if I'll get that money back."

"You will. How about this," he says, leaning forward, placing both forearms on the table, getting close to my face and even more serious. "You can take a picture of me. I'll give you my address, a photo of my driver's license, whatever you think you'll need. Go back to the place you've rented, stare at the mushrooms for a bit, and then when you realize you definitely have to take my offer, call me."

He is so confident that I'll give in, I almost decline completely. But what's the harm in taking his information, just in case?

I scoop up the phone and turn the camera around, taking a selfie with Chris. I grin because . . . well, because that's what you do.

Chris does not smile.

"The least you could do is smile," I tell him crossly. "You look like a murderer."

"Sorry to disappoint," he says, pulling out his wallet and shuffling around until he finds a license, and holds it up to me. "This is me."

I take a picture, but the address is in London, so I have to write his local address and his phone number.

Chris has long, callused fingers, and the nail beds are darkened with something black—nail polish? Ink? I'm not sure.

I tap on the finger holding his ID. "What's that?"

He flexes his hand, following my gaze. "Ink. I was drawing earlier."

That leads to a dozen more questions, just further enforcing that I know nothing about this man.

"If one of my friends were telling me this story, I would tell them to run the hell away," I grumble.

"But," Chris says, "what would your friends tell you to do? Maybe you're the overly cautious one in your group, and you need to live a little."

I ignore that because . . . well, he's pretty goddamn accurate. Maybe I am overly cautious, but since my husband, Kit, died seventeen years ago, if I wasn't cautious, my daughter would become an orphan. Yes, she's grown up now, but she still needs me. I pay her tuition, and aside from my in-laws, who still live in Argentina where my late husband grew up, Zoe has no other family—except for her three "cool aunts."

I would do anything for my daughter, including upend my entire life. Over the last few months, I got a passport, put my stuff in storage, rented out my house, quit my job, and traveled all the way here to Baden-Baden.

As for my friends, Jade would tell me he's cute, and I should sleep with him. Tessa, who is probably the most reasonable of the group, would tell me it's better than staying in my cottage and I can always leave tomorrow.

Emma, mother of three, gets it, though. She'd probably be just as cautious as I am.

"I'm not going to call you," I tell Chris instead of answering. "Probably. I'll figure something else out. I'm still quite certain only serial killers offer to house strange women out of the blue."

"Serial killers and perverts," he agrees amiably. Then he raps his knuckles on the table. "Call me when you change your mind."

I watch him walk away, tapping my fingernail on the tabletop. He's got a swimmer's build, those big shoulders that loomed earlier tapering down to a trim waist.

Hm. Cute butt, too.

When he disappears out of sight, I weigh my options.

This move was supposed to be an adventurous, try-anything, dream-big year for Zoe and me. I quit my job teaching yoga in the suburbs of Austin, Texas, to focus on offering classes and private sessions online. I wasn't starting from scratch, as I'd been posting videos with Zoe's help for two years, but my income took a significant hit.

For the first time, I wonder if this is all too much. It would be easier to go back home.

I'd struggled from the start with the logistics of this trip.

Jade, the first of us to decide to move abroad, had gotten an opportunity through her job as a chemist to work in Madrid for a year.

After getting dumped by her long-term boyfriend, Tessa got a digital nomad visa for Portugal where she could live as an expat and work for her magazine from home.

Recently divorced with three grown kids, Emma wanted to get her MBA. With the encouragement of her kids and us, she found a program in Rome that coordinated her visa and housing.

Zoe, inspired by listening to Aunt Jade's stories of traveling her whole life, got accepted to the architecture school's study abroad program, and the university in Munich made the arrangements.

I was the last one to make plans. I wanted to be near Zoe, but German visas and the rules of Schengen are complicated.

And now I have an apartment situation.

I could just forget it all and go home, but I'd miss a lot. I'd miss getting together every month in a new city with my friends. The yoga studio back home could only get me so far —I was limited by the hours I could teach and the number of students for each session. Sure, I was taking a hit financially now, but when my business gets rolling, I'll be able to make more money and help Zoe chip away at student loans.

I down the rest of my now-cool tea and stand, throwing my tote over my shoulder. I pick up my phone and text my friends.

SARA

I'm fine. I'm headed back to the (shitty) apartment. I'm going to look at listings. Tessa, have a great date with Luc, and we can talk in the morning.

What would I be teaching my daughter if I just gave up, anyway? The lesson hiding in this is to make the best of any situation and stand on your own two feet. That's what I did when her dad died, and that's what I'll do now.

How bad can a little fungus be?

———

THE FUNGUS IS THE LEAST OF MY PROBLEMS.

After returning to my apartment with a renewed focus, I find basic cleaning supplies and scrub until my back aches. I unpack, order a vegan meal from a delivery service, and eat dinner.

As soon as I roll out my yoga mat for an evening meditation, a heavy bass and screaming lyrics start up next door.

"You've got to be kidding me," I grumble.

I sit for no more than ten seconds before I realize there's no way I can practice mindfulness here. My resolve crumbling, I pick up my phone and send Chris's information—address, selfie, photo of his driver's license—to my friends.

JADE

Um, Sara, who are you stalking?

SARA

This guy, Chris, has a room for me to rent.

JADE

Wait, what happened to your apartment?

I fill Jade, and eventually Emma, in on the fungus-and-mold situation. Together, we weigh the pros and cons of the apartment and debate stranger danger versus the kindness of humanity.

TESSA

What do we know about this guy?

SARA

> I searched online, but his name is common, so the results are mostly about an MP in Britain's Parliament and a goth-punk rock star.
>
> Wait, how was your date with Luc? Is he still there?

TESSA

It was great. He's back at his hotel.

JADE

Did your date end with a bang?

TESSA

Jade, focus. Sara's housing crisis.

JADE

Yes, right, sorry.

SARA

> I can't believe I'm doing this, but I'm taking Chris up on it.

EMMA

Are you sure? I know odds are tiny that he would hurt you, but still. Is it worth the risk? You could just come here.

Jade's brushing her teeth right now, but she says there's room, and she'd love to have you.

But she's also asking if Chris is as cute in person as in the pictures.

WHICH IS NOT A FACTOR.

TESSA

It's going to be fine. Just keep us up to date.

EMMA

If anything feels off, dial 112 first.

SARA

Did you just look up the 911 equivalent for Germany?

EMMA

Well, I wasn't sure if it was the same in every European country.

A dot of white flutters past my eye. I glance up to see that the ceiling is flaking with every beat of the bass. I scrub my hands over my face and navigate to Chris's contact info.

Staying with a stranger has got to be better than this.

2

Chris

OFFERING A RANDOM WOMAN A PLACE TO LIVE CERTAINLY IS unusual, but with my bandmates' voices echoing in my head, it seemed like the right thing to do.

Just this morning, I'd talked to Ram, complaining about writer's block. Actually, I hadn't complained about writer's block, per se; I'd complained about everything but writer's block.

My place was too quiet.

The summer had been too short.

Really fucking inane shit.

But of course, Ram had asked how the writing was coming along, and I had avoided the fact that I hadn't written anything. The words weren't there; the music wasn't there.

Going stir-crazy, I ventured out of my house to find something different from the quiet emptiness of the mansion. Then I had stumbled upon a gorgeous American woman, clearly just trying to pull herself together.

It seemed like fate that I had a giant fucking house that was too quiet, and she needed a place to stay.

I'd even felt a thrill of excitement when she didn't recognize me at the café. That rarely happens now, even though we perform in stage costumes and makeup. The barista had complimented my music and asked for my signature, but I don't think the American was paying the least bit of attention to us.

Fuck, I didn't even get her name.

Now it's ten o'clock at night. My house is depressingly quiet, and I'm rattling through the rooms.

If the media could see me now. See? Rock stars aren't all sex, drugs, and rock 'n' roll.

Erm. Well, not *all* of the time.

I'm staring out into the back patio when the phone rings. The number's unknown, and I don't usually answer those, but I've been obsessing over the woman from the café today, and so I press the green button. "Hallo?"

I'm hit with a very surreal moment where my own voice is blaring on the other side of the call. I'm singing backup, and I hear Ram's drumming, too, and the wail of June's bass.

I also hear someone grumbling, and then a door slams shut, and the music quiets.

"Chris?" comes a tentative voice, feminine and American, with a hint of an accent that I think is Southern.

"Hey," I say gruffly.

"Did I wake you?"

I nearly snort but rein in my amusement. "No."

There's a beat of silence. "My neighbors like to play loud, terrible punk rock music, apparently."

The irony settles in deep, and I try to keep my voice neutral. "Are you going to take me up on my offer, then?"

Another beat of a pause. "Just for a few days. Until I figure something else out."

"Where are you?" I ask. "I'll come pick you up."

She rattles off an address as I type it into my phone. "I'll be there in thirty minutes," I tell her and hang up.

Half an hour later, I park in front of a small cottage. The party next door is in full swing—not one of my songs this time, thankfully—and I pull my hat farther down my head.

She must have been watching for me because the door opens, the lights inside go out, and she struggles down the walkway with two large rolling bags.

I hop out of the car and come around to help her. She hesitates when she sees me and peers at my face. "Chris?"

"Yeah, it's me." I don't want to explain that I'm hoping not to be recognized. I take one handle from her and roll the suitcase out and lift it into the boot. I grab the second one and load it up, too, while she climbs into the car.

I get in the driver's seat and glance over, expecting her to be sitting in the passenger side, but she's not there.

She's in the backseat.

Like I'm a hired driver.

When I meet her eyes in the rearview mirror, I keep my face as stern as possible to not laugh, and she glances away quickly.

The drive is quiet until the houses start to thin, and she breaks the silence.

"I sent my friends your ID and photo."

"Good."

"Do you even know my name?" she asks.

"No."

She lets that digest for a minute. "You don't know my name."

"That is correct."

There's a pause.

"What if *I'm* the murderer?"

I'm so surprised I cough, and she huffs indignantly behind me. "Women can be murderers."

"I know."

"And you aren't worried about your own safety at all?"

I don't know if it's that she's American or something else,

but her no-holds-barred teasing is refreshing. It reminds me of the way the rest of the band and I are together. "Okay, let's say you are a murderer. Maybe I should pull over and take a picture of your ID."

"A little late for that."

"True. I'm in a confined space with a murderer who refuses to tell me her name."

She gasps, but a glance in the mirror shows that she's fighting a smile. "I am not refusing; you never asked!"

"Okay." I peer at her. "What's your name?"

"That's better. It's Sara. Sara Wallace."

I pull my phone out of my pocket and press the voice-to-text icon, keeping my eyes on the road. I've barely seen a dozen cars since we left Sara's place, but you never know with these dark roads. I speak slowly and enunciate. "If I die, look for Sara Wallace. She's American, vegan, yogi, and on holiday."

With a tap, I sent the message to our band manager, Marcus, and put my phone back in the center console.

"That should be enough for my friends to avenge my death," I tell her.

The side of her mouth quirks up.

"So, Sara the vegan yoga instructor. How long have you been in Baden-Baden?"

"Just today," she says, sighing and looking out the window.

She watches the forest roll by, and I let the silence fall over us. It's dark, and we've made our way out of town now, the houses becoming sparse and the land wooded. Sara stifles a few yawns.

When I make the turn into the driveway, Sara sits up. The lights from the house shine brightly on her face, enough that I can see her eyes narrowing and focusing on the building.

"This is your place?" she asks.

"Yeah," I say. I can imagine what she's thinking as we

approach. The landscaping is uplit, the shades are all open, and the lights are on inside. It's like a beacon in the Black Forest.

I pull into the covered entrance and park. When I look over at Sara, her mouth is open, eyes wide, taking everything in.

Wordlessly, she gets out and stares at the house. I unload the luggage, having a flashback to when I had to lug my own gear around with the band.

I wheel one of the bags over to her and offer her the handle.

"Sara?" I ask when she doesn't notice.

She glances at me, her eyebrows knitted together in confusion. "You're renting me a room in this house?" she repeats.

"Yes."

"For the same rate as that shitty apartment in town?"

"Yes."

She says nothing but turns back to look at the house. I stand next to her quietly until she whispers, "It's like in *The Holiday*."

"What?"

"You know, the movie with Kate Winslet and Cameron Diaz. I guess, in this scenario, I'm Kate Winslet discovering the house she's swapped for in LA."

"Come on, Kate," I say. "I'll show you your room."

Sara follows, gaping at everything. I don't bother with a tour, figuring she'll want to look more thoroughly tomorrow, but for now, the bedroom is the most important part.

"Here's your room," I say, pushing the door open. Like every room in the house, it's clean, the bed freshly made for guests. I'm not sure who Marcus expected to sleep in these rooms when he booked the house for me—my bandmates?—but I'm glad to have the space.

"The bathroom is in here." I point at the cracked-open door on the side wall.

"This is my room?" Sara asks, pointing at her feet, which are barely inside the door frame.

"Yes."

"This is where I'm sleeping tonight?"

"Yes. Would you like to take a flying leap onto the bed?"

She cuts her eyes at me. "So you have seen it?" I can see the wheels turning in her head, and I can tell that she wants to. But she shakes her head. "No, I'm good."

"All right then. Sleep well. I'll see you tomorrow, and we can get the rest sorted out."

The door is nearly closed when Sara whirls toward me. "Wait. Chris?"

"Yes?" I say, pausing.

"Danke." Her pronunciation is atrocious, but she tries, and the grin that accompanies her words makes up for it.

I nod. "Bitte."

The door clicks closed behind me, and I stand in the hall for a moment, waiting until I hear a girlish squeal and the *foomph* of a belly flop onto the bed.

3

———

Sara

THIS MIGHT BE THE BEST BED I'VE EVER SLEPT ON. UNLIKE KATE Winslet, though, I'm already used to the time difference, and I don't need any blackout curtains—when I wake up, chipper and ready to start my day, it's still dark outside.

Yesterday, when I'd met my landlord, and he'd shown me the cottage I'd rented, I had deflated like a sad balloon. But now, in this beautiful guest bedroom, things are looking way, way up, and my spirits lift too.

I check my messages. After Chris had left me to settle in, I'd messaged Zoe.

SARA

> Change of plans for my accommodations.
> Here's my new address.

I haven't gotten a response from her yet.

I have new messages from my girlfriends. We'd texted last night through the ride to Chris's house, and I had told them briefly about my new room.

There are tassels and decorative pillows, and as I pointed out to my friends, Chris hadn't seemed like the fancy duvet kind of guy.

Tessa had suggested that maybe he was married. Which, yikes. I hadn't even thought of that.

The house, or what I saw of it, is nothing like what I expected. It's huge. A mansion. A professional decorated this room—or a wife did.

Chris was hard to get a read on. Despite his deadpan demeanor, I got the sense last night that he found me amusing, but it was very subtle.

The metaphorical wrench of the shitty apartment has negated any plans I had for the day, so I dress in comfortable clothing and tiptoe down the hallway, wondering which room is Chris's. I refrain from opening doors and poking my head inside, figuring that walking in on my new roommate would definitely be improper behavior. Though, who am I to know proper roommate behavior? I haven't ever lived with anyone who didn't already love me.

A grandfather clock ticks in the foyer as I make my way down the stairs. The decor is beautiful but stuffy. The furniture is mostly button-back dark leather, and the floors are light wood parquet. Exposed beams run along the ceiling of the great room. I wonder why Chris lives here. After realizing that my bedroom door had a deadbolt on it, I thought maybe this was a rental, and the rest of the house looks that way, too. It doesn't seem like his style, though I remind myself that I really don't know him at all. He seems more artistic than this stuffy place, and I'd imagined him in a modern, white, and tidy space.

My breath catches as I turn the corner and find the main living area. Dead ahead are large windows, showing a gray, pre-dawn landscape that will be stunning later. On the left is a family room, a large TV and couches surrounding it, a fireplace integrated into the support beams, the same dark wood as the ceiling.

On the right is my dream kitchen. It's huge, with gleaming white marble. An island counter separates it from the great room, with hanging pots above it. I step into the space and see that everything is top of the line, from the copper pans to the pot-filler faucet above the stove to the refrigerator.

I throw my hands out and spin around the kitchen space, Julie Andrews-style. Forget girls in white dresses with blue satin sashes and brown paper packages tied up with string. This kitchen is my new favorite thing.

The cottage I'd picked out claimed "well-stocked kitchen" in the ad. Well-stocked, my ass. It didn't even have a blender.

I open every cabinet in this kitchen and squeal with delight at each new item I discover. Immersion blender? Check. Food processor? Check. There are even some things that are foreign to me. I don't know their purpose or how to use them, but I'll learn.

Giddy, I throw open the doors of the double-wide, stainless-steel refrigerator and gasp in shock. Sad condiments, leftover containers, and a carton of milk stare back at me.

I tsk to myself. Such a waste to have a kitchen like this and not have it stocked with wonderful food.

I open the freezer, and it's like a flashback to twenty years ago. Frozen pizzas and French fries and comfort-food snacks sit on the shelves. Just the kind of stuff I used to rely on to survive when Zoe was little and before Kit died.

The pantry fares a little better, but not much. Neatly organized staples line the shelves, mixed with bags of chips and cookies.

At the far side of the kitchen is a small breakfast nook, and on the other side of that, a backdoor leads out to the porch. On the table is the first sign of Chris—or any personal effects of his: a laptop, a few pads of paper with scribbles on them, and dishes with crumbs.

The signs of my roommate snatch me back to reality and routine. I locate a kettle and heat water, darting upstairs for the satchels of green tea I brought.

Within a few minutes, I have a mug of tea warming my hands, and step out onto the deck. My eyes widen as I take in the scenery. From the windows, I could barely see anything, but now that the sky is getting lighter, the details reveal themselves; there is a gazebo to one side with a stone fireplace, seating for at least twenty, and a hot tub. Beyond the luxurious patio stretches trees and mountains as far as the eye can see.

I sip my tea while I take in the view and pick out the best spot to practice yoga on the deck. Once my tea is gone, I return inside to make breakfast. There's a thick, crusty, rustic loaf of bread in the back of the freezer that I toast and drizzle with olive oil. Not ideal, but it'll hold me.

I definitely have to ask Chris to take me to town for some food—assuming I stay, of course.

Then I retrace my steps up to my room, retrieve my yoga mat, and settle down on the deck for some practice.

I THOUGHT CHRIS WOULD BE UP BY THE TIME MY NINETY-MINUTE practice was done, but all was still quiet. I shower and settle into an upholstered chair in the great room with a John Green novel until my phone rings next to me. The morning has flown by—it's one p.m. in Spain, time for Jade's lunch break and a chat.

We don't talk every day, but with Tessa and I moving to our respective cities and Emma staying with Jade, there's a lot to catch up on.

I leave my book behind and run as quietly as I can to the breakfast nook, where I've left my headphones. I answer while they connect, and I'm the last to join.

"Hi!" I say, keeping my voice low.

I get a chorus of hellos back.

From her kitchen, Tessa calls out, "Sorry, I'm still making a sandwich. My video call ran long." She is an editor for a travel magazine and often has calls with writers, photographers, and her fellow staff.

"No worries," I whisper.

Jade leans closer to her camera and whispers back, "Why are you talking so quietly?" The youngest of us at forty, Jade is in her office. She's Mexican-American, with long dark hair and a bright white mallen streak that's accentuated by the high ponytail she wears most of the time. Smart as hell, Jade has worked in the pharmaceutical industry since she graduated with a degree in biochemistry. She's wearing a button-up blouse and munching on her lunch.

"My, uh, roommate? I guess? He's not awake yet."

Everyone's eyes dart to check their clocks.

"Wow, he really sleeps in," Tessa says.

"How do you know he's there and asleep? Could he have left the house?" Emma asks. She's somewhere in Jade's apartment, a corkboard behind her head with Jade's Polaroid collection tiling it. There are shots of Jade all over the world: the Great Wall of China, Sydney, San Francisco, and the newest one, a shot of all four of us in Paris that Luc took.

Emma is a tall white woman whose hair has gone almost entirely gray, which she jokingly blames on her kids. She has a round face and light crow's feet around her eyes.

"Good point." I stand up and walk over to the breakfast room, peering out into the driveway. "The car's still here," I say.

"Hold up." Tessa's voice is firm. "Is that his kitchen?"

I look down at my phone, which is in my left hand and no longer pointed at me. "Oh my god, Tessa, you would love this kitchen."

I give them a tour, showing them the rest of the house; my room, the living room, the backyard.

"What's down that hallway?" Emma asks.

She's talking about a hallway coming off the main great room. From the outside, I know that there's a lot of house over there, so it feels like it could be a wing.

I duck my head in. It's short, with three closed doors and an open one, which reveals a half bath.

"I don't know," I say. "I'm trying to be a good houseguest and not open any doors. And if Chris is here, I don't want to disturb him."

"Don't want to accidentally find the bodies?" Jade jokes.

The three of us make a face at her.

"Kidding, obviously." She holds her hands up. "I'm sure he's very nice."

"It looks like an old man's house," Tessa says. "How old is this guy?"

"His ID says he's thirty-eight. I think he's renting this place," I answer.

"Still, it seems like an odd choice to rent a stuffy mansion out in the countryside."

"That's what I thought, too," Jade says. "But that doesn't mean you can't enjoy the crap out of this place while you are there. Get your ass in that hot tub."

I laugh. Jade's the adventurous one out of all of us. She takes every opportunity to travel that she can, and this is her second time living overseas—she lived in Shanghai for a year. When she suggested we all move to Europe together, I don't think she expected any of us to take her up on it—after all, none of us visited when she lived in China five years ago, but that was different. The rest of us had partners or kids or jobs that kept us pinned down.

Now we're more flexible.

"I will definitely be getting into the hot tub. Maybe when it gets colder."

"You think you'll be there that long?" Tessa asks.

I bite my lip and think before responding.

"Too soon to tell. I'll try a few days and see how it goes. Plus, I need to work on getting the money back from the cottage. If I can get that back, I can rent a different place sooner. In the meantime, I've never lived with a stranger. Any advice?"

My friends chime in with tips and advice, most of which is useless. Since Chris and I aren't sharing a bathroom, I don't have to worry too much about my stray hairs in the tub or leaving toothpaste in the sink—not that I would, anyway.

But it gets me thinking about sharing the kitchen, dividing up utilities, and giving each other space.

Before we can get an update on Jade, she's got to get back to work. One by one, my friends hang up to go about their lives. I'd avoided eating because there wasn't much that I wanted to eat here, but without the distraction of my friends, my stomach makes it clear that it does not appreciate being empty. I nibble on some bread again and drink more tea while standing at the kitchen island, wishing that I'd grocery shopped yesterday. Then I curl back up with my book in the chair.

Finally, a door opens somewhere, and a few moments later, Chris shuffles in from that small hallway.

His mouth stretches in a giant yawn.

He's only wearing boxer briefs.

The bun at the top of his head has wilted in his sleep.

There's an enormous tattoo across his chest of a wolf with its head resting on his pec.

A deep V in his body runs from the shoulders down to a bulge that I try not to stare at for fear of blindness.

One can be sun-blinded. Can one be dick-blinded?

I take it all in and try to keep my face neutral. I'm no stranger to half-naked men. There were a few who would come into my yoga studio and practice shirtless, especially when I taught Bikram yoga. But this feels a little different. This is most definitely not a professional setting.

I don't even know if Chris has a partner, and why the hell would I be wondering that, anyway?

Chris catches sight of me and startles.

"Hello," he says. With his accent, the e is low and thick. "Are you all right?"

I am honestly not sure what my face is broadcasting. I feel a mix of emotions, and trying to parcel them out sounds like too much work, so I just swallow it all and clear my throat. "Yes, hi. Did you forget I was here?"

"No," he says. Then his eyes drift toward the ceiling. "Kind of." Before I can say anything, Chris turns around and wanders away.

In a few minutes, he returns, more awake and more clothed, with a T-shirt and lounge pants on. He pads barefoot into the kitchen, and there are rummaging noises and then the smell of coffee percolating.

Without the distraction of too much fair skin, Chris reminds me of a cat someone shooed out of a sunny patch by the window; just pure indignation at having to be awake.

A door opens and closes, and Chris passes by the big windows, settling into one of the outdoor couches.

I get up, abandoning my book, and make myself another cup of tea and carry it outside, but when I catch sight of Chris out the window, I stop dead in my tracks.

He's smoking a cigarette.

I wrinkle my nose.

Some part of me is deeply relieved that he's a smoker. Going from scorching-hot, tattooed nudity to someone who smokes is like whiplash for my libido, but that's probably a good thing.

A roommate who smokes, even outside, is almost a deal breaker in the roommate department.

A hot guy who smokes is most definitely a deal breaker in the romance department.

But I'm not in the romance department. I'm in the roommate department. It puts Chris firmly back into the box of a guy I barely know and have no interest in seeing naked.

4

Chris

THE SCREEN DOOR SQUEAKS AS SARA OPENS IT AND STEPS outside. I truly had forgotten about her when I woke up; sleep always sloughs off slowly, and every morning I use coffee and a cigarette to hasten it.

She's holding a steaming cup and folds herself into a cushioned chair opposite mine. She eyes my cigarette, and a moue of distaste forms on her face.

I take a deep puff, and she watches, which is hot. I've always found disapproval intriguing. It's what fed my fucked-up drive to be a musician, even when the odds are stacked against me.

Sara lightly shakes herself. "I'm going to go grocery shopping. Is there anything you need? Should I call up a rideshare, or do you want to come with me?"

I exhale. "You can take my car. Keys are in the kitchen somewhere."

The disapproval deepens. "What about insurance? And I don't have an international driver's license."

I wave it away. "It'll be fine."

Sara huffs at me. "It'll be fine," she echoes under her breath, but when she says it, it sounds irresponsible and dumb. She pulls out her phone and types away for a few minutes.

"Okay," she announces. "Your insurance most likely covers me, and I can drive for six months in Germany before I have to apply for a license." She peers at the screen, and her eyes widen. She lifts her chin to stare at me, horrified. "Your highways have no speed limit?"

"Are you a good driver?"

She straightens. "I'm an excellent driver. I take a defensive driving course and a performance driving course at one of the local race tracks every two years."

At my stare, she continues. "It's a leading cause of death, at least in the US, and most of them are single-car accidents."

"So, you can drive my car."

She chews on her bottom lip, and her eyes drift off to the side. "Okay," she says finally. "But I'll fill your gas tank."

I shrug, and she sips from her cup, watching me. The smell of green tea mixes with my cigarette smoke.

"What's that noise?"

I sit up straighter, listening. "What noise?"

Sara gestures to my face. "You were making a weird clicking sound. Were you popping your jaw?"

"Oh." I stick my tongue out so Sara can see the barbell that goes through the middle of my tongue. Her eyes widen, and I pull it back into my mouth. "I must have been tapping my teeth with it. Bad habit."

I can't read the look on her face. She takes another sip of her tea. "Anyway . . ."

I suspect she has a mental list that she's checking off.

"I know I'm only here for a few days—hopefully, if I can find a new apartment—but it would be nice to have a place to work that's out of your way."

I hook a thumb over my shoulder, pointing at my wing of

the house. "I have an office that I work in most of the day, so you can set up whatever you need anywhere you like. Anything else?"

My tone is short to keep her from arguing about that too. It's too early to discuss complicated logistics. I just want a coffee and a smoke.

Though, this is the point, right? A little human interaction here and there to change things up and get the creative juices flowing.

"Do you own this house?"

"No, it's a rental."

She gets a contemplative look on her face and studies the house for a moment. Then her muscular legs unfold as she stands. "That's it for now. I'll go to the store in a couple of hours and let you know when I find a new place."

I nod, but she's already walking away.

While I sit out back working on my second cigarette, Sara clatters around inside. When I shift to lean against the armrest to see what the hell she's doing, I see that she's taking over the kitchen table.

That's fine by me. I hardly spend time in there.

She makes several trips in and out of the kitchen, bringing a laptop, cords, a second monitor, and other various computer stuff.

Just like yesterday, Sara's wearing tight-fitting pants and a tank top. It's early fall, and just starting to be cool out. The pants are tight enough to reveal her fit body: toned thighs, sculpted calf muscles, and a lusciously curved ass.

I know she can see me through the glass, but she ignores me, which is good because I have to adjust my dick when I stare at her for too long.

I've been in this secluded house for three weeks. Sex went from being available everywhere I looked to being a solo act, and my body is cranky with sexual frustration already.

When I come inside, Sara's seated at the table, over-ear

headphones on while she clicks around on her laptop. I put my mug in the sink, grab a protein shake, and retreat to my studio.

My "studio" is the theatre room that I've taken over with my instruments and computer, and the "work" I do today is extremely unproductive. I vacillate between watching videos online, reading poetry, and—my favorite way to waste time—doodling.

Normally I spread my procrastination around the house, but Sara's just made a nest in the kitchen, and I don't feel like disturbing her or being watched, so I stay in my studio. When I get hungry, I eat some of the junk food I have stashed around here.

When I finally emerge, it's night, and Sara's nowhere to be seen, her laptop and accouterments folded up and tucked to the side next to one of my spiral notebooks. I think there were some dirty plates in here that I forgot about, but Sara must have cleaned them.

In fact, there are a lot of clean dishes in the drain, including pots, pans, knives, and some things I can't even identify. When I open the fridge, there are more signs of Sara—it's overflowing with food.

Anything that was in here previously is on the top shelf, which is a pathetic collection of stuff that I should probably throw away—a half-eaten snack bar I chucked in the fridge when I had an idea for a song title and some sauce containers from takeaway orders stretching back to when I first arrived.

The rest of the fridge is Marie Kondo's wet dream. Sara stacked and labeled storage containers with things like 'Mexican kale salad' and 'rye berry bowl.'

What the fuck are rye berries?

Then there are two shelves that are organized by color. Red raspberries, diced yellow melon, sliced orange mangoes, and all the other colors stare back at me, everything washed and ready to eat. The green section is the biggest, with multiple boxes of spinach and a drawer of kale that springs out when I open it like a jack-in-the-box of cruciferous vegetables.

"Jesus fucking Christ," I say, slamming the fridge closed.

Paper flutters, and I see a note attached to the door via a magnet.

Help yourself to veggies :)

I pluck the magnet up and pull the paper away, flipping it over. There's a pen by my notepad, so I grab it and hunch over the counter, sketching a variety of vegetables with stick arms and legs and open mouths with sharp pointy teeth.

The magnet clicks as I pin my drawing to the door. I open the freezer, which is mostly unchanged, and pull out a frozen pizza. Much tastier than that colorful crap.

THE NEXT DAY, SARA'S WORKING IN THE KITCHEN WHEN I COME in for coffee and food. This time, she doesn't join me out on the patio—probably avoiding my cigarette smoke—and I do the same thing as yesterday. I retreat to my studio.

Later, in the early evening, when I get too bored to work, I walk out into the main room. Sara's practicing yoga out on the back deck, a camera filming her, facing away from the house.

I watch her for a few minutes. Soft music comes from her phone, and a sheen of sweat covers her bare skin. Instead of leggings and a tank top, she's wearing shorts that barely cover the swell of her ass and a sports bra.

Her voice is low and calming, a stark contrast from the hoarse, grating vocals our band does. It's a soothing balm instead of sandpaper. I creep closer, leaning against the window.

"Now press up into a plank and hold the pose here. Close your eyes and take a deep breath. We're going to do a thirty-second body scan here, bringing mindfulness into our practice."

Sara's facing away from me, her strong arms holding her body off the hot pink mat. I listen as she walks her viewers through a breathing exercise, and as I lean against the door, I breathe with her.

Breathe into my toes and out of the top of my head. When that time is up, Sara continues through more movements and positions with crazy names—downward dog, tree pose, happy baby, the last of which makes me shift against the doorframe and ask my cock to relax.

Is this what having her as a roommate is going to be like? Seeing her half-naked and watching her body flex and move is like waving a juicy steak in front of a hungry dog.

Despite her health-nut lifestyle—or maybe because of it—Sara is fucking hot.

At night, when I emerge from another unproductive day for a hot meal, there's another note from Sara on the fridge.

What are you, a carnivore?

I take the new sheet of paper down and draw two figures. The first is a wolf, which I label "me". The second is a rabbit chewing on a carrot, which I label "you".

For the entire week, these notes become the extent of our communication. She responds with:

Even wolves eat vegetables.

I reply with a drawing of a wolf sitting on its haunches, holding up its middle finger.

The next day, I bark a sharp laugh when I see that she added a cigarette to the wolf's mouth.

Having a roommate is not exactly the change I expected. Sara and I operate on opposite schedules. When I wake up, she's working on her laptop in the breakfast room. She gives me a little wave, her big headphones on, while I pass through the kitchen to make coffee and go out to the porch for a smoke.

She's working hard at something, so I succumb to peer pressure and try to write in my studio. I'm also hiding—after watching Sara practice yoga a few days ago, I jerked off to memories of her flexing and stretching body and then got pissed at myself for lusting after her.

It's best if I stay in my studio for the afternoon.

In the early evenings, Sara spends at least an hour cooking. If she thinks I'm out of earshot, she plays music, gentle guitar-heavy songs with poetic lyrics. She dines outside.

After she's gone to her room for the night, usually around eight or nine, the only signs of her are the neat stack of her stuff in the kitchen and the surplus of fresh produce in the fridge.

I know she's trying to be a good roommate, but she's almost too perfect at it.

That night, I draw a rabbit doing a yoga pose—the one that has the bunny's legs stretched out behind it and the front legs pushing off the ground. Downward dog? I don't know the fucking names of the poses.

Saturday, when I come out of my wing in the afternoon, the note reads:

So I'm cute and fluffy?

Is that flirting? The bunny is going to flirt with the big bad wolf?

Even a few days in, I know Sara is ridiculously wholesome. We have nothing in common. If she knew the real me, the one the rest of the world knows, she wouldn't flirt with me. She'd know I'm not the kind of guy for her.

I used to attract a certain kind of woman: dark clothes, heavy makeup, piercings. But since the band took off, it seems like all kinds of women are interested in me.

But Sara doesn't want to trade mushrooms for a roommate who makes her uncomfortable.

Sara is forbidden fruit. A very healthy one.

A lyric pops into my head, and I freeze, like if I scare it, it'll disappear. My notepad is still on the kitchen counter, so I grab it and the pen. Instead of drawing a response to Sara's note, I write a line down. It's a riff on the big bad wolf motif, innocent victim, blood-red imagery—pomegranates? That takes me down a rabbit hole of a Persephone-Hades concept, and I walk on autopilot back to my studio before I lose the inspiration.

I forget to draw something for Sara, and the next day the note is utilitarian:

Need anything from the store?

Part of me is chastened, but the rest of me—a majority of me—just doesn't fucking care because I may have written something worthwhile yesterday and halle-fucking-lelluh.

I draw a pizza, and when I wake up the next day and have my coffee and smoke, Sara's not in the house and the car is gone from the driveway.

That night, there's no note, but the freezer is full of the brand of frozen pizzas I like, so I write:

How much do I owe you?

There's no response the next day, and I worry that I've insulted her. That might be projecting my own hurt. I thought our notes were funny, but maybe I insulted Sara with the rabbit thing.

This is why you don't flirt with your roommate, I remind myself. *You get butt-hurt over stupid shit.*

I wake up on Wednesday extra grouchy. When I come into the great room, Sara's laptop sits on the table, but she's not there. Movement catches my eye, and I see her out on the back deck, pacing. She's hunched over, holding her phone to one side of her head and the other hand covering the opposite ear as if she's trying to hear someone in a crowded room.

I step out, concerned. Sara whirls around, and my heart plummets when I see that she's got tears in her eyes. She's not crying yet, but it's incoming.

"I sent you the pictures," she says. She's quiet for a moment, listening, brows drawn together in concentration. "I can't understand you."

I gesture at the phone, and she says, "Hold on," to whoever she's talking to. Pressing the phone to her chest, she explains. "It's that landlord. I'm trying to get my money back, but I can't . . ."

"That fucker still pretending not to speak English? Give me the phone," I say.

She lifts it to her ear. "Mr. Leitz? Hello? Argh! He hung up on me."

I pull my phone out of my pocket. "What's the number?"

Sara reads the digits out, and I dial.

"Hallo?" a gruff voice answers.

I speak in German. "I'm calling on behalf of Sara Wallace. You owe her the rent and deposit she paid on the apartment."

"Who are you?"

"The guy that's going to call the tenants' association and my lawyer if you don't pay up."

Silence falls on the line, and that was an easy victory. Dickwads like this are just taking advantage of people, and once you push back with enough force, there's a quick back down. I'm not lying either. The record label has a legal team for personal cases. But I am lying with the threat—regardless of whether this asshole pays, I'm calling the tenants' association.

"Fine, I'll refund the money."

"Good. Hopefully, you'll never have to hear from me again."

I hang up the phone. "He'll refund the money."

Despondence morphs into shock and then gratitude. Unfortunately, that also causes the tears to spill over and leave behind fat, glistening trails on her cheeks. "Really?"

"Yes, really. There are legal rights for tenants, and he knows that he's liable. Every town has a mietervereine, an organization that helps tenants, and I threatened to call the local one."

She clutches her hands under her chin and she hastily wipes the tears away. "Thank you so much. I . . . . Can I hug you?"

I suppress a sigh. Really? I do a nice thing and have to subject myself to Sara's body pressing up against mine and her smell getting all up in my nose? "Sure," I mumble, expecting a quick, fleeting hug, but Sara all but leaps at me. Her arms wrap around my waist, and her cheek presses into my breastbone. When I get over my surprise, I wrap my arms around her shoulders, resting my chin lightly on her head.

Just like I thought, Sara's body is warm and fits perfectly against mine. She smells like coconut and baby powder, and goddamn it, the hug changes, and my dick starts to get ideas.

I pull back first, taking a step back to get some fresh air.

"Sorry." She wipes her face again. "It was just really scary.

Logically, I know that I have enough money to survive for a little while, but it was such a big risk to build up my business while also paying for Zoe's college, though, of course, she's so smart she got scholarships and financial aid, so it's not like I have a huge amount of expenses, but I'm definitely not earning enough yet, and I was so worried I was going to be spending two or three times as much on rent than I was expecting." She snaps her mouth closed. "Sorry, now I'm rambling. My money troubles are definitely not your concern." Her gaze drifts over to the monstrosity of a house that I'm renting. "But thanks for helping me with this." She smiles cheekily. "Danke."

Still charmingly terrible pronunciation.

"Bitte." She's still looking at me, reminding me of adoring fans, which sours my mood. Adoring fans come with expectations and pressure. I cross my arms. "I grew up with a working mom who struggled to pay bills, and rent was always difficult. But she was smart, and we learned quickly about tenants' rights."

Pity flashes on Sara's face, and that's better than adoration. "Oh. I should have thought of that. I mean, I've owned my house for a long time. It was a wedding gift from my in-laws, so I never had to deal with renter's rights."

She's married? Oh shit.

There's no ring on her finger, and I just assumed she was single.

I've slept with plenty of women, but I do draw a line—I don't fuck married women.

Not that I was going to fuck Sara.

Sara sees the surprise on my face, and she explains. "My husband passed away a long time ago. It's just been me and Zoe, my daughter, in our starter house all those years."

"I'm sorry for your loss," I say, and ignore the part of me that's relieved.

"Thank you. Anyway," she says with the practice of

someone who's long had to brush off platitudes. "I suppose I should start getting ready to move out once I get the refund—look for another place and sign a lease. I'm definitely going to pay more this time if it means I have a mushroom-free bathroom."

She glances back at the house and frowns. This arrangement was not what I expected when I suggested she move in here, but it works. We rarely see each other, and I actually wrote one halfway-decent song this week.

I fold my arms over my chest. "What else do you need?"

Her finger taps her chin as she thinks. "I need a two-bedroom place so that I have a better location to practice and film yoga. I was going to move as much out of one bedroom as I could. The previous place—" She waves her phone to indicate the mushroom farm. "—also had a proper office chair." She puts a hand on the small of her back and stretches, looking up at the sky and thrusting her breasts toward me. They're smushed into a tight sports bra, giving her deep and high cleavage, and I unfocus my eyes so I don't stare at them. "The kitchen chair is killing me."

When she relaxes back to standing, I avert my eyes. None of those things are impossible here. She's a quiet roommate, and the most I see of her are signs of her cooking. She definitely won't find a kitchen that equals this one. Nor a place with a room so suitable for her yoga practice.

"Stay here," I say. "We can get you a desk and a chair, and you can use any of the rooms to do yoga. You've been a great roommate."

"You don't know that. We hardly ever see each other," she protests.

"That, I think, makes for a pretty good roommate," I point out. "Besides, I'm used to having people around. It's too quiet out here."

"Quiet is a good thing." Sara screws up her face. "I would have to pay rent. I mean it," she says when I open my mouth to protest. "If you don't tell me how to pay you, I'll just start leaving hundred-euro bills around."

"Fine, you pay me what you would have paid for the mushroom apartment."

"That's too little," she argues.

"It was also your own place. Here you're just renting a room instead of the entire building."

Sara's mouth opens and then closes. "I know you're making me a really good offer, but I feel like I'm supposed to protest more."

"I'm inclined to blame the patriarchy."

Her dark eyebrows lift. "You know what? Me too. Why should I turn down such an excellent offer when it's really going to help me out? Screw that." She holds her hand out for me. "Roommates?"

"Roommates." We shake on it.

5

Sara

After agreeing to continue our roommate situation, an office chair magically appears in the kitchen the next day, which is definitely going to help with some of the tightness in my lower back as a result of sitting in a wooden chair for nearly a week while working.

Two days later, there's a note on the fridge. I get excited thinking it is going to be another adorable drawing from Chris—the previous ones are in my room on the dresser—but it's a note.

Movers coming at ten to clear out the front room for you.

Around ten, I leave my headphones off so I'll hear them knock. When I open the door, there are two burly men with a van parked behind them.

The one on the right grumbles something at me in German, and I smile at him. "Entschuldigung, ich spreche kein Deutsch." I have been trying to get in an hour of my

41

language classes every night, but being able to name the colors or ask where the bathroom is located isn't super helpful right now. At least I can apologize for not speaking German.

They look at each other, and I wish Chris was awake. After a minor hesitation, I move aside to let them in. They head straight for the door to their left, one that's been closed ever since I moved in and I haven't peeked into.

Chris told me to expect movers, but what if it's an elaborate heist? What if one of these paintings is worth a lot of money and . . .

I open my mouth to protest but snap it shut as soon as I see the contents of the room. It's a dining room with a long, polished, wooden table and high-back chairs all the way down. The wood floor matches the rest of the house, and there's a set of chandeliers over the table, the center one slightly larger than the flanking pair. It looks like the table from Beauty and the Beast, but instead of a dark, cavernous room, it's light and intimate.

What really grabs my attention, though, is the wall on the right. The floor-to-ceiling mirrors reflect the opposite windows. The lighting right now is perfect, indirect and soft.

The movers pick up the furniture, making trips in and out. Since the van is right up at the front door and the dining room is against that wall, in no time, there's a spacious, empty room.

Literally my dream yoga room.

The movers make one trip in the reverse direction, delivering a modern glass desk into the room.

One guy waves before exiting and closing the door behind him.

I watch the reflection in the mirror as the van pulls away.

Then I Julie-Andrews spin again.

After that silliness, I move my work stuff into the room. I've been filming on the back deck and also using some footage I recorded back home to publish videos on a regular schedule. But this room is going to be perfect, not only to record but to set up my live sessions and have an office to edit so that I don't have to work in the kitchen.

And I need to get my backlog built up. It's Saturday, and Zoe is coming to visit me Tuesday night and staying till Friday morning.

One appeal of this program for her is that the class schedule is pretty compressed, so she should have time to explore Europe. She has one class Monday and Tuesday for four hours a day, but the class only goes for four weeks. She has Wednesday and Thursday off right now, but that changes later in the semester.

When Zoe leaves Friday morning, I'll travel with her to Munich, where I catch my flight to Rome to meet Tessa, Jade, and Emma.

My chest tightens, thinking about Rome. I know that it's good for me to take breaks and to spend time with my friends, especially since I'm turning into a recluse in this giant house with no one to talk to except a moody artist who keeps a weird schedule.

While I've been super productive with the videos, I'm not actually seeing much in terms of results. Sure, I've got an uptick in subscribers and Patreons, but nothing as drastic as I'd hoped. I need something catchy, something viral, that will help me gain the numbers I want to see to make this more sustainable.

Although, now that I've agreed to live here with Chris, that number is a lot closer than it would have been. Plus, the refund for the mycelium-filled apartment hit my bank account yesterday.

Visiting Rome means paying for a flight and a hotel. After our trip to Paris, when we accidentally walked in on Tessa and her solo session, we agreed we should at least get two rooms.

Plus wine, dinners out, tours, transportation . . .

This is what I agreed to, though, and one reason why I came to Europe. And this week, Tessa and Luc had a crisis, one that finally got Tessa to admit that she wants Luc to be more than a fake relationship. We need to celebrate.

A knock interrupts my thoughts. Chris stands in the open doorway, leaning against the frame with his arms crossed, dressed in his usual band shirt and lounge pants.

"What do you think?" he asks, voice still thick with sleep.

I've just unrolled my yoga mat and am kneeling at one end. I smile up at him from the floor. "It's perfect."

He nods and pushes off, wandering away, presumably for coffee and a smoke outside like usual. My stomach rumbles, and I think I've missed lunch, busy moving and thinking unproductive thoughts.

Chris makes coffee in the kitchen. I hang back by the table, giving him the space to do his own thing. I flip open my content planner next to my laptop and run my fingers along the upcoming week. There's a circle the weekend Zoe's going to come in big, red ink. I see it every time I open my monthly calendar, a reminder of why I've got to make my business profitable.

"It's just that my friends are all going, and it would be a lot of fun. I should have realized that it would conflict with our weekend together," Zoe says. I can picture her giving me puppy dog eyes and pressing her palms together, pleading with me.

It's Tuesday, the day Zoe is supposed to take the train to visit me, and I'm outside at the table having an al fresco lunch.

"That's okay," I say, swallowing back my disappointment that Zoe is canceling. Her schedule at school may be fairly open, but her social calendar has gotten remarkably busier. Back home, I saw Zoe at least two or three times a month—she would come home for a weekend, or I would do something in Austin, so I'd take her out to lunch or coffee. Now, it's going to be over a month by the time I see her.

Granted, this weekend I am the one not available, but still.

And there's a festival her friends are going to, and I can understand wanting to attend. She's young, I remind myself; these years are supposed to be about independence and fun.

"Are you sure?" she says, and the barely-constrained hope in her voice has me fake-smiling and infusing as much enthusiasm into my words as I can.

"Of course. Have a great time and be safe, nena." The term of endearment is from her father, and I've kept that part of his memory going.

"I will. I totally will."

She gabs for a little while in excitement, telling me about her plans and some of the artists performing at the festival. I haven't heard of any of them.

"Maybe I should come to Munich?" I suggest.

"Oh. Uhhh . . ." That uh kills me, and a sinking feeling settles in my stomach.

"No, I can't do that. I have to record videos to publish this weekend. Ha, silly me," I say, totally backtracking. It's a lie—I've already filmed enough for this weekend so I could take it off.

"Okay," Zoe says too quickly. "We'll plan something else. I promise. I'll get out there soon."

"Sure," I say, trying to keep the shakiness out of my voice.

"I watched your latest video yesterday."

"Oh?" I say, achingly pleased for any little sign of interest from Zoe. "Did you follow along?"

"Of course," she says and fills me in on how her yoga practice is going. We talk for a few more minutes, and then she has to go.

I hang up and slump onto the table. I've been getting up later and later lately, and aside from my phone call with Zoe and eating my overnight oats, I have done nothing productive.

And I don't really want to.

But I do, anyway. I slog through filming a few short videos for my patrons, but I have a suspicion they're all crap. I guess I'll find out when I go to edit them this afternoon.

I can't get my mind off the idea that Zoe doesn't have time for me.

Maybe I shouldn't have come to Germany. Maybe Zoe needs more space, and I'm too close.

My mood deteriorates, and I give up on getting any more work done. Instead, I declare a Level Five Emergency and raid the kitchen.

Here's a benefit of having a roommate that seems to live exclusively on junk food: I can raid his stash. I'll go to the store first thing tomorrow to replace everything, but for right now, these sea salt potato chips and Oreos are going to fill the aching hole in my chest.

Oh, and a bottle of wine.

6

Chris

I WALK INTO THE MAIN ROOM AND DO A DOUBLE TAKE.

Sara is in the armchair asleep.

I lean against the wall, crossing my arms and taking in the glory that is this tableau.

She's not just asleep, she's conked-out, mouth-open asleep, an empty family-size bag of potato chips on the table and a mostly-empty bottle of wine sitting in a puddle of its own condensation.

If I couldn't already tell that something was up, Sara's giant sweatshirt is another clue. It's two sizes too big and has stains on the front and a stretched-out neckline. Her fit body is swimming in it.

She might be drooling on the leather armrest, too.

There's a perfectly good couch less than a meter over, but Sara has curled up in a ball, her head at an awkward angle and one foot pointing skyward.

It shouldn't be cute, but it is.

I sigh. I've slept in worse places—when I was in my twenties touring with the band, I woke up several times in bathtubs—but I know Sara was struggling with her back before we got her the office chair, so I don't think I should leave her like this.

Pushing off the wall, I crouch down in front of the chair. I reach out but pause, my hand hovering over the lock of thick dark hair that hangs in her face.

When I wake her up, there's no telling what she'll be like; groggy and quiet or drunk and upset or any other flurry of emotions that are hard to navigate.

Right now, her face is serene, and I consider not waking her. Whatever has upset her, whatever broke her routine, isn't going to be magically fixed when she wakes up. Her dreams might be better.

Sara snorts slightly, her mouth closing and nose wrinkling while she stretches and shifts around. When she's done, that one foot is still up in the air and the other leg is hooked over the back of the chair. Her head dangles off the seat, and I can see the roof of her mouth through her once-again open lips.

"Sara," I whisper.

There is indeed a pool of drool on the leather where her head was.

It's gross, I tell myself. *Gross and not at all adorable.*

I hide my smile behind my hand and try again. "Sara."

My voice penetrates this time, and she blinks at me upside down. Brown eyes flecked with shades of gold and umber focus on me. Grogginess and confusion fill her face, and then recognition kicks in.

"Oh. Hi," she says sheepishly. Even when she's embarrassed, her lips tip up in that perpetual smile. There's a line of circles on her cheek where the buttons of the armchair left their imprint. "Am I in your way?"

"No, but I thought you might be more comfortable in your bed."

I back away while Sara struggles to stand, un-pretzeling

herself. When she straightens, she catches her head. "Oh." This oh is less "oh hi" and more "oh my head."

I brace myself to catch her as she wobbles, but she sinks back down onto the chair with a moan, her head in her hands.

I perch on the corner of the low table across from her and wait.

"I am such a lightweight." She drags her hands down her face. Her index finger gets caught on the imprints in her skin, and she groans again.

"Are you okay?"

She laughs, but it's sad and husky. "My daughter canceled on me."

My elbows rest on my knees, and I clasp my hands between them. "I'm sorry. I know you had big plans.

"A spa day." She sniffles. "We'd cook her favorite meal together. Picnic at the park. Go hiking."

"You can still do those things," I suggest.

She scoffs.

"It won't be the same," I amend, "but you'd still have fun, I'm sure."

"We were going to have a picnic and practice yoga on the back deck." Sara flings her arms out, slumping against the chair. Her eyes are unfocused. "It's warm enough, but it's supposed to get brisk again on Monday. It's probably the last time I will practice outdoors. Oh," she says softly. "Zoe was going to be in one of my videos."

I eye the wine. Did Sara really get drunk off of less than a bottle?

When I glance back, her eyes are closed. "Sara?"

"Shhh . . . ." She holds a finger up, her eyes slitting open while she aims for my mouth. It takes two tries, but then her finger presses against my lips with more force than necessary, digging them into my teeth.

Sara's leaning out of the chair now, balancing herself

between us and staring at my lips. Her finger is cold against my skin.

She sways back a bit, her head resting on the armrest and the pressure of her finger easing.

The tip of that finger traces my bottom lip, and my heart climbs in my chest.

"You have pretty lips."

A laugh escapes, and Sara's eyes widen as her finger touches the interior of my lip, the dampness preventing our skin from sliding apart as if we're magnetized.

I still and watch Sara's face. It mirrors the desire rushing through me. She's mesmerized, a flush on her cheeks that has nothing to do with the alcohol or sleep.

But she is drunk.

And even if she wasn't, it's too complicated. I don't know what she wants, but Sara doesn't seem like the kind of person who's looking for a quick fuck, which is my expertise.

She's sparkles and happiness, and if things got awkward and I saw her dim, I'd hate myself.

When her finger lightly touches my teeth, I know I need to stop her.

I pull away, and her arm falls in the space between my body and her chair.

"Come on," I say, rising to my feet. "I'll help you to your room."

Sara stands but immediately sways, and I wrap an arm around her waist to prevent her from sliding back down. She leans on me, her head fitting just right under my ear.

"Is it dinner time?" Sara asks, concerned.

"Not yet."

"I mean my dinner time. Do you even eat dinner?"

She tilts her head to look up at me while I navigate her out of the room and to the stairs. Now that she's moving, the gold flecks I noticed earlier are brighter. Maybe it's because she's more awake now, or maybe she's just out of the shadowy corner of the room.

"I eat dinner. Just a lot later than you, so you've already gone to bed."

"Oh. I haven't made anything yet."

"Are you hungry?"

I look down at our feet while I help her up the stairs. Out of the corner of my eyes, I can see her wrinkle her nose. "I should be."

"How about this? We'll get you upstairs for a nap, and I'll order something for us to eat. I'll find something vegan."

Sara gasps, and her free hand comes up to my chest. We pause at the top of the stairs. "Can we have something Asian? Like pad Thai or mapo?"

Her eyes are definitely brighter now, and it's not the lighting. Of course, talking about food perks her up.

"I'll find something, okay?"

Sara nods and then leans her head to rest on my shoulder, tired again.

I give myself a moment to enjoy the feeling of her body against mine. My fingers lightly press into her upper arm. Despite how muscular she is, Sara is still soft and smooth.

And tempting.

———

An hour and a half later, I've just returned from picking up our takeaway. I did manage to find a vegan tofu mapo, which I set on the counter and unpack before going upstairs to wake Sleeping Beauty.

Sara had crawled into bed and flopped down over the covers. That was the first time I'd been in her room since she moved in, and as I expected, it was meticulously tidy. There were only a few things out on the dresser and nightstand—

including a small stack of papers that I recognized as the cartoons I'd drawn for her.

I had left the door slightly ajar, so now I knock and wait for Sara's mumbled, "Come in." A few moments later, the bedside light clicks on.

"Hey. How are you feeling?"

Sara sits up and blinks at me. Her jaw moves around, lips and cheeks bulging slightly while she runs her tongue over her teeth. "Thirsty."

I point to her nightstand and the still-full glass of water I placed there. Sara sighs in relief and chugs the glass, swinging her legs over the side of the bed.

"I got you some mapo tofu."

Sober Sara has less enthusiasm, but she comes downstairs and plunks herself down at the counter.

I open the containers and set hers in front of her. "Chopsticks or fork?"

"Chopsticks," she says, and then halfheartedly uses them to poke a piece of tofu.

"Do you want to talk about it?" I ask.

She looks at me from under her brows. "Do you really want to hear me complain about my daughter?"

I shrug. "If it helps, sure."

"I just . . ." She puts her head in her hands, and her fingers thread through her hair. Sara's hair is dark brown, but a few grays here and there hint at her age. "Moving here was so overwhelming. It reminds me of when I took Zoe to college, except I'm going off to college too."

"How old is your daughter?"

Sara sighs. "Twenty-one. We've always been so close, but I feel like moving here has made us drift apart. And I know it's only been a couple of weeks. But still. There's a distance between us that wasn't there before. It's been a hard day for me. I'll get over it." She eyes me as she picks up a bell pepper. "Do you have kids?"

I choke on my Kung Pao chicken. "Definitely not," I say after clearing my airways.

"Ever been married?"

"Also, no." We eat for a few moments before I ask the looming question. "How did your husband die?"

"He was very unlucky. He had a fast-growing brain tumor at the same time as having a fussy and irritable toddler. He was having symptoms that we thought were just lack of sleep and stress, and by the time we found the tumor, it was too late." Sara crams a block of tofu into her mouth.

"My mom died of cancer."

Sara stops mid-chew and stares at me. Her hand covers her mouth while she swallows enough to talk. "I'm sorry to hear that."

"Thanks. It was breast cancer. She didn't tell me about it until after her first round of chemo because I was out of the country." My band was doing its first tour, and it devastated me to not be there when she needed help.

Sara's eyes sadden. "She was alone?"

"No, thank god," I say, scooping more rice into the chicken. "Her live-in girlfriend helped her a lot. It was messy, though. Opened my eyes to caretaker burnout when Elise left my mom before the second round of chemo. I was there for that one, but it didn't do any good."

Sara reaches over and squeezes my forearm. "I'm sorry. People often told me we were lucky the cancer was so fast, but there's really no good amount of time for that kind of thing. Yes, we had a few weeks with him, but he suffered. I'm sure it was hard to see your mom go through chemo."

She removes her hand, and we continue eating. It bothers me that Sara's so upset over her daughter not coming to visit —maybe leftover guilt over not spending enough time with my mom.

"What if you and I did all the things you had planned with your daughter?"

Sara pushes her half-eaten container of food away. "You want to picnic and hike with me?"

"It could be fun."

She squints. "Your mouth is saying yes, but this—" She gestures to my face. "—is saying hell no."

I bark out a laugh, and Sara's eyes widen.

"Jesus Christ, I made you laugh." She's staring at me like I'm an alien.

"What?" I ask.

"I didn't know you laughed, honestly. You've got the—" She waves at me again. "—brooding recluse in the Black Forest thing."

"You've made me laugh before."

An eyebrow raises. "I did? When?"

"The notes we exchanged on the fridge."

It's the first time we've talked about it, and Sara blushes. It's charming and sweet, her eyes flicking to the fridge and back to me.

Our smiles fade until we're watching each other. Maybe I didn't misread the flirtiness in the note.

Sara's eyes dance around my face. We're both trying to get a read on the other.

After a flick down to my mouth, Sara swallows and turns forward again. With a little shake of her head, Sara claps her hands.

"Okay, so tomorrow, the plan was to shop in town, hike, go to the baths, and cook dinner together."

It's my turn to raise an eyebrow. "You want to go to the baths with me?" My gaze involuntarily drops to her chest, and I get a vision of Sara naked in the slick water of the baths, relaxed and warm, and I really don't need the scandal of getting kicked out for inappropriate behavior. Or to make Sara uncomfortable. Can I trust myself to go to the baths with Sara and behave?

"Sure," she says breezily. "I'm thinking that I don't want

to take up too much of your time, and I could get more work done, but I've already got the tickets for the baths and the food to cook. So why don't we just do those two?"

"Umm . . ." I had no idea Sara would be so casual about nudity. Americans are usually so uptight about this stuff.

Sara misreads my hesitation. "I promise, you'll like the food, even though it's vegan," she says with a smirk.

I very much doubt that I'm going to dislike anything about our day tomorrow.

7

Sara

I'M LOOKING FORWARD TO MY DAY WITH CHRIS. IT'S GOING TO BE a roommate-bonding experience, I tell myself. An insight into the man I've been living with for over two weeks and hardly know.

I'm in the living room with my laptop when Chris comes into the kitchen in the early afternoon. I pull my headphones off and tease him. "Good morning."

He nods at me and starts the coffee machine.

"Our tickets are for four p.m., and I was wondering. What do people wear to the baths?"

He blinks at me for a moment. "What?"

"What should I wear to the baths? The website doesn't have any advice on that."

Chris crosses his arms on his chest, and then one hand goes up to cover his mouth, and I think he might be laughing, though I'm not sure why this is funny.

"What?" I ask, but he just looks up at the ceiling. "What?" I get a little louder and try to poke him with a finger, but he twists out of my way.

"It's a nude bath," he finally says.

"What?"

"It's a nude bath." He says it a little slower, and at first, I think he's teasing me, but no, he's definitely serious. The blood drains out of my face.

"It doesn't say that anywhere!" I click over to the open browser, and Chris moves around to look over my shoulder. This close, I can smell him, just the natural scent before he's had coffee and cigarettes. He smells like detergent and cotton and warmth.

"Right here," he says, pointing down at the small text at the bottom.

I squint and read it out loud. "Joint, textile-free Roman-Irish bathing. Textile-free? Can't they just say nude?"

"I think your browser is translating the words," he suggests.

"Oh, that makes sense. Wait, what do they mean by joint?"

Chris coughs and really can't hide his laugh now. "It means . . . I think you might say unisex?"

I take a step back. "Excuse me? I'm going to be naked in front of you?" The end of the sentence pitches up into hysteria territory, and now Chris really is laughing.

"Stop laughing!" I insist and smack his arm with the back side of my hand. "I didn't know!" He just doubles over, and I'm pretty sure his eyes are tearing up.

"Oh my god," I say, another thought hitting me. "I was going to do this with Zoe."

It's mildly horrifying, but also, I have to admit as Chris wipes his eyes, very funny.

Finally, I join Chris's laughter, and my laughing starts Chris back up again.

Once we get control of ourselves, he asks me, "Are we still going to the baths?"

I pause, feeling like uncool and uptight. But do I really

want to spend a few hours in close proximity to a wet, naked Chris? My body clenches just thinking about it.

I shake my head adamantly. "Absolutely not."

————

After canceling my tickets to the bath—no refunds—I try to get back to work. The embarrassment lingers, though, one of those moments in life that's going to pop up in my head at unexpected times.

Part of me wonders, though, what would have happened if we had gone.

Of course, in real life, I would have spun around the moment I realized we would be naked, but in my mind, I play out what it would be like if I was comfortable and casual with it.

I would see Chris naked. He would see me naked.

I've already seen him shirtless, and that image stuck in my mind more than I would like to admit. Granted, it has been a very long time since I've had sex.

When Zoe was a teenager, Tessa and Jade encouraged me to go on dates. I went on a few, but considering men romantically while having a teenage daughter in the back of your mind was distracting. I was constantly thinking, would I introduce this guy to her? Would I want him around her? Would he be a good influence?

The nuances of raising a human being that you wanted to someday find a healthy relationship were complex.

And the answers were usually no. The quality of the men I went out with was terrible. They were definitely not worthy of being in my daughter's life.

Vibrators are more reliable, and I've got a good one.

However, vibrators don't have tattoos and tongue piercing and that V of muscles that I'd really like to run my tongue along.

Not Chris's. Just . . . a hot guy.

After several hours of distracted work, it's time to start dinner. The first course is crudites with hummus—which I've already made—followed by kale and mushroom crepes with a white sauce and Zoe's favorite chocolate mousse—also already made.

I'm pulling out the vegetables when Chris comes in.

"Okay," he says, clapping his hands. "Put me to work."

I point to the counter. "You can slice the cucumbers and make carrot sticks. I'll get started on the mushrooms."

He gives me a thumbs-up and opens the cabinet closest to him. Then closes it and opens the next one.

"Looking for the cutting board?"

He nods.

"The drawer under the knife block. Grab me one too."

I put my head in the fridge, looking for the mushrooms which have fallen back behind the spinach. I hear the drawer opening and closing and then the slick of the knives coming out of the knife block.

I grab two containers of mushrooms, then open the drawer and pull out the giant bundle of curly kale.

I nudge the door closed with my hip and put my produce to the left of my cutting board. I glance over at Chris and freeze.

He's got a steak knife in one hand and a look of pure concentration on his face as he bends over the counter, slicing the unpeeled cucumber into rounds of varying thickness.

I clear my throat. "Do you like cucumbers?"

"Sure," he responds absentmindedly, in a way I'm learning means "not really."

He's put a steak knife on my cutting board too. I pick it up and sweep around him. "I prefer a chef's knife for work like this. Do you want one too?"

Chris straightens up and frowns at the knife block.

"Sure?"

I give him the chef's knife and take the santoku knife for myself.

He holds it up and, in a terrible Australian accent, says, "Now that's a knife." His smile is mischievous, and I can't help but return it. He holds the steak knife up to the chef's knife. "You know they swear size doesn't matter, but I'm getting a different vibe here."

I tilt my head at him. "Are you making jokes because you don't know what you're doing?"

"Yes."

I pause. "Would you rather be in charge of the wine?"

"Also, yes."

I laugh and gesture with my chin at the fridge. "Bottle of Riesling on the door."

Chris finds glasses, opens the wine, and sits at the counter, a safe distance away from knife activity, while I work on the vegetables.

I glance up from my pile of minced mushrooms and see Chris staring at me. "What?"

"Are you a trained chef? Because I would be missing two fingers if I tried to do that."

"No, but I took a knife skills course. Actually, Zoe and I took it together."

"Okay, smarty pants," he says, twisting the cap off the wine. "Why do you use that knife?"

I explain while I work, and Chris pours me a glass, leaning across the counter to put it next to my workstation. He asks questions while I work and listens intently. The topic wanders from my knife skills to cooking, my yoga, my plans.

It's domestic in a way that I've never experienced before. Kit and I were high school sweethearts, and before Zoe was born, we lived with my parents. When we moved out and Zoe was young, meals were quick. I wasn't a vegan, and it was all about whatever I could get on the table the fastest.

Then, when Zoe was growing up and I was trying to eat

healthy foods, it was all about teaching her good habits. Just the two of us. She loves cooking just as much as I do now, and while I expect she isn't a strict vegan, when she's home from college, we try out new recipes together and work in the kitchen, a well-oiled machine.

This here, with Chris, is something different. His gaze is intense like I'm under scrutiny. It's almost too much. It feels intimate, cooking for him.

I try to ease his attention. "If you're renting this place, where do you actually live?"

He thinks about it for a bit too long, just enough to make it weird. "London," he finally says.

"Is that for work?"

"Yeah. There's a lot going on in London, and it's a bit of an epicenter. Plus, I can fly anywhere from there."

"But you're German?"

"Yes."

"What brings you here, then? Why rent a place out in the middle of nowhere?"

Chris raises his voice as I scrape the onions and mushrooms into the pan, and it sizzles. I turn the heat down, not used to a fancy copper pot like this one. "I've been struggling with my creativity lately. And I thought I could use a change of pace."

"How long have you been here?"

He grimaces. "Four weeks."

"And I take it things aren't going well?"

"No," he says. "But I'll figure it out." He says it with confidence, but I wonder how much he believes himself.

8

Chris

Watching Sara cook is amazing. I had no idea everyday people cooked like this.

With her focusing on what she's doing, she's more willing to talk about herself, too, so I pepper her with questions. She tells me about her yoga videos and her friends, who she chats with almost every day—I've seen her sitting out on the back deck and video chatting in the early evenings sometimes.

The past few years of my life have been . . . not exactly isolating, because I am surrounded by people all the time, but the people I'm around are always demanding something of me. They're my bandmates who want leadership and cooperation, or the roadies just trying to do their jobs, or the fans and media, people whose expectations are heavy.

Sara is the opposite. She's fascinating, and her passion for yoga shines through. I remember once feeling that kind of passion. Hell, three months ago, I felt that kind of passion during our first tour after winning Eurovision, playing to packed venues and screaming fans.

That passion has slipped out of my fingers as I try to hold it tighter and tighter.

Sara puts a plate in front of me with a flourish. The chopped veggies and hummus are ready. She plucks a carrot up and scoops it into the hummus.

She talks about her Patreon and the struggle to get followers on YouTube, which parallels a little with the band and how we were putting songs out on music platforms before we got popular with smaller venues.

When there's a lull, I ask a question that I've been wondering since I met her. "Why are you vegan?"

"So, I'm not a super strict vegan, and I actually consider myself plant-based, not vegan, but hardly anyone knows what that means. There's a surprisingly large amount of food with animal products in it. I was super strict for a long time, but now I don't worry about it too much. I don't eat flesh or dairy or eggs. I don't stress over wine." She pauses and takes a sip. "Or cosmetics, or a variety of smaller things. As to why, there are a lot of reasons. Meat is bad for the environment. It's bad for the animals. But mostly," she continues as she stirs something thick and white on the stove, "it's for my health. There are a lot of studies out there correlating meat to lower life expectancy."

"My mom changed her diet when she got sick. Or she tried to. She wasn't much of a cook, so taking care of herself that way was hard."

Sara nods. "It is a lot of work. Hence the knife skills class and such. Okay." She switches off the stove. "You're about to have your first vegan meal, the perk of being my roommate."

I watch as she assembles dinner and then presents with a flourish. The savory, umami smell of sautéed mushrooms hits me first, then the richness of the sauce.

Sara climbs onto the barstool next to me and angles her wine glass toward me.

"Cheers."

"Prost."

The food is freaking delicious. "Fuck, how are you not a chef?"

Sara laughs. "Turning a beloved passion into a job is a surefire way to start hating it."

That's fair.

Sara talks while we eat, and I try to slow down to enjoy the taste. She's telling me about substitutions and cooking techniques, but it just feels like magic to me.

She tries to gather our plates when they're empty, but I beat her to it. "You cook, I clean."

"Are you sure?"

"Hey, I may not be able to cook, but I *am* capable of cleaning."

"All right, then I'm going to go meditate. Unless you want to join?"

"This was healthy enough for one day."

She laughs. "It was nice having dinner with you, Chris." She pats my shoulder before leaving the kitchen.

———

"Hey, man!" Ram says as soon as I answer the phone. Our drummer calling at one in the morning probably isn't a good sign, and he sounds drunk as fuck.

"Ram, how's it going?"

Tonight, I'm sitting out on the patio in the cold air, a cigarette keeping me company on an otherwise empty night. Sara's bedroom light went out hours ago, and I have hardly moved since.

"I have a song idea."

I grimace. This isn't the first time since the tour ended that I've fielded a call like this from him—or from any of our band members, actually.

"Yeah?" I say.

"Yeah, hang on, hang on. I wrote something down." There are the sounds of people talking, low music, and chair scraping. "Yeah, yeah, here it is."

I wait while he clears his throat.

"Upside-down and underwater. And that's all we are," he reads aloud.

It takes me a few beats of silence to realize he's finished, that those two lines are all he's got for me.

But then again, that's maybe two more lines than I have after weeks of working before Sara moved in.

"Say it to me again." I put him on speaker phone and open a notes app to write them down.

"You think you could do something with it?" he asks excitedly. "Work your magic?"

I used to love it when someone called it my magic, but now I just wince. If it was magic, it's left me, and the void in its place is glaringly obvious to me, but no one else, it seems.

Ram and the rest of the band know that I have nothing. And yet there are still these expectations that I'm going to come up with a whole second album worth of hits.

"Yeah, I'll figure something out," I tell him, because that's what's expected.

We chat for a few more minutes while I smoke another cigarette. Ram sounds like he's enjoying the fame that our Eurovision win has brought. He tells me he's in Amsterdam and that I should join him because the drugs are mind-opening.

"Lyrics will just pour out, man."

Of course, the problem is they won't be any good.

A few minutes later, we say goodbye, and I stub out the butt of my cigarette. I wonder briefly about the other band members: last I heard, June, our bassist, was in London, and Alwin, our lead singer, was in Berlin.

There's a thunk from inside, and I get up, cautiously opening the back door into the kitchen. My first thought is that there's either a fan or paparazzi trespassing, though our manager has done a pretty good job of keeping my location a secret. And I've been careful, too. People know I'm in the area, but they'd assume it was for a short visit because what kind of rock star would hang out in the country near a spa town? It's not on-brand for us.

But as the door opens, I see that it's only Sara. She's at the sink, drinking a glass of water and staring out into the night or her own reflection in the window.

"Hey," I say quietly, but she still jumps and lets out a squeak.

"Oh!" She puts a hand to her chest. "Chris, you scared me."

"Sorry. Are you all right?"

"Yeah," she says, turning to face me and holding up her glass. "Just thirsty."

I lean against the counter and look her over. She's wearing yoga pants and a sports bra, like usual. The yoga pants are a gray camouflage, and the sports bra is bright pink. Does she sleep in these clothes too?

"Do you own any outfits other than your workout gear?"

She blushes and crosses her arms over her chest, and I feel like a bit of a cad for asking.

"I do," she insists. "I just don't have a reason to wear anything else."

"I suppose my company doesn't warrant anything nicer. I just always feel extra lazy in your presence. Like you could pop off for a jog at any time, and I'm . . ." I wave at my own outfit, thick cotton track pants and a hoodie. I suppose I could technically go running in this, but I don't have underwear on, and I'd have a hard time with everything swinging about.

Like she's reading my mind, Sara says, "I like the support."

It pulls my eyes right to her chest, which I try not to linger on, but she brought them up. Sara's breasts are small, a perfect handful—not that I've measured. The sports bra keeps them high and tight against her chest, and I shift slightly and feel my own support-less situation.

"I prefer to free-ball."

Sara's blush deepens, and her eyes flick to my groin, which gives a twitch at even this slight bit of attention.

"Yes, well . . . to each his own, I suppose."

I smirk, and Sara gives me a begrudging smile.

"All right," I say. "I'm off to bed. Sleep well."

"Sleep well," Sara echoes, and I wander to my room, another day in the books with no forward progress.

9

Sara

"Cheers," says Tessa on our Saturday night in Rome. "To the fantastic weekend we've had exploring Emma's new home!"

We all click our glasses together at the chic Italian wine bar. It is warm and cozy; candlelight and soft Classical music fill the space.

Rome has been an absolute dream. My friends and I have had two packed days of playing tourist, drinking wine, and staying in a lovely, ritzy hotel.

I worried that things would be weird since Tessa had a new boyfriend, and a long-distance one at that, but Luc was in Paris, and while Tessa did occasionally spend time on her phone with him, she was mostly present with us.

It's been one month since that weekend in Paris, our first wine tour weekend. Emma and Jade have been living together in Madrid, but that's coming to an end. Emma's semester at business school starts next week, so we took the opportunity to visit what would become her new home.

Tomorrow, Jade would head back to Madrid, and she looked a bit melancholy at the prospect of losing her roommate.

"I'll miss having you live with me," she tells Emma.

"I know. I'll miss it too. We had so much fun together."

"I was wondering how you two would match up. I was sure that Jade was going to be a bad influence." I wink at her to let her know I am teasing, but Jade preens, taking it as a compliment.

"Emma was undeterred in my attempts to get her to break the seal." Jade ruefully shakes her head. "Actually, I think it worked the other way, Emma was more of an influence on me. I didn't bang a single guy while Emma was visiting."

We laugh and tease and drink our wine, ordering appetizers and enjoying a very slow Italian dinner. We picked this place because they have a few vegan selections, and I'm thankful that Tessa put the work in to find it.

Emma downs the last sip of her Prosecco and stands. "I'm going to get us another round."

She wanders off to the bar, and I turn back to my conversation with Jade about Zoe's classes. However, within a few minutes, I've definitely lost Jade's attention to something behind me.

"What?" I ask, turning in my seat to look. Tessa's typing on her phone, and Jade has a thoughtful look on her face, the end of her long, dark ponytail in her fingers.

"Watch the guy at the corner of the bar," she says.

"The one in the polo?"

"No," she says. "The one in the jacket and jeans. Older, salt and pepper hair."

I spot him just as he looks at Emma. She's oblivious, playing with a cardstock drink menu on the counter. His eyes warm looking at her, and when she glances up, he smiles at her. While I can't see her face, I can imagine the look she has as she ducks her head; she has absolutely no idea what to do with an interested man.

Once the bartender pours our wine, Jade leaps up to help Emma carry them back to our table. On the way, Jade leans in and whispers to Emma conspiratorially.

They both glance back at the man at the corner of the bar; Em's glance is quick while Jade smiles and waves. Tessa puts her phone away, and we glance at each other, amused.

"Stop encouraging him," Em hisses, pushing Jade's hand down.

"Why?"

"You're giving him false hope," Em says.

"Honey, men are going to always hope to sleep with you. You're beautiful and charming. Hope isn't something you give them; they already have it. And any guy worth going home with is going to know that having a conversation or flirtation with you is not a consolation prize. A man should be so honored."

Emma blushes and glances at the man again. "It's not that I don't want to sleep with someone." She leans in and drops her voice to a whisper. "It's just that it's been so long. It feels like . . . like being revirginized."

"That's definitely not a thing," Jade interjects.

"I know, I know. You've made us all read the book, Jade." Emma's referring to *Come As You Are*, a self-help book written by a sex therapist, which is Jade's favorite. She'd sell it door to door if she could, but instead, she's just made the three of us read it. We all learned something about our own sexuality, stuff that, frankly, I should have learned a lot sooner.

It's not that my sex life with Kit was bad. But it wasn't inspired. Jade shares stories—enthusiastically—of toe-curling sex and swears that we're entering the prime of our sex life. Turns out that is something the *American Pie* movie franchise got right; sex is supposed to get better as we get older.

Tessa is in agreement, and Luc, her much younger boyfriend, stars in our gossip fests lately.

"I'm just saying," Jade points out, "that you have us all here. If you want to go talk to that guy, we can have a signal. An eye roll if we need to rescue you from the conversation, or a wink if you're going to go home with him."

"And then we can make sure we have his information, just like y'all did with my roommate. And if anything goes wrong, we can help you," I say.

Jade blinks at me, possibly surprised that I agree with her.

"But only if you're comfortable with it," I add.

"Thanks, Sara," Emma says, but Jade hasn't taken her eyes off me.

"Hang on," Jade says, and now I have the full brunt of her attention. "Sara's been awfully relaxed this weekend," Jade twists her mouth to the side and wiggles an eyebrow. "Are you getting some frustration out somehow?"

"No!" I protest. "I am not sleeping with my roommate."

"Wow," Tessa says, leaning her elbow on the table and propping her chin in her hand, mirroring Jade. "Jade didn't say anything about your roommate."

"That's not . . . I just meant . . ."

Emma claps a hand over her mouth to hide her giggle.

"You!" I say, pointing at her. "Go talk to him!" I jab my thumb over my shoulder to indicate the gentleman at the bar.

Emma groans and pouts for a moment, but her eyes glance back over my shoulder. "Okay," she says, drawing in a breath and then taking a sip of her bubbling wine. "What do I say?"

"I always start with hi," Jade says helpfully, and Emma pinches Jade's bicep. Jade yelps and rubs her arm but laughs as Emma stands, straightens her shoulders, and walks toward the bar.

Tessa and Jade both watch, not subtle at all. "What's happening?" I ask.

Jade flicks her gaze at me and smirks. "She's walking to the bar. He sees her. I'm guessing Emma's just said hi. He's saying something . . ."

Tessa and Jade both whip their heads at me. "He just looked at us. Busted," Jade says.

Tessa snickers.

That's how we pass the next hour or so, talking about our work and Jade occasionally providing commentary on the situation at the bar.

"Oh, they're standing up," Jade interrupts my possibly-too-thorough analysis of my YouTube statistics.

"She just winked!" Tessa squeals, grabbing Jade's arm excitedly.

All three of us watch as Emma and her handsome stranger weave their way through the tables. Emma stops at the back of her chair and leans in toward us. "We're going to his place," she whispers, and I have to clap my hand over my mouth to not giggle.

The man stops to her right, and as Emma gathers her things, he smiles at us. "Hello," he says, Italian accent thick.

I clear my throat and straighten up. "Can I see some ID, please?"

Jade guffaws next to me, but the man just smiles and pulls out his identification card. I snap a picture.

"Where are you going?" He rattles off an address which I write down. "Are you driving?"

"Okay, Mama Bear," Jade interrupts.

"It's okay," he says to Jade and then turns back to me. "We will take an Uber."

"That she'll order and share the ride with us."

He smiles, bright white teeth against olive skin. "Yes, signora. I will take very good care of her."

At his low, flirty words, Emma's already pink cheeks deepen in color, and she ducks her head. She rolls her eyes when Jade lets out a low whistle and then blows us all air kisses. "That's enough. Love you, see you later."

When Emma and her man depart, Jade, Tessa, and I look at each other. Jade's smug and offers us a hand for a high-five.

Tessa smacks her palm, and after an eye roll, I do too.

"Here's to Emma," Jade says, holding her almost empty glass up. "And to her many orgasms tonight."

10

Sara

WE HAVE A FEW MORE GLASSES OF WINE. I MAKE SURE EMMA AND her man—Santo—get to his place. Jade wanders off to chat with a guy at the bar, and Tessa and I talk about Luc's work. When we met him, he was balancing three jobs and stressed about trying to care for his grandmother, the woman who raised him. Now, though, he's whittled most of his time into two jobs: bartending and ride-share driving.

"I think I'm about ready to head back to the hotel," Tessa says after an immense yawn. "Where's Jade?"

"I'm sure your desire to leave has nothing to do with getting your boyfriend on the phone to say goodnight," I tease. "You said he gets off work in about thirty minutes, so . . ."

"Hush, you. I'll let Jade know we're leaving and pay the bill."

I stack some of our empty plates and gather my things. To my surprise, Jade joins me.

"You're coming back to the hotel with us?" I ask.

"Yup," Jade says, flipping her long, dark hair over her shoulder. "I'd rather hang with y'all in the hotel room."

When Tessa returns, we step out into the cooler night air. My feet are tired from walking so much the past few days, and I'm slightly tipsy. The combination of our heels and the cobblestone streets of Rome make our trip back to the hotel difficult.

"I don't know how Italian women do it," Tessa gasps, laughing and leaning against me after nearly turning her ankle. We probably look like drunk American tourists to all the people sitting out on the sidewalk cafés enjoying the evening.

We make it back to our hotel without too much damage. Tessa peels off in the lobby, waving her phone and saying she's going to call Luc.

Jade and I split up inside our room. She closes the bathroom door behind her, and the shower starts.

I sit on the bed, the linens made since the cleaning service came. Pulling out my phone, I ignore notifications for anything work-related—comments on social media and my evening reminders to meditate and go to bed.

There are two messages I don't ignore.

ZOE

I hope you are having a great time in Rome.
Tell my aunts I say hi.

SARA

They say hi and they miss you.

ZOE

I can't wait to visit Jade in Madrid.

The thought of Jade and Zoe getting together makes me nervous. Jade's a fantastic friend to me, supportive and fun. But when Zoe got old enough that I wasn't a "fun mom" anymore, Jade became the cool aunt. While Jade wasn't great with our kids when they were growing up, she's Zoe and Emma's kids' favorite now. They love going bar hopping with her, and I cringe to think about the sex advice—no matter how accurate and sex-positive Jade is—that my daughter is getting. I gave her the basics, of course, made sure she was safe and healthy and knew that her body and her pleasure are beautiful.

If I know Jade, the conversations with my daughter go a bit further than that.

But I trust Jade. And of course, I trust Zoe, too.

SARA

Y'all are going to have a great time.

It's the best reply I can muster up. The check boxes turn green, but Zoe doesn't respond.

The second message is from Chris.

CHRIS

I tried to make that cauliflower and lentil
curry tonight and fucked it up.

Chris had loved my dinner Wednesday night so much, I made enough to share Thursday with leftovers. And then I did a bunch of prep work and left a recipe on the fridge in case Chris wanted to try his hand at cooking. All he had to do was mix a bunch of stuff and simmer it on the stove.

There's a picture, too, of Chris making a face at his bowl.

SARA

How did you mess it up?

CHRIS

It was kind of . . . soupy? So I let it cook a bit
longer than your directions, and the
cauliflower is mushy.

SARA

Did you measure the water out?

CHRIS

Yeah. I used a cup.

SARA

Oh no. Like a one-cup measurement or a cup
you would drink out of?

CHRIS

What's the difference?

SARA

A cup is a standard measurement, not
whatever glass you have lying around.

CHRIS

How was I supposed to know?!

That's all right. I won't starve.

How's the weekend going? Why are you
chatting with me instead of spending time
with your friends?

I explain where everyone is and that I'm all alone in the
hotel room. When I reread my text, it sounds more suggestive
than I intended.

SARA

Not that I'm like, alone alone. Jade is in the
shower. And Tessa will be up any minute. I'm
not doing anything.

CHRIS

Like what? What would you be doing all
alone in your hotel room? :-D

I roll my eyes at the flirting, and a door opens. I expect it's
either Jade coming out of the shower or Tessa coming in from
the lobby, but instead, when I glance up, Emma is coming
through the door.

"Hey," I say in surprise. "What are you doing back?"

She throws her bag on the desk and flops face-first onto the bed and whimpers. "I couldn't do it." Well, the comforter muffles her face, but I think that's what she says.

I slip off my bed and kneel next to her, a gentle hand on her shoulder. "Couldn't do what?"

She toes her shoes off where her feet hang off the edge of the bed, and we both wiggle up to the headboard.

"He wanted to go down on me. I mean, he did go down on me. But it was . . ."

When the silence hangs, I try to guess. "It wasn't good?"

"I don't know," she admits. "Do you know how long it's been since a man has gone down on me?" She winces. "Sorry. I should remember who I'm talking to."

"It's okay," I say, and grab her hand and pull it into my lap, patting it. "How long has it been?"

Emma thinks for a minute and then shakes her head. "I honestly don't remember the last time Bruce did that. Years. He never did like it anyway."

I laugh. "It's been a long time for me too, so my memory might be a little hazy. But I don't remember Kit being all that good at it. I mean, we were so young everything was just rolled up with enthusiasm. And after Zoe was born, there were a lot of quickies as we could catch them."

"What about some of the guys you've dated recently?"

"I think we either never got to that part or skipped the foreplay." My mind goes to Chris. Would he skip the foreplay?

"You should never skip the foreplay," Jade interrupts as the door to the bathroom swings open. She's wrapped her hair up in a towel and has a T-shirt and shorts on for sleeping. "Emma," she says, eyebrow raising in surprise. "Is everything okay?"

The door to the hallway opens, and Tessa joins us. Before she can say anything, Jade waves a hand. "Come on, we're getting the scoop on what's-his-name."

"Oh," Tessa says, sitting at the foot of the bed and giving Emma's bare foot a squeeze. "Are you going to see him again?"

Emma shakes her head hard. "Definitely not." She recaps the story for Jade and Tessa. "I basically just ran out of his apartment, and he probably thinks there's something wrong with me."

"Why did you run out?" Jade asks.

"Because it was embarrassing. I wasn't expecting that!"

"What?" Jade asks, her brow wrinkling.

"I wasn't expecting him to put his mouth down there! I just thought . . . I don't know! I couldn't stop thinking about how it had been a few hours since I'd showered and I had just peed at the bar and I haven't done any upkeep down there because, obviously, I wasn't planning to go home with a guy and . . ." Her voice chokes off, and she wipes a stray tear from her left cheek. "I guess I'm just not ready yet."

"Hey," Tessa coos. "That's okay. It's all taking steps and trying something new, right?"

"Emma, babe, I'm so sorry. I didn't mean to pressure you." Jade sucks her bottom lip into her mouth, the skin under her teeth turning white as she worries it.

"You didn't pressure me. Really. I thought I wanted it at the bar, but when he was actually . . . you know . . . I just couldn't turn my brain off and enjoy it."

"You definitely have to be in the right headspace for it," Tessa says. "A bit of confidence goes a long way."

Emma sits up, wiping her eyes and giving us a wobbly smile. "It gets better, right?"

And even though none of us have been in Emma's exact scenario—or anyone else's, for that matter—we all agree with her vehemently.

Because it has to get better.

11

Chris

THERE'S A KNOCK ON MY BEDROOM DOOR, AND BASED ON THE light filtering through the blinds, it's morning. Very morning. Like so morning, I usually see this kind of light when I'm going to bed.

"Chris?" Sara's voice comes through the door. "Someone's here to see you." Sara got back from Rome two days ago. For someone I don't actually see much at all, I missed having her in the house.

That jerks me up and out of bed. Not many people know where I am, and a visit from those who do can't be a good thing. I flashback to last year when Ram overdosed at a party, and Marcus had to find the rest of us, one by one, throughout the night.

"I'm up," I say to Sara and check my phone. No messages giving me any kind of clue who this might be.

I put on clothes and meet Sara at the front door. It's closed, and when I look at her, she says, "I didn't want to just let some random person in," and gets out of my way.

When the door opens, the man standing on my front

porch turns around, a wicked grin on his face. "Well, well, well, Chris," he says to me in German. "I definitely did not expect this when I decided to drive out to see you."

Alwin, the lead singer of our band, looks between me and Sara. "I would say personal trainer," he guesses, and I look over at Sara. She's wearing yoga pants and a sports bra, like usual. "Did he interrupt your video?" I ask her in English.

She shakes her head. "I hadn't started yet. You know him, I guess?"

I grit my teeth. A visit from Alwin is a reminder that the clock is ticking to put our next album together. "Alwin, Sara. Sara, Alwin."

Alwin steps in as Sara backs up from the door, and he shakes her hand, looking smug. "Pleasure to meet you."

Of all the people to have at my door, Alwin has got to be the worst. According to most of the media, he's actually "the hot one." While I am "brooding and trouble," Alwin is "charming." He's the one most likely to bed a groupie—or groupies all at once, in a few instances—and he's also the most likely to preen and brag about the band.

"Would you like some coffee? Or tea?" Sara asks, and I thank god with my next breath. It's too early to deal with Alwin without coffee.

"Coffee would be great," I say, closing the door. "Someone is going to need it on his drive back to wherever he came from." I glare at Alwin.

"No problem," Sara says, turning and walking to the kitchen.

Alwin watches her go with a tilt of his head.

I move to block his view and switch back to German. "What are you doing here?"

"Me? What are *you* doing? Do you have an American girlfriend? Did you meet her on tour?"

"She's not my girlfriend," I say. "And she doesn't know about Verduistering."

Alwin's eyebrows nearly shoot off his face. "What?"

"She doesn't know I'm in—"

Alwin claps his hand on his mouth, sheer delight on his face, and I know I'm going to get a ribbing about this forever. "I am so glad I drove from Berlin."

I snort and tug on his sleeve, leading him back toward the kitchen.

Sara, despite not being a coffee drinker herself, has the machine on and is pouring two mugs when we get into the kitchen.

"Thank you, Sara," Alwin says and takes a seat at the table. "Join us, yes?"

She glances at me, and I nod.

"I'll just make myself another cup of tea."

"So, I'm sorry, you two are . . .?" Alwin trails off to let us fill in the blank. He's needling me since I already told him we're not together; he just wants me to say it in front of her.

"Roommates," I say firmly.

"And how do you know Chris?" Sara asks Alwin.

"We're colleagues," he says smoothly and winks at me while she's not looking.

He probably thinks I'm doing something seedy—well, seedier than hiding my fame from Sara—and is ready to jump in feet-first to back me up.

I'm reminded of all the times we had to bullshit our way through the industry. Fake it till you make it is very apt, and we often told tales of grandeur to people—promoters, groupies, radio DJs, anyone who would listen and might get us a foot in the door.

"Where are you from, Sara?"

"A small town in Texas," she says. "But lately, I've been living outside of Austin. Still a small town, but near the big city."

"Ah." Alwin puts on a terrible Southern drawl. "Everything's bigger in Texas."

Sara laughs. "That's actually pretty good," she fibs, and there we go. Alwin has charmed her, and I'm just sitting here hoping that he won't try to take her from me. She's not even mine, I think, and then mentally slap myself because I sound like a possessive idiot when in reality, I'm a one-hit wonder.

Because if Alwin's not here to tell me bad news, then he's undoubtedly here to check on my work.

"Have you been to Texas?" Sara asks, and she might take the glint in his eye as flirting—which it is, of course—but it's also Alwin finding this whole thing hilarious.

"I have," he says. "For work."

The work was a sold-out concert in Houston, but Alwin doesn't say that. They do talk about his visit, though, as short as it was, and then about Baden-Baden and the touring around Sara's done, which, she admits, isn't much.

"Listen, I'm going to let you two get to work, or whatever. I'll be in the front room if you need me." She stands up and then pauses, like she's got something to say but changes her mind.

When she disappears into the hallway, Alwin and I both watch her go. He whips his head toward me and switches back to German. "What the hell is going on here?"

I run a hand down my face because any words I put together in my head sound a little crazy. "I met her in town, she needed a place to stay, and I have a shit ton of rooms."

"And she doesn't know who you are?"

"No."

"You bumbled upon the one person in the world who doesn't know who you are and offered her a place to live?"

"To be fair, most Americans don't know who I am," I point out. "They may have heard of the band but not of me. And that is true for a lot of Europeans too."

Alwin leans closer. "What do you get out of this arrangement?"

"I told you."

"No," he says, shaking his head. "Don't tell me she needed a place to stay because while I'm sure it's true, there's more to it than that. What are you getting out of this?"

"I'm not sleeping with her."

"I didn't say you were, but thanks for the heads up." He grins, and I throw my spoon at him, and it clatters against the wall when he ducks.

"She's not for you either."

He fixes me with a look. It's a look that reminds me of when he convinced me to join the band. He was at me for months trying to get me busking with him, and I know that Alwin is stubborn as a mule.

"Fine." I sigh. "This place is big and lonely and empty, and I thought that having someone around might unlock some secret deep inside my brain."

He laughs, the fucker. "Aw, you missed us. Is she your muse?"

"No."

I don't tell him that, lately, it's kind of felt like she is. I've written a few things that aren't total crap, but I know I can do better. I have to do better. How could I follow up the hit single that won us Eurovision with something that is mediocre? Despite Marcus telling me there's nothing wrong with hiring an outside songwriter, I worry that our band is *special* and *no one would do us justice.*

It's not fucking rational, okay?

"Come on," I tell him. "Let's go make some noise."

Back in our early days, "make some noise" was literal. Now, at least today, anyway, it means let's read each other's lyrics over and over again, playing with intonations and cadences until we're exhausted.

"This one's not bad," Alwin says for the third time today. It makes me want to fucking smack him.

"What's this one?" he asks and holds a slip of paper toward me.

I lean into it and squint, reading the two lines. "Ah, Ram got drunk and called me with that suggestion."

Alwin flips the paper over, looking for more. "Just that?"

"Yeah."

He balls the paper up and tosses it over his shoulder. "Next."

Eventually, we grab guitars from their stands and play. There are no amplifiers, just two guys with guitars in a sound-proof room. It reminds me of the start of my career with Alwin, fresh off a failed ska band and looking for something with more edge.

But that was ten years ago. It's been a long slog since then.

"Fuck it," Alwin finally says. "I'm tired. And starving."

I lead Alwin back to the kitchen, and he opens the fridge.

"Help yourself to anything in there," I say, struggling to contain a laugh.

His eyes almost pop out of his head. "What the fuck is this shit? Since when do you eat green things?"

"Ha, ha."

"Seriously, are you a health nut now? Last time I checked, you had the eating habits of my four-year-old nephew."

"Sara's vegan. And she cooks."

"Speaking of Sara," Alwin says, letting the fridge fall closed and looking around as if she'll magically appear.

"Leave her alone," I say. "Want me to order food?"

"You're in the woods out here. What can you get?"

I place a call to a takeaway shop in Baden-Baden, and when I look up, the kitchen's empty. I find Alwin leaning against the door to Sara's yoga studio. She's on her elbows and knees, facing away from us but at an angle, her ass up in the air. My gaze roams over those perky butt cheeks and the bow of her thighs.

I watched some of Sara's videos online. I have a new appreciation for how hard it is but also how fucking sexy Sara is.

And then I remember Alwin is there. He's watching Sara, too, that same appreciation reflected in his eyes.

I tug his shirt to pull him away from the room, but he resists me. "She might be filming," I whisper. Or worse, live, and I don't want to fuck up her videos.

"Hey, y'all," Sara says, projecting her voice. It's not the calm and reserved voice she uses for the camera, but casual. She's raised her ass up into the air, rested her head on the floor, and is walking her toes toward her hands. "I'm not filming," she tells us.

"You're very flexible," Alwin comments.

"And strong," I add on, feeling like I should compliment her too.

"Thanks," she says and grins while still upside-down. Her toes barely touch the ground now, and she carefully bends her knees, which are tucked into her chest, and points her toes at the sky. After a few beats, she gracefully extends one leg and then the other straight up.

"Whoa," Alwin mutters.

Then she folds one leg and then the other, knotting them together.

"Now you're just showing off," Alwin teases her. "What's that pose called?"

Sara makes it look smooth and elegant, but there is a bit of strain in her voice when she answers Alwin. "Lotus Handstand."

We're quiet as she breathes and then carefully untangles her legs and, in an even more impressive display of control, straightens them to the ceiling for a brief moment and then lowers them to the floor, finally taking her weight off her arms. She's sweating and breathing hard, and I'm definitely turned on . . . and I'm sure Alwin is too.

"We've ordered lunch," I say, doing whatever I can to turn our attention away from the V of her legs. "I ordered an extra veggie stir fry if you want it."

"Thanks," she says.

Alwin starts toward her. "You know, maybe I should take yoga lessons."

I grab his shirt and yank him out of the room. "All right, that's enough. Leave Sara alone."

When lunch comes, Alwin and I unpack it in the kitchen.

"Hey Sara," Alwin says in a sing-song voice capped with a winsome smile. "Here's your veggie dish I ordered."

"Thank you."

"Excuse me, I ordered for her."

Alwin ignores me and laces his fingers together, tucking them under his chin and batting his eyelashes at her. I'm often just blown away by how pretty Alwin is when he turns on the charm. His cheekbones stand out, and combined with his pointed chin, he has an elfin quality about him. Right now, his dark hair is chin-length and silky, heightening the androgyny Alwin leans into. "Stay and eat with us."

Sara glances out the window. "We could eat outside."

Alwin hums when he stands and shoots me a look. "How outdoorsy."

Over lunch, Alwin peppers Sara with questions, hopping from one topic to the next. He's fascinated by her life raising Zoe as a single mom, and in turn, he tells Sara stories of party hopping. He name-drops a lot, clearly amusing himself by heightening Sara's curiosity.

Sara says she has to get back to work. She thanks us again, stacks her dishes, and goes back into the house. We both watch her go, and then Alwin's head snaps back to me.

"You are so into her." He smirks.

I roll my eyes. "I'm not. Come on. We're entirely different people."

"True. That woman is a minivan away from a suburban American soccer mom, and you're the least attractive member of a super-star punk rock band."

"The least? Please. I'm hotter than Ram."

"Not before he opens his mouth." Alwin's knee jiggles under the table. "I bet she hates that you smoke."

"She does," I agree.

"You should quit. She'll never want to kiss you when you taste like an ashtray. It's disgusting. You would think that being pan would mean that I've doubled my potential hookups, but, in our lifestyle, since I don't want a smoker's mouth on my dick, I've cut the pool by like seventy-five percent."

"That makes no sense. You can't taste from your dick."

He shrugs. "It's mental. The smoke permeates their mouths. Maybe they have cancer breath. I don't know. But if you want any chance of kissing her, maybe you should cut it back. Like, nicotine patches or gum or, I don't know, replace it with some other oral fixation."

He grins. But the stupid fucker has a point. I change the subject rather than concede. "Are you staying the night?"

"Nah, I'm headed back to Berlin today." He rises. "In fact, now that I can tell Marcus we've actually done some work, I think I'll take off and leave you with your future wife."

"Fucker. Stop being afraid of a little hard work."

He points at me. "Pot." Then points at himself. "Kettle. Twenty euros says that we've already done more today than you do most days."

I throw a balled-up napkin at him, but it falls uselessly to the table.

He grins. "Love you. Talk soon."

I flip him off, but just before the door closes behind him, I shout, "Love you too."

12

Sara

MY DAY IS NOT GOING WELL. AFTER ALWIN'S VISIT YESTERDAY, I recorded two more yoga sessions, but this morning, when I went to edit, I realized that I accidentally nudged a setting on my camera that meant I was just slightly out of focus the entire time.

It wasn't super obvious. But you could tell. And the perfectionist in me was having a hard time convincing myself it would be fine. The part of me that really wanted to get a new video out was trying to say no one could tell.

I think my brain is melting. I have been staring at my computer way too long.

Keeping up with this schedule is hard work. Publishing videos more often is so time-consuming, and I'm not quite getting the traction I thought I would. Yeah, I'm growing, but not as much as I was hoping.

My phone dings next to me, but I am almost done with this video on deep breathing, so I ignore it.

Until it dings again.

And again.

And again.

My curiosity peaked, I unlock my phone and look at the messages.

EMMA

Holy shit, holy shit, holy shit. The guy from the bar is my professor! Red alert! This is not a drill!

JADE

What guy from the bar? When did you pick someone up???

NOOOOOOO

The guy who went down on you???

EMMA

YES! Help! What should I do?

JADE

Ask him for a do-over?

EMMA

JADE!!!

JADE

Okay, okay, where are you now?

EMMA

In an empty classroom. Class is over.

SARA

Did you talk to him?

EMMA

No! What would I say? Hi, remember me? The woman who freaked out when you tried to . . . ARGH. See, I can't even finish that sentence in a text!

SARA

Did he know who you were?

EMMA

Definitely.

JADE

Oh boy.

SARA

> Emma, you are both adults. There's nothing
> to be embarrassed about.

EMMA

There is definitely something to be
embarrassed about. My professor, who I
have to stare at for several hours a week for
the next ten weeks, knows what I taste like.

What I TASTE LIKE.

This is very disturbing.

Eventually, Jade and I coax Emma out of the room she's hiding in so she can go home. I don't blame her for freaking out.

I work for nearly another hour before my phone starts dinging again.

EMMA

I pepper-sprayed him.

FML

JADE

What? How? I don't . . .

EMMA. WHAT IS HAPPENING RIGHT NOW?

EMMA

I thought he was following me. I didn't mean
to pepper-spray him. It just happened.

JADE

Your pepper spray magically fell out of your
purse and aimed itself at him and fired itself?

EMMA

I got scared!

SARA

I think we need to video chat.

It takes much longer to talk Emma down this time. She's having a shit day, which puts my day into perspective.

I'm being unproductive, and it's frustrating me.

She pepper-sprayed someone who's going to help determine whether she gets her degree or not.

When we convince her to calm down and go home, we hang up, and I get back to work.

Fifteen minutes later, there's a knock on the open door to my studio.

I drop my head into my hands. This is not my day.

"Is this a bad time?"

I lift my head. Chris leans against the doorframe.

"No, it's fine. Sorry. I'm just taking a dozen steps backward today and getting nothing done." I rub my forehead. "Did you need something?"

"Have you eaten?"

I glance at the clock. Jesus. It's almost eight. "No, I haven't."

"Well . . ." Chris pulls his hand out from behind his body and reveals a sandwich on a plate. "Ta-da."

I push back my office chair, feeling lighter already. "You made me a sandwich?"

"Yes." He enters the room, setting the plate to the side of my keyboard. "I didn't do as good of a job as you did, but unlike curry, sandwiches are hard to overcook."

The sandwich looks good—spinach, hummus, some leftover roasted vegetables.

"Thank you, Chris. Really."

He leaves, and I dig into the sandwich. I'm about halfway through it when my phone rings. I expect it's going to be some other dramatic thing with Emma, but instead, it's Zoe.

"Hey, nena, how's it going?"

"Hi, Mom! It's great. I just got back from that trip I told you about, in Innsbruck? The one with the Zaha Hadid designs, remember?"

I eat while Zoe chatters. Since we've come here, these updates are so school-focused. I don't hear much about friends or cute classmates.

Zoe winds down a story about building a model for her latest studio project.

"I was thinking that I might visit Aunt Emma in Rome next month. RHI, DID YOU TURN OFF THE BURNER?"

I wince and hold the phone away from my ear as my daughter shouts at her roommate, Rhianna.

She must get a response because she's back to me. "There's a lot of architecture programs in Rome, so I might be able to connect with someone from my school to go touring with."

"Emma would love to have you, of course. Does that mean you might have some time to come and visit me too?"

"Yes, and that's the real reason why I called," she says. "What are you doing a week from today?"

"It better be hanging out with you, or I hate this game."

"You're hanging out with me." She makes a noise like I've won a prize on a game show.

Okay, *now* I'm having a great day. "Yay! I'll put that in my calendar. I've been researching things we can do here, and there's a hotel with this amazing classical architecture. We can have a nice time at the spa and then come back here and cook. I'll make your favorite meal."

"A spa?" she asks, brightening even more. "That sounds fun."

"And lots of nice walking. The temperature is really comfortable right now. And you'll have your own room."

"We could use the hot tub too," Zoe says, enthusiasm infusing her voice.

"Yes! Oh, nena, it's going to be so good to see you."

"RI ARE YOU SURE YOU TURNED THE STOVE OFF? THEN WHY DO I SMELL SMOKE? Damn it, Mom, I've got to go."

"Wait, what's going on—" She hangs up.

My daughter is killing me.

SARA

Please tell me that the burner is off and the smoke was a false alarm.

ZOE

The burner is off and the smoke was a false alarm.

SARA

Sigh.

I love you.

ZOE

Love you too, mom.

13

Chris

I PICKED A HELL OF A TIME TO STOP SMOKING.

It's only been a few days, but it's fucked with my sleep, I'm jittery, and I've apparently picked up a bad habit of picking at the calluses on my thumbs just for something to do with my hands.

To compound all that, I need a fuck.

Badly.

Ever since Alwin and his stupid, flirty face left, I can't stop thinking about Sara. As in naked, sweaty Sara, who showers in my house and thrusts her ass up in the air and is insanely flexible.

I'm sitting out back drinking a coffee—I'm drinking like eight a day now that I'm trying to quit smoking—and it's early afternoon. A chill has settled in, the signs of summer sucked out by a cold front.

Why haven't I been able to write anything good? I see lyrics all around me, the rustle of leaves or the sheen of water on a surface, but when I write them down, they're all crap.

The back door behind me opens, and I turn. Sara steps

out, and my eyes do this dance over her exposed skin—face, shoulder, cleavage, bare stomach with her cute little belly button I want to stick my tongue in, hand holding a steaming mug, her other shoulder for good measure and back on her face.

"Hey," she says, leaning against the exterior wall. "I just wanted to ask real quick if I could use the hot tub tonight since it's kind of chilly?"

Goddamn, I need a cigarette.

"Yeah, sure."

She asks about logistics of getting it going, and fuck if I know, so we investigate, lifting the lid. Steam escapes with the smell of chlorinated water.

"Well, looks promising," she says. Experimentally, she presses one of the buttons on the side, and despite the daylight, the tub turns a soft blue color. The lights go off with another press, and the next one causes the tub to erupt in bubbles.

She looks at me, grinning, her cheeks flushed from the warmth with wisps of hair curling in the humidity.

"I guess the landscapers that come keep up with it."

"Awesome."

We set the lid back down.

"I'll use it after dinner, so I won't be in your way."

I shrug, but in my head, I'm thinking about how she's going to be wearing a bathing suit. Will it be one piece or two? Sexy as fuck boy shorts? A teasing sporty top like she wears around the house?

In fact, it's kind of all I can think about as we separate and work for the day—well, Sara works. I fantasize about her in a bikini.

I'm trying to come up with the next line for a chorus that needs to rhyme with "dorn," but my eyes keep drifting to the clock. Six fourteen. Six twenty-three.

Is she having an early dinner?

I crack open the door to my studio and sniff the air. It smells good, like cumin and onions. *Banana Pancakes* by Jack Johnson plays, and Sara hums along with it while kitchenware clatters.

Twenty minutes later, I crack the door again. The smell still lingers, but the kitchen is quiet.

I'm not sneaking. I'm just walking casually in my own house, glancing out the window . . .

"Hey."

I suppress a jump at Sara's voice behind me. She's sitting in the corner of the room, reading, looking at me with her eyebrows drawn in confusion.

"Are you all right?"

"Yup," I say, "Just, uh, getting some water."

"Okay." She looks back down at her e-reader.

In the kitchen, I pour myself a glass of cold water. Sara has cleaned, and several things sit in the drying rack, and she has wiped the counters. On the stove, a pot gently simmers, the steam barely escaping.

Okay, I've probably got at least a half hour before she's out in the hot tub.

"Smells good," I say while walking back from the kitchen, glass in hand.

After half an hour, I crack the door again. Dishes clattering and water running.

Fifteen minutes later, all is quiet. The daylight is giving way to gray outside, the dishes from Sara's dinner are in the drain, and there's no sign of Sara.

Fuck it. I'm having a smoke.

I sit outside and light up my cigarette, body sagging with relief. The night is still and quiet, the lights from the house forming a perimeter of bright lights and harsh shadows before rapidly fading to darkness.

I try to make the cigarette last. Just this one, I tell myself. Surely Sara will be out soon, and then I can go back inside.

She's not out by the time I get to the last bit.

Okay, one more.

Because I'm a shit human with no self-control, it's four cigarettes by the time the door opens behind me. Sara doesn't say anything at first, and I close my eyes. I've been lingering, waiting to catch a glimpse of Sara before she gets in the hot tub because it's all I have been able to think about today.

"Chris?" Sara's voice comes from in front of me. I open my eyes, and, fuck, the waiting and the guilt over the cigarettes are worth it.

Knotted on the top of her head, her hair reflects the harsh lighting. The bathing suit is a one-piece that is modest up top, wide straps that come down to a high-cut neckline, but it's cut high at her thighs too.

Sara leans in, peering at me, and I realize she can't see my face in the shadows. Probably for the best.

"Is it still all right if I use the hot tub?" One arm holds a bath towel and her e-reader, the other a glass of wine.

"Yeah, of course," I gesture with my half-burnt cigarette and then snub it out, rising to help her remove the cover. I turn my back as she sets her things up on the shelf in arm's reach.

I should go inside. I've had four cigarettes and wasted most of my day, and I've seen what I wanted to see.

There's a small splash of water and then a moan. It's small, almost more of a sigh, but my body responds. My pants do nothing to hide my erection, so I face the yard, staring into the darkness and willing my feet to move.

What am I waiting for? The willpower to walk away or the lapse of control to turn around and look at Sara?

I give in.

Sara sits up to her chin in the water, her eyes closed. A lump of disappointment sits in my chest.

Wet, slippery women have invited me to join them countless times in hot tubs. My hot tub memories are full of drunken Ram and women making out and the slide of skin and casual fucks.

This moment is anything but. With her eyes closed, head tilted back, tension leaching off of her, Sara could be a nymph or sprite.

And here I stand, staring at her, the big bad wolf.

Out of all the women I could lust after, I've picked my sweet, wholesome roommate.

14

Sara

It's a little hard to pay attention to my cooking when Chris is outside looking all broody and contemplative.

Last night, the hot tub was supposed to be relaxing. The cool air had nipped at me, the heated water soaking my body that was sore from a particularly grueling advanced class I had recorded the day before.

But that was nothing compared to catching Chris staring at me. He looked away quickly, but it was enough for me to tighten with need.

I've seen more of Chris in the week since I returned from Rome than I had the three weeks prior. While we're not exactly doing stuff together, we both seem to be gravitating toward spending time around each other. Instead of being back in his studio, Chris often sits on the couch and writes while I sit at the kitchen table. We're in sight of each other, and sometimes, when he's not paying attention, I look up and watch him work.

He doodles a lot. I find spiral notebooks everywhere or

pages he ripped out, his frustration apparent even in the drawings.

Tonight, while I'm preparing my dinner, he's outside again. It's dark out, the days getting shorter. His notebooks cover the table, the floodlights illuminating the space of the patio but not much else. The Black Forest beyond is a void that the light can't touch.

Chris tilts his head back in the chair, and I wonder if he can see the stars or if the lights are blinding him. His hair is in a bun, which is how he usually wears it when he's working. Earlier in the day, it's up at the top, but as time moves on, it gets looser and migrates down his scalp. He redoes it constantly, but he also lets his hands wander and play with the bun, tug at it, absentmindedly pull it apart.

My phone pings with a message from Tessa. Luc's visiting her this weekend, and they've been doing fun things around Tavira.

TESSA

You won't believe what I did today

I went to a topless beach! With Luc!

There's a picture attached, though it's PG—Tessa and Luc from the shoulders up, with a wide beach and giant cliffs behind them.

TESSA

I knew this was a thing, but I've never done it
before.

EMMA

Were there a lot of people around?

TESSA

Some. Now that summer is over, it's not as
crowded as it was.

Honestly, I only lasted about five minutes
before I put my top back on again.

But Luc's having a good time . . .

LOL

Movement catches my eye.

Chris is standing up, ripping page after page from his notebook and flinging it away. Of course, it's paper, so it doesn't go far, but then he picks up his mug and flings it out into the darkness. Apparently, that's more satisfying, so he grabs the closest thing with some weight—his chair—and flings it too.

I sprint for the door and get outside in time to hear the second chair crash into the bushes.

"Chris!" I shout, and he startles.

He's breathing hard, wide-eyed, angry at himself, the world, something.

"What are you doing?" I strive to keep my voice calm.

"Fucking shit up." He gestures out to the lawn and turns to glare at me. "Fucking everything up."

"You're not—"

"You." Chris takes a step toward me and then another. I swallow at the look on his face, the heat in his gaze. I've drawn his anger away, pulled his emotions outward instead of inward, but as he stalks toward me, that anger cracks and fizzles into desire.

"Me?" The word is breathy, and the band of my sports bra is too tight around me. I can't get enough air. Chris draws near until we're toe-to-toe.

"Yes, you," he says, and it's low and careful. "With your sports bras and your wholesomeness and your cheerful attitude."

He's looking down, those cheekbones angled at me, and

those lips, the lips that I touched when my curiosity got the better of me, are right at my eye level. I take a deep breath, my breasts brushing against Chris's chest.

"Do you hate those things?" I whisper.

"No," he rumbles. "I fucking love them."

His hand snakes up to cup the back of my neck and pull me toward him, crushing my mouth against his. This kiss is demanding and hot, all tongue and teeth and anger and frustration, and instead of tempering him, forcing him to slow down so we can both realize what a colossal mistake this is, I bite his lip.

Chris groans, pressing me back into the door. That vibration echoes through him and into me as he presses his body against mine. His cock is hard on my belly. His other hand comes to my neck, and his two thumbs press into the soft underside of my chin and tilt my face up.

His tongue is in my mouth, the barbell a strange invasion. It clacks against my teeth and shocks me out of my lusty haze.

What am I doing?

All the things that lust blocked out roar in: the faint hint of cigarettes, the metallic taste, the fact that this kiss is not born of emotions I invite into my life. Anger and frustration only lead to bad decisions.

My hands grip Chris's forearms between us. The skin shifts underneath my palm as Chris grows more restless.

I have to stop him now.

I push hard, but Chris gives at the slightest pressure, and I thank god the door is holding me up; otherwise, I would have stumbled.

We stand there panting at each other.

Chris swallows. His gaze flutters all over me, over my kiss-swollen mouth, my heaving breasts, my hand on the doorknob.

"Shit." He runs a hand over his head. "Sara, I'm sorry."

"It's fine," I say quickly. I swallow and hold out a hand, trying to calm my thoughts. "It's fine." That sounded calmer and more collected. "I'm going to get back to work, okay?"

Without waiting for an answer, I twist the knob and escape, power walking to my desk and putting my headphones on. I go through the motions, opening up a file in my editing software and hitting play, but my eyes unfocus right away.

My body is screaming at me to go back out there and kiss Chris again. The desire that shot through me was like being woken up from a deep sleep by fireworks, a desire that had laid dormant all this time.

But I don't go back out there. Kissing Chris would be a mistake. That one kiss shouldn't have even happened.

Except I replay that kiss in my head over and over and over.

———

CHRIS COMES INTO THE KITCHEN THAT NIGHT WHILE I'M cooking. I look up from the vegetables I'm chopping, watching as he braces himself against the island counter.

"Sara, I'm sorry. I didn't mean to scare you." His bun is sagging, hair falling loose around his face, signs that he's been messing with it.

"You didn't scare me. I'm worried."

He presses the heels of his hands into his eyes and mutters, "Me too."

I put the knife down and cross my arms. "Let's talk it out," I urge. "Maybe I can help."

Chris lets out a long breath. "Okay."

I open the fridge. "Wine?" I ask as I pull out a half-drunk bottle of Riesling.

He shakes his head and disappears to the mini bar in the living room. Glasses clink, and he returns with a glass tumbler with an inch of dark liquid and a bottle of whiskey. He straddles the bar stool, and I hold my wine glass up. "Prost."

"Prost." He clinks his glass to mine, and while I take a sip, he knocks the whole thing back. I lean against the counter while Chris pours himself another finger of whiskey.

"What's going on?"

He's quiet for so long I think he might not answer, but then he sighs and confesses. "I'm stuck."

"I gathered," I tease, giving him a small smile, but he's not ready for that yet, so he lets out a noise like a harrumph and looks away.

"I made this thing, and it was so good, and people loved it, and they want more from me, but I don't know if I have more. Everything I work on is crap now. I'll just be some guy who did a thing and then disappeared into obscurity again. Not a guy who . . . who . . ."

He fishes around for the right words and says something in German. "I want to be the guy who leaves a mark. I can't do that if I don't do more than just this one thing."

"Okay," I say slowly. "What have you done to get yourself out of the rut?"

Chris gestures to the house. "I came here to remove myself from distractions, to get out of the city and . . . I don't know. Get in a better headspace?"

"It sounds more like you are trying to change who you are. Why do you think you need to change yourself?"

He glares at me. "I just know. I just feel the emptiness inside my brain that tells me I need to change if I want to be good enough for the band."

Well, that's a can of worms to open. "Okay, but what did you actually change? You moved your person in regards to space, but you are still the same you. How can you change things up and become a different you?"

"I don't know!" he says, anger and frustration coloring his voice.

He glares into his drink while I heat a bit of broth in a wok, allowing bubbles to form at the edges before I toss in my vegetables.

"I heard once that impostor syndrome is your brain getting ready to level up," I tell Chris.

"Impostor syndrome?"

"Yeah, like when you think everything you do is crap and you aren't a success and nothing's good enough. It's just your brain working out how to do things better. Starting over and over again and practicing to get better."

Chris is quiet, and I let the sizzle of the vegetables be the only noise.

"How do you get out of it?" he asks quietly.

I shrug. "I guess you keep going. Power through. But it doesn't hurt to change things, right?"

"I don't know what to change," he admits.

"Look, I'm going to offer these suggestions because they're things I can help you with. Maybe the answer is, like, skydiving or fried Twinkies, but you're stuck with me, so I'm going to suggest you try meditation or yoga."

I can see that he tries not to wrinkle his nose at the suggestion.

"Look, do fifteen minutes of mindfulness with me every day for a week. What is there to lose?"

"That doesn't seem like enough."

I pick the wok up and shake the vegetables, flicking them around in the pan to cook them evenly. "Okay, well then, do an hour of yoga, fifteen minutes of mindfulness, wake up at six a.m. every morning, go for a run, and switch to clean eating."

Chris finally smiles. "Okay, fifteen minutes of mindfulness it is."

I laugh. "Have dinner with me, and then we can do fifteen minutes of mindfulness."

His smile is still there, and he slips into teasing me. "I guess it's better than throwing chairs."

"Cheaper, for sure. You may have just lost your security deposit on this place."

15

Chris

Mindfulness isn't what I expected it to be. I thought it would be boring as fuck, but it's hard.

Sara and I sit in her yoga studio, cross-legged on the ground. Or, at least, she sits cross-legged. When she sees how inflexible I am, my ankles barely crossed and my knees up in the air, she suggests I sit against the wall and on a towel to 'elevate my hips.'

"You have really tight hip flexors," she says. "Maybe you should be doing yoga."

"Baby steps," I grumble, and she flashes a smile at me.

"Fine, fine. Mindfulness and healthy foods are a good start."

I nearly say that a few meals don't mean I'm committing to healthy foods, but I keep my mouth shut.

"Okay. We're going to do a body scan, and the point is to focus on your body and the things you are feeling and sensing. If your mind wanders, it's okay. Don't feel bad about it, but gently guide yourself back to the practice. We'll start by paying attention to our breath."

We sit there, eyes closed, as Sara narrates in a calming tone, taking deep breaths. My mind does wander a lot, especially to the lyrics I'm trying to work on, but she magically seems to know when it does and reminds me to return my attention to my breath. I fidget, too, popping knuckles and scratching itches, but aside from speaking, she doesn't move at all.

Next, we focus on different parts of our body from the top down, visualizing breathing into and out of that part.

"Okay, you can open your eyes now."

I do, and she smiles at me.

"How do you feel?"

"Like I'm really bad at mindfulness."

She laughs. "Like everything else, you'll get better with practice."

I bite my tongue against saying that the last thing I need to add to my to-do list is another thing to fail at; I'm already failing the band.

When we leave the studio together, Sara turns off the lights and closes the door behind her. She retreats to her room, and I sit down to try to write more. I don't feel different. Nothing changes, really, the words are still crap, but I keep trying.

The next day, when I get up and walk into the kitchen in the early afternoon, there's a note on the fridge.

Try something different today . . . like this sandwich.

There's a plate in the fridge with a colorful sandwich on it, thick with green, red, and yellow. I eat it for my breakfast with some coffee and have a one-man jam session in the studio until dinner, when I eat with Sara, and we do mindfulness again.

And this becomes our routine.

On the second day, I write something that I don't think is half bad. Something I might be able to pass on to Alwin or Marcus, and they might say it's usable.

On the third day, we finish our post-dinner mindfulness, and Sara moves over to sit against the wall with me. "How do you feel?"

"Well," I start, "I'm still absolute crap at this mindfulness."

"Has your work improved at all?"

"A little. And I'm definitely less angry about it, so that's a start."

She lifts an eyebrow. "So, not fully converted yet, but maybe you want to keep going?"

I pluck at the bracelet around my left wrist, a leather braid June gave me once. I think about Sara's yoga practice and how I'm more intrigued by it now. It might be a combination of having seen her practice and a desire to watch her do more, or maybe it's that I have actually written something worthwhile. Even if it was just the one song.

"We can keep going," I allow.

Her face lights up, and okay, that was worth it. I might regret it tomorrow, but I'm inexplicably pleased to have made Sara happy.

She claps her hands together and wiggles, nudging me. "Okay, new after-dinner routine: fifteen minutes of mindfulness."

"All right," I agree.

Sara puts a hand on my arm and squeezes. "I think it'll be good for you." Before I can respond, though, she's up and stretching, throwing her arms over her head and on her tiptoes. Now that the weather is getting cooler, she's taken to wearing a large hoodie with her yoga pants, and it's disappointing not to see her in sports bras anymore. I suppose I could turn the temperature up.

"I'm off to bed," she says, interrupting my thoughts. "Good job today. See you tomorrow."

16

Sara

I'M AN HOUR EARLY TO PICK ZOE UP FROM THE TRAIN, AND I'M too excited. It's been a month since I last saw her in Munich.

For the past three days, Chris and I have had a more solid routine together. In the evenings, I cook us both dinner, and then we practice mindfulness. I'm not expecting any miracles, and it's only been three days, but there's been no more chair-throwing.

Or kissing.

I park Chris's car and spend some time walking through the area around the train station. The station itself is quaint, with a large clock above the entrance and an open-air platform. Some signs are in German and English, telling me where to buy tickets or smoke—which makes me think of Chris—but there are also advertisements in German for the local museums and other destinations served by Deutsche Bahn, the national railway company. Zoe took the first train after her Tuesday class was over, so it's late afternoon, and there are some commuters around.

I wait inside, impatiently tapping my foot. I check my

phone. I order a chai tea with almond milk from the nearby coffee shop.

I haven't been able to get the kiss out of my head. Aside from the faint taste of cigarettes, it was a good kiss. A really good kiss.

Actually, what was even better was the lead-up to it. I replay in my head over and over again the way Chris stared at me while he approached, the press of his thumbs under my chin, that moment just before the kiss when everything coiled inside of me.

In the train station, I clench my thighs together. I've used my vibrator every night since that kiss, but I'm still so goddamn horny.

I need a distraction, which is why it's perfect that Zoe is here. We can finally do all the things I wanted to do with her, and I'll get a break from thinking about my roommate. It's chilly, but we'll picnic anyway. I'm making those mushroom crepes again, but we are not going to the baths.

Finally, finally, my baby girl is one of the people coming out of the stream from the platform, and all the worries that have been niggling in the back of my head melt away because Zoe shrieks and launches herself at me.

"Oh, I missed you," I say into her hair as we hold each other tight. For so long, it's been just the two of us against the world, and even though I know we both have to go do our own things, it's felt like a part of myself is missing.

"I missed you too, Mom," Zoe says, pulling back and sweeping her hair out of her face. It's her father's hair, thick and dark, wavy at the length she keeps it at, just past her shoulders. It's been amazing and heartbreaking to watch my girl grow up and show more and more of the Argentinian heritage her father gave her.

"Is this all you brought?" I gesture to her cross-body bag. She's got a reusable water bottle clipped to it, but otherwise, everything she brought fits into a bag the size of a laptop.

She shrugs. "Yeah. It's only a weekend, and I didn't want to bring any of my schoolwork with me. And I figured if I need anything clothes-wise, I can borrow yours."

That makes me smile. Ever since she was about sixteen, we've been about the same size, so as Zoe got older, our two closets became absolute mayhem. When she went off to college, most of my favorite pieces of clothing disappeared.

I lead us toward Chris's car while asking about her trip here. As we approach, I press the clicker to unlock it.

"Whoa, Mom. What are you driving?" Zoe stops and stares.

"This is Chris's car," I say. Yeah, it's definitely not my taste in cars, and I cringe every time I fill it up at the gas station. The first time I had to call Chris because while I could guess that diesel in German was diesel in English, I wanted to make sure that benzin was gasoline before I filled the tank.

"Okay, one: this is a gas-guzzler, so picturing you behind the wheel is making my brain explode. Two: this is a G-Wagon."

"A G-Wagon?" I stop and look at the car, tilting my head. It's one of those kinds of cars that looks like it should be off-roading, but I'm one hundred percent confident it's never even touched mud, like most Jeep-looking SUVs I've seen around Austin. While I haven't enjoyed the gas mileage, I have enjoyed the space in the back for groceries, but I am completely baffled by the lack of cup holders. The manufacturer is Mercedes, but other than that, I know just as much about cars as you would expect from someone who, until recently, had owned a Honda Accord for the past ten years.

"What's a G-Wagon? And, excuse me, when did you become car savvy?" I open my door and climb in, starting the car up while Zoe gets in her side. We both have to stretch a little to climb into our seats.

"One of my roommate's friends is big into cars." Zoe wiggles in the seat. Once she has her seatbelt on, I pull out of the spot. "Leather. Fancy. Mom, Chris just lets you drive this car? You know it's like a hundred-and-fifty-thousand-dollar car, right?"

Zoe and I both pitch forward when I accidentally press on the brakes too hard. I'm half in, half out of the parking spot.

"What?"

"You know Chris is rich. Your guest room is so fancy."

"Yeah, but I can't crash his guest room!"

"Challenge accepted," Zoe teases—I hope. She reaches forward and presses on a flat surface of the console, which pops up and reveals two tiny cup holders.

"How did you know that was there?" I ask as I inch the car forward—carefully—and do an approximately twelve-point turn to get out of the spot without coming too close to any other cars.

Zoe shrugs. "Lucky guess." After a few moments of fussing with it, she can't get her water bottle to fit in the cupholder, so she closes it up and holds the bottle in her lap. "What did you say Chris does again?" she asks while running a hand over the dashboard.

"He's an artist. The place he's renting is pretty nice, so I guess it makes sense that he has a fancy car too."

"What kind of art?" For part of her architecture coursework, Zoe has had to take art and art history classes, though I'm sure that nothing she's studied has been modern, so what are the odds that she would be familiar with Chris's work?

"You can ask him all about it," I tell her as we pull onto the B500.

The trip is quiet, Zoe taking in the sights and scenery. I want to point out everything I can to her, wanting her to like this little town I've chosen to be my home for the time being. Instead of taking the Michaelstunnel, which goes underground, I drive through town, pointing out the architecture as we pass by and asking questions.

She does her best to answer them but laughs when I ask

her about the style. "Mom, I'm studying environmental design. And my classes on the History of Architecture have been very classic-centric so far—Roman and Greek ancient stuff. I don't know much about German styles."

"Okay, okay," I say. "As long as you're learning something."

"I am," she assures me and then tells me about her latest studio project.

When we pull into the driveway of the house, Zoe gawks. "What. Is. Happening. This isn't where you've been living."

I laugh and get out of the car.

"Shut up. Oh my god. This guy is so rich." She turns to me. "Mom, you have to date him."

"Hush," I say, glancing at the windows like Chris is lurking in one watching us and listening. "I'm not dating him."

"But he's rich. And you told me he's hot." Zoe slams the car door.

"I did not say hot. And we have absolutely nothing in common," I say as I open the door into the kitchen.

"Okay, Aunt Jade says he's hot. Have you at least seen him naked?"

"Oh my god! Hush, you. You've been spending too much time with Aunt Jade."

"You have seen him naked," she crows.

I ignore my daughter. "Chris?" I call out. He doesn't answer, and the house is quiet. It's early evening, so he's usually in his studio anyway. "He's probably working. You'll meet him later, but for now, let me show you your room."

There's a lot of gawking and squealing, though, at one point, Zoe wrinkles her nose. "How old is this guy? You'd have to be, like, in your sixties to enjoy this decorating style."

"It's a rental," I say as I lead her up the stairs. I show her the guest room and let her freshen up while I go back downstairs. When Zoe joins me, I've got a bottle of wine open and am prepping for dinner.

"What are we making tonight?" Zoe asks, helping herself to the second glass I poured.

"Those wild mushroom crepes you love and some roasted veggies."

"Yum." Her eyes light up. "What can I do?"

An hour later, the vegetables are in the oven, we have a stack of crepes, and Zoe is starting the vegan Bechamel sauce. A door opens and closes in Chris's wing over the soft music we've got playing on the Bluetooth stereo.

"Chris!" I call out. "Zoe's here."

"Coming," he calls back.

The pan for the sauce is just hot enough, so I add the flour into the oil and stir. I have to keep a close eye on this lest the flour burn. Zoe's sitting at the counter, sipping her second glass of wine, when Chris steps into the room behind her. "Chris, this is my daughter, Zoe," I say, turning my attention back to the pan. "Zoe, this is my roommate, Chris."

Chris's low voice says, "Hello," and a glass shatters.

17

Chris

glass all over the kitchen floor, but Sara steps into mom mode.

"Oh my god," Zoe says. Sara doesn't notice that Zoe's looking at me and not the glass on the floor.

"Don't move. I'll get the broom."

"Oh my god," Zoe repeats, her fingers pressed into her lips, and I don't know why it didn't occur to me that this would be a thing this weekend. Having Sara treat me like a normal person has lulled me into a false sense of security, and that security is being yanked out from underneath me.

"Mom," Zoe says, her tone soft. When her mother doesn't respond—can't hear her over the music and the clatter of cleaning supplies in the utility closet, I assume—Zoe raises her voice. "Mom! MOM!"

"I'm coming. Relax, sweetie."

Zoe stands up abruptly and then shrieks when her bare feet come in contact with a piece of glass. I don't have shoes on either.

"Stop!" Sara cries. "You're not wearing shoes. Why is no

one wearing shoes?" she laments, never mind that she herself is barefoot.

Zoe's back on the stool, fanning herself and quietly chanting under her breath, "Oh my god, oh my god, oh my god." I think she's forgotten about the glass in her foot now.

Brusque and business-like, Sara sweeps a path from the closet to where I stand, and then she hands me the broom and the dustpan. "You, sweep."

I sweep. Zoe stares at me. And Sara bends down to attend to her daughter's injured foot.

"Mom," Zoe whispers.

"Yeah, sweetie?"

"Why is Chris Rächer here?"

Sara's brow wrinkles. "Who's Chris Rächer?"

I clear my throat. "That's my stage name."

"Your stage name?"

I bend down to sweep the glass into the dustpan, and Zoe answers for me. "Mom, he's the guitarist for Verduistering."

"You're a guitarist?" Now Sara looks up at me. "In a band?"

Zoe's looking a little pale, and I'm not sure if it's the small amount of blood on the paper towel Sara's pulled away from her foot or the sheer mortification over her mom not knowing who I am. "Verduistering won Eurovision last year," she whispers to her mother.

"Oh, wait. I think I remember Jade telling me about that. It's like American Idol, right?"

"Mom," Zoe wails, broken out of her shock by her mother's lack of coolness. "You've been living with one of the members of the hottest rock band in the world, and you didn't even know! This is so unfair."

Sara ignores her daughter. "Chris, can you get a first aid kit for me? I think there's one under my bathroom sink."

I know there's one in the half bath off the front entrance,

so I grab that instead, and when I step back into the kitchen, Sara and Zoe are having an argument via whispers.

Sara thanks me with a tight smile. "Can you give us a few minutes?"

"Sure," I say. "It was nice to meet you, Zoe."

A noise vaguely resembling a titter comes out of her mouth, and her cheeks darken in a blush.

I retreat back to my studio and leave the door open. Sara's never been in here, but I guess there's no reason to close it now. I pick up one of the four guitars and play absent-mindedly.

I should have said something to Sara before Zoe arrived. It was lucky for me that I went as long as I did without her knowing, but now this is going to be a problem. Zoe's clearly a fan, and I close my eyes when I realize I should have asked her not to say anything to anyone before I left the kitchen. The last thing I want is to have my location splashed all over social media.

Zoe wouldn't mean any harm by it, but it would definitely ruin this small, quiet thing that Sara and I have had going here.

There's a knock, and I look up to see Sara in the doorway. Her gaze roams around the room, taking in the dark wallpaper, the computer, the mixing board, and various paraphernalia I have strewn around, including a lot of scratched-out papers.

"I'm sorry," I start. "I should have told you."

She steps in and leans against a bare spot on the wall, her hands behind her back. Her eyes drift down to where my hands rest on the guitar. "Yeah, you should have." Sara's voice is tight with confusion and hurt. "And I should have asked you. I feel like an idiot. I assumed it was a visual art. Acrylics or oils or something. Didn't you say you did paintings?"

"I do. Just as a hobby, though. And not here."

"But those sketches you did. Those were fantastic."

"They were just sketches."

"Well, I assumed. And you know what they say about assumptions."

"No?"

"It makes an ass out of you and me."

It takes me a moment to figure it out in my head, and when I do, I want to smile, but Sara's glowering. "I hadn't heard that one before."

"It's a weird idiom. I bet German is full of weird idioms too."

"Yes," I say, and then I try to think of one, but before I can continue, she interrupts.

"Can you play something for me?"

I suspect that Sara will not be a fan of my music, and that's okay. She listens to mellow songs: Jack Johnson, Matt Kearny, Death Cab for Cutie. I strum a few chords of *Passenger Side,* and she smiles at me.

"How about some of your music?"

I look at my guitar, too uncomfortable to meet her eyes, and play a few cords from the song that won us Eurovision. The song I wrote.

When I let it trail off, she's still watching me. It feels like a judgment being passed, and I know I've fallen short. My life here with Sara is not the real world. The real world, in the form of Zoe, has crashed into our little bubble.

"You look pretty different when you're in the band," she says. "Zoe showed me some videos. I asked her not to say anything to anyone else, by the way."

"Thank you." I set the guitar down on its stand and swivel the stool around to face her again. "We have stage personas, I guess you could say."

Her eyes travel to my hair, which is swept up in a tidy bun at the back of my neck. It's a sandy blonde now, my natural color, but it's usually dyed black. My clothing choices for as long as Sara's known me have been sedate. If she watched the video of our performance at Eurovision, Sara would have seen me with contouring, vibrant eyeshadow, painted nails, and an all-black outfit.

I wonder what she thinks of it, but I can't open my mouth to ask.

"I feel stupid," she admits. "Why didn't you tell me?"

"I liked you not knowing." Her face falls, and I try to explain. "You and I have been here in this"—I wave my hand around to encompass the entire house—"domestic life. At first, it was refreshing, but then I thought you knowing who I am would change things." When Sara just stares at me, I add, "For the worse."

I guess we'll find out how bad the change will be.

Then the smoke alarm goes off.

18

Sara

THE BECHAMEL SAUCE IS A BURNT CRUST IN THE PAN. BY THE time we get the doors and windows open, the pan outside, the alarm turned off, I give up, and we eat peanut butter sandwiches.

Chris eats his quickly and then leaves, and I don't blame him. My daughter has no chill. She's been staring at him and pretty much ignoring any attempt Chris or I make at polite conversation.

"Tomorrow we'll go get mani-pedis and then have lunch out," I say, trying to talk about—think about—anything other than Chris.

"You would tell me if you were sleeping with him, right?"

"No! I mean, no, I'm not sleeping with him. Yes, I would tell you if I was." Well, I would have told her before, but if I started sleeping with him now, I'm not so sure I'd tell her anymore. But that's a ridiculous thought because I'm not going to sleep with him.

"Have you met any of his bandmates?"

"I haven't—" I cut myself off when I realize who Alwin must be. "Yeah, I met this guy, Alwin."

Zoe puts her hands over her face. "You met," her finger twitches next to her eyebrow, "the lead singer?"

"Oh, for Pete's sake, Zoe. They are just people." I pick up my plate, empty save breadcrumbs, and stalk over to the sink.

"No, Mom, they are definitely not just people. Alwin was on the cover of *Vogue*. Chris is incredibly talented, obviously rich, and he's in a rock band. They party a lot. His drummer OD-ed last year. Why the hell is Chris Rächer here playing house with you?"

The way she delivers the last word has me fuming. "What is that supposed to mean, Zoe?"

"Exactly what I said," she shoots back. "Why is he here with you in the middle of bum fuck Germany taking on roommates he doesn't even know and doing yoga and eating vegan food? You're not exactly—"

Zoe bites her tongue. I take a deep breath and count to ten. "I'm going to go to bed." It's early, so early that Zoe opens and closes her mouth in surprise before she nods. "Come on to your room, so you'll be out of Chris's way." I can picture Zoe lingering downstairs until Chris comes out for a smoke break or—heaven forbid—poking around in his wing.

I turn on my heel. Zoe better leave him alone.

When we get upstairs to the guest bedrooms, Zoe flops down on her bed and whips out her phone.

"Don't tell anyone about him, okay?"

"You already said that," she mutters under her breath.

I look up at the ceiling and take a deep breath. "I love you," I say, and she grumbles a vague "I love you" back.

When I get to my room, I know I should shower and get ready for bed, but I bypass all the normalcy and slip under the covers with my phone.

For the next several hours, I go down an insane rabbit hole reading about Chris's career, his personal life, his bandmates.

That there is so much information about one person on the internet is astounding.

And so is Chris. I had vaguely heard of Eurovision before, but it's not a reality show. It's way bigger than that, and Chris's band winning is a huge deal. According to some articles, they toured for several months before returning to Germany to write their next album.

I watch videos of the band, of Chris, until I hear the shower across the hall start up. It's late, and I lay back, trying to clear my mind so I can fall asleep and not think about my rock-star roommate.

———

ZOE'S VISIT WAS OVER TOO QUICKLY. WE DID ALL THE THINGS WE wanted to do; a spa day with manicures and pedicures, hiking, picnicking, shopping.

But every time we came back to the house, Zoe got nervous. She'd try to casually walk through the house to see if Chris was around, only to be disappointed when he wasn't.

I kept us out of the house as much as I could, but when we were home, Chris stayed in his studio with the door shut. I would feel bad under normal circumstances, but I'm still upset.

When I return from taking Zoe to the train station, I drop the keys in the bowl on the kitchen counter and stare out the window. I'm in a bad mood, the specter of Chris's fame hanging over me. I weigh my options: do I try to get some work done or completely give up on the day and binge-watch something?

A binge sounds good.

When I spin toward the stairs, my eye catches on a piece of paper pinned to the fridge.

It's a drawing of a bunny sitting up. There are little movement lines that make me think the bunny is wiggling its nose.

In front of it, the wolf lays on its back, belly exposed and tail tucked.

I'M SORRY.

I HOPE YOU HAD FUN WITH ZOE.

I HAVE AN IDEA. COME SEE ME WHEN YOU'RE READY TO TALK.

The studio door is open and Chris is working on his laptop, so I knock on the frame. He wears over-ear headphones similar to mine, so he can't hear me.

I shift to the side to catch his eye and freeze. On the screen in front of him is one of my videos.

Chris scribbles something on the notepad in front of him, and his foot taps a beat. When I've watched him work before, whatever's been happening is in his head. Right now, it's happening on paper.

I shift again, and Chris catches sight of me. He leans back and pulls off the headphones.

"Hey," he says. "Did Zoe get to the train okay?"

I lean against the doorframe and nod. "Yup." I wave the sketch in front of me. "You have an idea?"

His office chair wheels back, and he reaches to pull a stool over and pats it. "Sit."

I sit.

"Here's what I'm thinking. You're looking for something to go viral to attract more clients for you, both for your Patreon and your private lessons, right?"

"Yeah." I eye him. "This sounds like you're procrastinating your own creative pursuits right now."

"One hundred percent. But I owe you."

"You don't owe me." I cross my arms on my chest. "I'm just mad that you didn't tell me about your job. You let me feel . . . stupid, I guess."

"Once again, I am so sorry. But hear me out. I didn't tell you I was famous, so let me use that fame to help you."

"I'm listening."

"What about some kind of interactive yoga where every move corresponds to a different note or something. Like a jam session?"

"That idea requires both the musician to be familiar with yoga and the yogi to be familiar with music. You're suggesting that I would basically create halfway decent music when I have no musical talent."

"I mean, we could plan something in advance. The yoga routines you do have a repetition to them. You run through a series of poses and then repeat them, not unlike a song with verses and a chorus and a bridge, right?"

I tilt my head to read the pages in front of him, but he nudges me away.

"Just listen. Here's where we could start; low and slow, deep and resonating for the breathing. We could actually lay tracks over each other, with a bass track for the breathing while my guitar plays, but that's up to you. I've written a few bars for different poses, kind of getting the feel for them. Like this one here, mountain pose."

Aw, he remembered mountain pose.

Chris grabs a guitar and plays a riff, then a long, low note, I guess? And again and again, and yeah, it feels like a breath, stretching up and tall.

"Wow," I say.

"Is that a good wow?" he asks.

"Yeah, that's a good wow."

"Good. I've got more."

He plays through several poses, pausing after each one to gauge my reaction. By the fifth one, I'm excited, and I can hardly let him finish before I blurt out, "You've never done yoga before? How did you pick up so much information?"

He tips his chin at his screen. "I watched your videos. Maybe not all of them but most of them. Didn't you notice a big new Patreon supporter a couple of nights ago?"

"Chris!" I smack his arm with the back of my hand. "You didn't have to do that! I would have given you access to the videos for free."

He strums the guitar, but it's absentminded this time. "I'm already getting free mindfulness sessions."

"You don't need me for that. There are podcasts that guide you through fifteen-minute meditations," I say.

"Doing it with you is peer pressure. I want to impress you, so I work harder."

My mouth drops open a little before I catch myself and shut it with a click. "So, what? You'll write music for a yoga video?"

"Yes, and then I'll do yoga with you. Six videos. They'd have to be beginner sessions, but maybe the last one or two you could do an advanced course, and I'll sit it out. Or something like that."

I rub my face with my hands. It's actually a pretty good idea. And for the later sessions, Chris can do the basic poses, and I can do the advanced ones, so we can appeal to a wider audience.

This is above and beyond our roommate agreement. He's offering me a lot of his time and energy and lending me a touch of his fame. I would be an idiot not to take this opportunity to collaborate with him, even if I know he's using it to avoid his own work. I don't think he realizes how much time this is going to take, both for him and for me.

"Six videos is too much. Why don't we do four short sessions?"

"You're the expert."

I still hesitate. This could be a big break, or I could be getting my hopes up too high. Either way, if Chris is willing to invest the time in me, I am too.

"Okay," I say, sticking out my hand. "I'm in."

<hr>

OVER THE NEXT FEW DAYS, WE REPURPOSE THE KITCHEN TABLE, sitting side by side several hours a day and going over the plan for each video. We decide to do one beginner session and three routine videos. We keep them short—fifteen-minute sessions—and also talk logistics.

I have to demonstrate a lot for Chris, and just like that time Alwin was here watching, I feel his eyes on my body. It's distracting.

After agreeing to film these sessions, I'd finally messaged my friends about Chris and the band. All week we've been talking about it, and I bet Emma's relieved we're no longer talking about her professor.

Jade came up with a name for our video series—Rock Steady.

This afternoon, Chris played the final recording of the music for session four. With that, everything was ready to go.

I leaned back in my office chair, which I'd moved from the front room while we worked in here. "We definitely need to film an announcement. Like a "Hey, here's what's coming up next week, be sure to tune in" kind of thing. And I've been wondering if I should do this on YouTube or put it behind the paywall of Patreon," I say.

"Why wouldn't you do Patreon?"

"I can offer Rock Steady for free because it'll be really popular, and then hopefully, people will pay for a private session or for the Patreon. Or I can offer Rock Steady under the Patreon and make money off of it. Which is better for long-term growth? But also, if it's on YouTube, then I'll get subscribers, and the people who really like my stuff will follow me to Patreon; funneling in, you know. But if I put it behind a paywall, then maybe I'll get a bunch of unrelated people, and they'll just leave once the four sessions are over. But then I'll have a boost of income anyway."

"I think you're undervaluing yourself." Chris gives me an

exasperated look. "Do you know how much I get paid per hour in the studio?"

"No, not really."

He tells me, and my jaw drops. "Well, shit." I cross my arms, that feeling like I'm taking up too much of his time resurfacing again. Also—damn. He makes way more hourly as a musician than I do teaching yoga. I squint at him. "This is keeping you from getting your own work done."

Chris shrugs, and I side-eye him. "How many of your own things have you written lately?"

Chris twists his mouth into mock contemplation. "Does being in a better mindset count?"

I make an air-whip and crack it at Chris.

He gives me a half-smile and leans back against his chair. "I was wondering what I should wear for these sessions."

"What do you mean?"

"Do you want," he gestures at himself, "Chris Rächer or Chris Müller?"

"What's the difference?"

"Well, apparently, one is not famous enough to be recognized by Americans," he teases, and I swat at him.

"I want you to do whatever you are comfortable with," I tell him. "Honestly."

He runs a hand over his jaw, thinking. "Maybe for the announcement video, I'll go as close to full-on Rächer as I can. But for the actual sessions, I'll dial it back."

Honestly, I can't picture either. I've seen photos of Chris as his stage persona, but it's a little disconnected and surreal for me. I don't know what to expect when I see this side of Chris in real life.

19

Chris

Working so closely with Sara the past three days, planning this series of videos, proves that my attraction to her hasn't died.

Today we're filming the announcement, so I'm getting ready in my room, applying eyeliner and contouring. We've been discussing yoga and music together, combining our interests, and it's sexy as fuck.

Especially when I watch Sara demonstrate.

My phone rings, which breaks me out of my memories of her bent over, ass up. It's Marcus. "Hello?"

"Hey Chris, how's it going?"

We go through the pleasantries for a few minutes, and then Marcus gets down to business.

"How's the writing?"

"Better," I say, and it's not a lie for the first time in a while. "I have a few songs written that I think might be worth something.

We take some time and go over the best ones I have, and it's an excellent distraction from thoughts of Sara.

"These are good," Marcus says with approval. "You've made a lot of progress lately. With the songs Alwin's got, we might really have something here."

"Alwin's got a song?" This is news to me.

"A few. Most of them might not shape up to much, but one's pretty good."

Marcus says a few lines, and I freeze. That's one of the songs I wrote, a song Alwin and I talked about while he was visiting. I had considered bringing it up to Marcus earlier in the call, but frankly, I thought my more recent stuff was better.

"Alwin wrote that?" I say, trying to keep my voice neutral.

"Yeah, he sent it to me last week. Listen, I think you've made great progress. You've got a few more weeks until the Berlin concert, so let's plan to spend an extra day all together and go over the possible songs for the album."

"Yeah, sure," I say, my thoughts reeling. Is Alwin trying to take credit for my song? Something doesn't sit right, the way Marcus said the lyrics, the way he said that it was Alwin's song.

"Speaking of which, do you need any passes?"

"What?" I ask, having lost the conversation.

"Backstage passes. Do you need any?"

"Uh . . ." I think for a minute, but there's only one person who comes to mind that I really want backstage: Sara. "Yes. One."

"You got it."

Marcus lets me go a few minutes later, and I sit for a while, my mind a jumbled mess.

———

WHILE SARA SETS UP THE CAMERA GEAR, I GET DRESSED IN MY room. While I can't replicate what my makeup artists do, I've tried my best. I dyed my hair a black that washes out, painted my nails black, drew on eyeliner with exaggerated wingtips. I pulled out a set of leather pants and a mesh long-sleeve top.

It's been too long. It's weird, but there's the spark of pre-performance energy here, in this mansion in the Black Forest.

I stop in the studio, grabbing my guitar. Just like a music video, the song is prerecorded, and I'll pretend to play my guitar.

When I step into Sara's studio, she looks up and does a double take.

"Wow," she says, and a different kind of energy sizzles up my spine. Sara's seeing me in the flesh as someone different, someone famous. And not to sing my own praises, but someone with a different "sexual energy"—that's the phrase all the magazines like to use, though I couldn't nail down exactly what it means.

Her gaze travels up and down my body, and I bite my lip to keep my broody musician look going. When she meets my eye again, she flushes.

"Sorry," she says. "It's just different, you know? You suddenly aren't my mild-mannered roommate who occasionally farts on the couch anymore."

"One time," I say. "And I didn't think you could hear me over all the noises you made while you were cooking."

Sara grins, turning her attention back to her camera. "Almost done here."

I have a thought and tilt my head. "Should we be filming this at night? You know, dark energy vibes?"

She snorts. "God, no. Filming at night is hard. It's all sharp shadows and harsh lighting. Besides, this video is supposed to be a bit of a surprise, right?"

"True. Business as usual until I bust in."

She smiles but doesn't take her eyes off the setup. "Can you stand just off the middle of my yoga mat?"

I stand a few places, and Sara makes sure she's backed the camera away enough to fit my whole body in the shot.

"Okay, I think we're ready." She brushes her hands together, then rubs them on the tops of her thighs. "Are you ready?"

I give her a thumbs up and get into position off-camera.

Sara hits record, turns on the music, and begins her sequence of movements.

At first, the music is just deep and resonating bass notes. Sara moves fluidly, gracefully with her breath. A guitar slide hits between notes, and that's the cue; something's different. It's time for me to step in.

I come in from the side, behind Sara, and play the notes. My guitar sits low, my head down, hair hanging in my face. As the music gets more complex, more intricate, so do Sara's poses.

I walk slowly to her other side, fingers moving faster. Standing next to Sara while I play and she practices puts dirty thoughts into my head. I wonder if I could play while she moved around me, curving around my guitar, stretching her foot up and over my shoulder.

But we don't do that now. We don't touch. Sara stays in the confines of her yoga mat, and I keep my eyes on my guitar until I strum the last note.

The final movements and poses are faster, and she's breathing hard next to me. She turns her head.

"What do you think? Should we do it again?"

I lift my chin to the camera. "Let's watch it."

"Okay," she says, nerves replaced with excitement, and prances to the camera. I come up behind her. Sara navigates to the video and hits play.

We both lean in. Sara's a little damp, a little sweaty, but her total focus is on the video.

My focus is on her. I can't look away.

"That came out great!" she says, interrupting my thoughts and nearly popping me in the chin when she straightens.

"Yeah? I mean, yeah, it did."

"Let's record one more time just to be sure."

We do it four more times, actually. The second time I miss my entrance queue, too busy watching her—why? I can watch her do yoga anytime I want. We live together, for fuck's sake—and the third time, Sara isn't happy with the way she placed her foot or her hand or something. The fourth and fifth times are good, I think.

"Okay," Sara says. "I release you from your duties."

"Do you think I should shower, or would you prefer to have Chris Rächer at your dinner table tonight?"

Sara flushes, and my heart skips a beat without my permission.

"Do you like this?" I gesture to myself.

She looks me over, shy suddenly, and shrugs. "It's another facet of you."

I think that's a yes.

20

Sara

CHRIS COMES INTO MY YOGA STUDIO, AND I GLANCE OVER MY shoulder at him and then do a double take. Again.

I'm a professional, I swear. But seeing Chris like this makes it hard to act like it.

On Monday, I edited the two-minute introduction video and posted it that night, announcing that the sessions would start on my Patreon today, Thursday, with a live introductory session. Chris shared it on his social media accounts, and it took off. I watched my Patreon double, triple, and then I stopped doing the math.

Chris dressed the same as before, maybe a little more subdued in the makeup department, but the long dark hair and black nails are still there.

And . . . tattoos. Lots of tattoos because he's shirtless. I haven't seen him bare-chested since my first morning here, and while just last week, for the intro video, he was in a see-through top, the combination of the mesh and tattoos made it easy to forget there was bare skin under there. Now, not so much.

He's also wearing tight yoga pants, which guys wear all the time. My yoga classes back in Texas definitely had more women than men, but there were guys who attended. Some of them were definitely in the hot and buff category, but Chris is something else, especially with the wolf tattoo that snakes around his shoulder to rest its head on his pectoral muscle.

"Is this okay?" Chris's question zaps me out of my staring contest with his tattoo. "I know tight clothes are best so people can see our bodies."

"Yes, thanks. I forgot to mention that."

He smiles. "I've paid attention."

"Um . . ." I gesture at his hair.

He lifts a hand and snaps the band on his wrist. "Man bun?"

"Sure," I say, and Chris grins, the flash of his tongue piercing winking at me.

We've decided to do these sessions live on Patreon. It'll feel more authentic and personable. It also means I'll get the videos out faster and do less editing.

Which is good, because my friends are arriving tomorrow.

Chris sits on his yoga mat—on top of a bolster to elevate his hips—and I make the final adjustments. Our yoga mats are perpendicular to the camera, parallel to each other, with Chris at the front left and me to the back right.

I check the setup one last time; there are already over a hundred people waiting, but I don't tell Chris that. I don't want him to be nervous trying something new in front of so many people.

A few more clicks, and the music is on. It's a simple, slow bass rhythm Chris recorded, just enough to feel electric but slow enough that it's not frantic.

It makes me feel a little badass, and I want to use it for all my yoga sessions now.

I've got my remote clicker, and I settle into Sukhasana,

cross-legged on the floor, and glance over at Chris, who's been watching me.

"Ready?" I ask.

"Ready." He nods and turns back to the camera.

I take a deep breath, in and out, relax my face, and smile. I click the button, the red light turns on, and I greet the watchers.

"Hello and welcome to our first session of Rock Steady. I'm Sara Wallace. Thank you for supporting my Patreon and this project. You may know this man next to me as Chris Rächer, but today he's my beginner student. Chris, have you done yoga before?"

"This is my first time." I can't see his face, but his voice is calm and natural. Of course, he's good at this; I've watched him in dozens of interviews.

"That makes me a yogi to the stars now."

"Someone call *People* magazine," Chris deadpans.

"Maybe work on your bandmates first. We can have a session together before your next concert." I wink at the camera. "All right, so given that Chris is new to yoga, we're going to go over a lot of basics. Session two will reinforce those basics and add some intermediate balance poses. Then we'll have four videos of yoga routines set to rock music, composed and played by Chris. He'll stick to basic moves, and I'll do more advanced options.

"I want to note that Chris has a lot of upper body strength —" He flexes in front of me and kisses his bicep. "—and I have more flexibility, so you'll be able to see the wide variety that yoga covers. Ready, Chris?"

He claps his hands together into prayer. "Ready."

I take us through breathing, some light stretching, and then into sun salutations. When Chris is in downward dog, I get up and gently adjust his poses, explaining to the viewers what I'm doing and why.

We expect that most people watching are pretty new to

yoga and may have come in just to watch Chris or hear the music, but that's okay. My goal is for these sessions to be entertaining and informative and for yoga to come across as badass.

Chris does great, holding poses without complaint, even when his muscles tremor slightly and sweat rolls down his temple.

"Okay, and now back to Warrior One," I say. Chris slowly raises his arms over his head, and I straighten them up. "You can see how we've still got a straight line here." I lean across his body to the side facing the camera and intend to trace a line from his hands to his hips without touching him, but my finger accidentally grazes just below his armpit, and Chris jerks toward me, flailing. "Argh!"

He tilts, and his arms windmill but I'm in the way, and we both end up on the floor, Chris nearly on top of me.

"Sorry! Sorry," I say.

"You tickled me," he accuses. His expression is dour but twitching. He's trying not to laugh.

"I didn't know you were so ticklish," I say from the floor beneath him.

I look at the camera from the ground. "Okay, well, we've learned two things there. One, Chris is ticklish, so use that information as you see fit, everyone, and two, it's okay to fall down as long as you get back up."

Chris takes the hint and stands up, offering me a hand.

"Back to Warrior One," I say, and Chris shakes his head.

We finish the rest of the session. There's no more tickling —accidental or otherwise—and Chris looks great in all the poses, as I knew he would.

"Finally, put your hands to your third eye, and bow. Namaste, and thank you for attending the first Rock Steady."

Chris waves while I grab the remote and turn the recording off.

I immediately flop onto my back. "Oh my god."

"You? You weren't the one doing all the hard work here." Chris rotates so he can look at me.

"Keeping you in line is hard work."

"Did I go off script too much?"

I shake my head. "No, I think that was great. The point is that yoga isn't all serious and quiet, right? Breaking the mold?"

Warm fingers wrap around my ankle and tug. "You did great. Do you want to close up, and then we can celebrate?"

"Celebrate?" I ask, sitting up. "What did you have in mind?"

He just smirks and gets up, wandering out of the room. I watch him go. I already admired his body before, but seeing those muscles work hard and getting up close to his tattoos kicked it up another level.

Honestly, I don't know how many more levels I have.

I stand and unplug everything, shutting the cameras off and spending a few minutes closing my laptop down. I'm sure there will be questions and comments for me to handle later, but if Chris wants to celebrate, I won't say no.

When I leave the studio, Chris is leaning against the kitchen counter, on his phone. Next to him, a chilled bottle of wine is just starting to sweat. He put a shirt on, though it's sleeveless, and having less of his skin exposed just seems to narrow my focus on his arms.

"Step one, wine. Step two . . ." he pulls the freezer open and pulls out a pint. "Vegan ice cream."

I gasp. "What a treat."

I pour while he scoops, and soon, we're seated next to each other at the island, clinking glasses.

"To Rock Steady," he says.

"To discovering you are ticklish live on camera."

Chris smiles and shakes his head. "Please tell me you are ticklish too."

I just smile and shake my head.

He mutters a curse in German, and my phone vibrates on the counter. I'd left it here while recording, so I haven't checked it in a while.

There's a flurry of messages from my friends, the most recent one showing:

JADE

DID HE HAVE A BONER???

I unlock my phone and scroll up to the first unread message in the chat.

TESSA

Everyone's logged on to watch Rock Steady, right?

EMMA

Yup!

JADE

Wow, I hope Sara is really enjoying those tattoos.

TESSA

Is it just me or are they really cute together?

JADE

It's not just you.

EMMA

Did you see the way he just looked at her??

JADE

Y'all, the comments section is going INSANE

"Is everything okay?" Chris asks.

"Um, yeah. My friends were watching the session and I guess the comments are entertaining."

JADE

People are shipping Sara and Chris!

EMMA

What does that mean?

TESSA

Like, people want to see them together.

JADE

Someone says Chris has a boner. They did a time stamp.

DID HE HAVE A BONER???

TESSA

I don't think so. I mean, it's hard to tell, but it just looks like a bulge.

JADE

Those pants don't really hide much tbh.

If he had a boner, we would KNOW he had a boner.

SARA

He did NOT have a boner.

JADE

Well, he should have.

My phone buzzes several times as my friends tell me how great the lesson was and how much they enjoyed our banter.

When I look up, Chris is watching me, a small smile on his face.

I blush and put the phone facedown on the counter. The last thing I need is for my roommate to know my friends were checking out his package and people are shipping us.

21

Sara

THE NEXT DAY, I'M BACK AT THE TRAIN STATION TO PICK MY BEST friends up for our ladies' weekend. It's only been three weeks since Rome, but Jade has a work thing next weekend, so we moved our visit up a week.

Jade and Emma are already here, and Tessa's train arrives in twenty minutes. We squeal and hug and get shushed by an old lady, but I'm just so glad to see them.

"How were your trains?" I ask.

"Fabulous," Jade says. "When are we getting a train from Austin to Houston is what I want to know."

"It was great, but the destination is even better," Emma says sweetly.

"I'm excited to meet your rock star, Sara. And he has single bandmates, so . . ." Jade bats her eyelashes at me. "Maybe you can work out an introduction to break my dry spell?"

I roll my eyes. "Get in line. Zoe vacillates between pining for Chris and asking me to set her up with Alwin."

"You need to tell her she can't have Chris. But also," Emma says, turning to Jade, "you're still in a dry spell?"

"Yes!" she groans. "I'm just not clicking with anyone, and I hate it. Is it the Spanish men? Is there some pheromone I'm giving off that repels them? I don't understand."

"We'll see what we can do here," I offer Jade.

We chat about Jade's work and Emma's classes until Tessa arrives, and there's more squealing.

Once it dies down, Jade clears her throat. "Okay, ladies, don't kill me. But I booked us a session at the baths."

Tessa laughs, and Emma looks mildly horrified. "The naked, co-ed baths?" Emma clarifies.

"Yes," Jade says as we step out the station doors. "You don't have to go if you don't want to. But the baths are open until ten, and I thought we could go after dinner to wind down and relax. It'll be fun, and I think it will help us all be more comfortable with our bodies."

"And their aging process," Tessa says glumly.

"Babe, you are fabulous," Jade quickly tells her.

"I know," Tessa says, making us laugh. "I mean, thank you. Sometimes though, being with a younger man has its downsides."

I pop open the back of the car—the very expensive car that I'm still handling with kid gloves now that I know just how much it costs—and start piling the luggage in, thankful for the gas-guzzler once again.

"Luc hasn't said anything to you, has he?" Jade squints at Tessa, possibly thinking about inflicting damage on Luc if the answer is yes.

"No, of course not. He's great. But it's harder than I thought it would be to be with a guy who's eleven years younger. He's very . . ." she trails off as if searching for the right word, but the look on her face quickly moves to lusty.

We all pause. "Hello, Tessa." Jade waves a hand in front of Tessa's face.

I smirk when her eyes refocus. "Luc is very what?"

"Hard is what I was thinking," she admits, and we laugh. "But not like that," she continues as we climb into the car. "His body is just so firm and his skin so young, and I'm feeling a bit like a wrinkled paper bag lately."

"You're not a wrinkled paper bag," I say firmly as I back out of the spot. "You're forty-two, for Christ's sake."

"I know, I know. At least Luc is an ass man."

"Your forty-two-year-old ass is a classic, babe. Everyone loves a good ass," Jade tells her.

Tessa smiles, and I let them chat while I focus on driving carefully.

I'm relieved when we pull up to the house. The ladies ooh and ahh over the mansion, though the wealth doesn't leave quite the impression on them that it did on Zoe or me. Jade makes great money at her job, and Tessa's from a wealthy family.

"Where's Chris?" Jade asks once we've walked through the quiet first floor to the stairs.

"He's probably in his studio. He's been in there a lot lately; I think his writing is going well. We'll see him soon enough, I'm sure."

I show my friends their rooms—we like to share rooms to spend time together, so I put Jade with me and Emma and Tessa in the room next door—and tell them to freshen up for dinner.

Jade disappears into the bathroom, and I pull out my favorite little black dress. I haven't worn it since Zoe was here and we went out to dinner. Tonight, we have a reservation at a bistro in one of the hotels, and then, apparently, we will be heading to the baths.

The bathroom door opens, and Jade emerges from a puff of steam, her long hair up in a tight bun to keep it dry, the gray streak peeking out from amongst the dark. I wipe the condensation off the vanity mirror the best I can and set to work on my hair and makeup. Jade joins me a few minutes later, and I zip up her dress for her.

"So," she says as we both face the mirror and work on various makeup applications. "Last month, we got Emma a hook-up—albeit an absolute disaster of one. But you claim you aren't banging Chris, so should we set you up tonight?"

"Are we picking out a man at dinner or a man at the bath?"

"Hmmm . . ." Jade ponders. "I suppose if we meet in the baths, you really know what you're getting."

We share a giggle in the mirror. "Pretty sure treating it as a hook-up meeting point would get us kicked out. We'd be those uncouth Americans."

"Surely it happens, though. Not hooking up at the baths, per se, but what if you slip into the bath and across the way, you see your soulmate?"

I lower the mascara wand, and I stare at Jade. "Soulmate? Since when do you believe in soulmates?"

"I don't," Jade says quickly. Too quickly. "It's just an expression."

I hum and give her some side-eye. "Unlikely to happen tonight for any of us, I suspect. But just in case, we should have a signal. Wink once for hook-up potential, wink twice for your soulmate," I tease.

"Shut up." Jade laughs and nudges me.

Ten minutes later, we're both ready, and there are voices coming from the hall, so I bet Tessa and Emma are too.

I slip on my favorite peep-toe heels and open the door. It's not just Emma and Tessa's voices that carry up from the stair-well, but I hear the timber of Chris's voice too.

Jade and I are halfway to the stairs when I remember I've left my lip stain in the bathroom. "Shoot. I'll be right down," I tell Jade as I dart back to the room.

It takes me a minute to find it since I threw everything haphazardly back into my makeup bag, but soon I'm at the top of the steps while the ladies and Chris laugh at some joke.

Chris is in his usual outfit of lounge pants and a rock band T-shirt—not his band, of course—and Jade's telling him a familiar story about her attempting to do yoga when her stomach wasn't feeling well. He's listening to her, smiling and nodding, when he catches sight of me.

And then we're the only two people in the room. His face changes, going from gentle amusement to surprise to wonder and then . . . lust? I watch those dark eyes travel down my body, and a shiver shoots up my spine.

My friends' chatter dies down, and a sudden bout of self-consciousness makes me stumble. I squeeze my eyes shut for two seconds and curse the fact that I, who have the strength and balance to do complicated yoga poses, can't walk down a pair of stairs under Chris's gaze.

When I open my eyes, I startle. Chris is right in front of me. "Are you okay?" he asks quietly.

"Yeah," I say, a blush heating my cheeks.

"Those shoes," he says, his voice fading to a whisper as he looks down. "Those shoes are beautiful."

Someone clears their throat, and that breaks the spell. "Here," Chris says, offering me his hand, "We can't have you twisting an ankle on my stairs. My yoga lessons must continue."

I slip my hand in his, telling myself that he's just being nice and helping me down, but my stomach—and parts lower —flutter at the warmth and firm grip. I wonder briefly what the calluses on his hands would feel like on other areas of my body, and once I get to the bottom of the stairs, I clench my thighs together.

More stable this way, I think.

"Okay, then," Tessa says. "Chris, lovely to meet you, and thank you for lending us your car and a place to stay."

"You are welcome," he says, crossing his arms over his chest. "Call me if you need anything."

The ladies are quiet as we leave the house—like the calm before the storm—as we pile into the car and four doors slam shut.

"Ho-ly shit," Jade says in the back seat, enunciating each syllable.

"Well, we know Chris is a leg man," Tessa says mildly.

"Stop it. It was nothing," I chide.

"Sure, sure," Jade says. "Nothing at all. Absolutely nothing about the way Chris was staring at you made me want to cream my panties."

"Oh my god," Emma says from the passenger seat. "Even I'm turned on now."

They erupt into laughter, and the bright red blush stays permanently on my face the entire drive to dinner.

22

Sara

"This is really nice," Jade says for about the hundredth time.

The four of us are at the baths. After initial awkwardness, completely on our part and not anyone else's, we slipped into the water and slowly got comfortable.

Yes, there's nudity everywhere, but everyone else is very chill about it. Jade's looking on with mild curiosity, Tessa has her eyes closed and is relaxed back against the wall of the pool, and Emma is more flushed than any of us and desperately trying to keep her eyes from meeting anyone else's.

I told her if she wanted, I could drive her back to Chris's and then return later to pick up Tessa and Jade, but she wanted to do it with us.

"You know, this is actually impeccable timing," Tessa says, her eyes still closed. "One of my frequent contributors sent me an article about a yoga retreat in Bali. It's all very zen, and I wanted to go myself." Tessa's magazine is all about travel, and she spends a lot of time working with the contributors.

"This is like my own little wellness retreat. But even better because I have you all with me."

"We'll even get to do yoga tomorrow," I say.

"If you ask nicely, Tess, I'll make some of those infused pitchers of water tomorrow, too," Jade says.

"It is a lot better with friends," Emma adds. "Even if I'm slightly uncomfortable having seen you three naked."

"She went alone to the retreat, and I kinda picked up on the fact that she was getting tired of traveling without her partner."

"That's gotta be tough," I say.

"It's not quite long-distance," Tessa says, "but I can see some parallels." It's been almost two months since Luc and Tessa met, and they're making the long-distance thing work.

"I don't know how you do it," Jade adds. It's tinged with a bit of bitterness. Her longest relationship dissolved when she accepted the job in China and they couldn't handle the distance.

Tessa hums. "Luc's worth it."

When our skin resembles prunes and we are starting to fall asleep in the water—the wine and baths are a potent combination—we get out and leave, rinsing off before we go. I look at myself in the mirror of the bathroom. I'm returning to Chris's house without my makeup, my hair pulled back in a sloppy bun. The only similarity to the Sara who walked down those stairs earlier is the dress and the heels, and I feel a twinge of regret that I won't get to see Chris's eyes light up when I walk in the door like they did earlier.

Now that my wine has worn off—Emma volunteered for sober driver duty tonight and drove us from the bistro to the baths—I drive us back to Chris's house. We're all quiet, sleepy, and relaxed, and I expect we will all slink into bed when we get home.

"I enjoyed the baths," Jade says, and I catch her eye in the rear-view mirror.

"Doesn't surprise me at all," I say. I drive for another moment and then bring up something I've been thinking about all night. "Okay, y'all have seen my boobs now. Do you think I should get a lift?"

I see movement in the rear-view mirror when Emma sits up straighter. Tessa glances at me from the passenger seat.

"Do you want a boob lift?" Jade asks cautiously.

"I've been thinking about it," I admit. "They're . . . not what they used to be, you know? Gravity is taking its toll. I'm not perky anymore."

"Does this have anything to do with the fact that Chris has probably seen a lot of young and surgically enhanced breasts in his lifetime?" Tessa asks.

"Or the fact that you want him to see you naked?" Jade chimes in.

I think back to the look in Chris's eyes when I came down the stairs. He's always looked at me in an appreciative way, but with the exception of tonight, I've always—always—been wearing a sports bra.

"Maybe," I admit.

We're quiet in the car while I make the turn down Chris's road.

"Well," Emma says. "I've started maintaining things down there. I know it's not like getting surgery, but it's something I was self-conscious about that night with Santo."

Jade looks over at Emma. "What are you doing? Waxing? Trimming? Brazilian?"

Emma's cheeks go pink. "Just trimming everything down. But I've thought about a Brazilian."

"I like mine. Everything's more sensitive, especially with my vibrator."

"Luc likes the airstrip," Tessa says.

"Jeez, I'm not doing anything," I say. "Maybe I need to book a wax or something."

Jade's voice is sly from the backseat. "Because Chris is going to see you naked?"

I roll my eyes at her, and she reaches forward to squeeze my shoulder. "Whether it's waxing or a boob lift, you should do whatever makes you happy. Don't do it to make a guy happy. I mean, the wax is a much easier place to start, but if you get a boob lift, I can make time to come help you recover."

"Aw, thanks," I say, and we pull into the carport.

Despite trying to be quiet, Chris still hears us as we enter the house and comes out of his studio. He must have left the door open.

"How was your night?" he asks us, leaning against the kitchen counter while we drink glasses of cold water. The baths made me thirsty, and I'm sure I'll end up waking up several times to pee tonight.

Tessa stretches and yawns. "The tamest ladies' night we've ever had. Despite all the nudity."

"Don't worry," Jade says, and I'm not sure who she thinks is worried, exactly. "Tomorrow night's going to be quite the party. On the agenda is a night of wine, Sara's delicious cooking, and a movie marathon."

"After a day of touring the town," I add.

"Yes, after we walk our asses off all day," Jade agrees.

"Report for breakfast at oh-eight-hundred," I say, and Jade salutes.

"I'm going to go outside and call Luc," Tessa announces, thumbs already tapping on her phone as she walks out the back door.

"Bed for me," Emma says and stifles another yawn while she stands from her stool.

"I guess I better go to bed too," Jade says. "But first, I'm going to take a very long shower, and it'll be at least half an hour, so you might as well hang out down here, Sara," she tells me with an exaggerated wink and a glance at Chris.

I roll my eyes. "Goodnight, you two."

Emma hugs me, and Jade blows me a kiss, and Chris and I are alone in the kitchen. Emma whispers as they walk up the stairs, "Why are you going to shower again? Didn't you just rinse off at the baths?"

The kitchen is quiet, and I take a moment to kick my shoes off and sigh in relief. I love those babies, but even with a break while we were in the baths, my feet are tired. I've gotten used to being barefoot around the house.

Chris's eyes flicker down to my feet with a little echo of the heat from earlier.

"What did you do tonight?" I ask. I know I could go upstairs and hang out in the bedroom while Jade's getting ready for bed or even use another bathroom to brush my teeth and wash my face, but I don't really want to. I want to have Chris's attention again. It's been a long time since someone has looked at me with that kind of want, and even though I don't know what I will do with it, the feeling is heady.

"I wrote tonight," he says, and it comes out with more smugness and confidence than I've ever heard before.

"Yeah? Good things, I assume."

"Yes. Do you want to hear one?"

My whole face lights up, and Chris smiles in response. "I would love to."

I leave my shoes on the kitchen floor and trail behind him into the studio. I haven't been in here since the day I discovered he was a musician, but it looks the same. Chris is still messy with his papers but tidy with his guitars, each in its own stand and glossy. Instead of the overhead lights being on, the room is only lit by the desk lamp. I imagine him here, hunched over the desk, writing until it got too dark and he had to turn on the lamp. Or, perhaps, he sat in the dark playing by feel until he heard us enter the house.

He picks up one of the guitars, an acoustic, plain wood

and simple. "I'm going to play one for you that the band probably won't ever use. It's not really our style, but you might like it."

He drags a small black stool over from the corner and sets it next to his—close together. It takes me a moment to figure out where to put my knees when we're sitting this close and he's got a guitar in his lap.

The blonde curtain of hair falls over his face, and he pauses for a moment, fingers held over the strings. Flicking his hair out of the way, he glances up at me. "This is rough, okay?"

I swallow. There's something in the way he says rough that catches me. Like this is a vulnerable side to Chris, and I think back on our conversation about impostor syndrome.

I know I'm going to like whatever it is that he's written. Already I can feel the emotion in it, and he hasn't strummed a cord.

And then he starts, and while last time I was looking at his hands and watching him play, this time I look at his face. His face, which already looks a little other-worldly to me, becomes achingly beautiful. He sings lightly, and it takes me a few rounds of the chorus to catch up with the lyrics.

It's about a woman who wears a dress bought by her lover. A dress that makes her feel beautiful, a dress that reminds him of why he loves her.

Chris is right; it's not something I could picture his band playing. This song should be played by a lone singer on a stool, in an intimate setting, with a quiet audience.

Or maybe not even that.

Maybe it's meant to be sung for just one person, the lyrics whispered in the dark with powerful emotions trembling within the words.

Chris's eyes open, and moments later, the music trails off. I don't think it was the end of the song. His words die, a note resonating between us even when the guitar string has stopped vibrating.

The space between us shrinks, me leaning in, and even though he couldn't see me when his eyes were closed, he has leaned in too. In the dark shadows of the room, Chris's eyes have lost the vibrancy they usually have, but the muted greens and golds and browns make me think of the woods surrounding his house.

His eyes flick down, and he kisses me.

It's like the song, slow and sweet and careful. Chris's mouth grazes mine, my breath hitches, and we move together. My eyes flutter closed, and his mouth eases mine open. Those lips that just sang to me, the ones that shaped the words, take on a new form, perfect and soft and warm and new.

With a swipe of his tongue, Chris asks for entrance, and I let him in. He tastes like fire, not a cigarette like I expected, but burning embers.

With the guitar between us, there's no way to get closer, no easy way to touch each other. The air shifts as he removes the guitar from between us, and then it gives a mild twang and thump as it hits the carpet.

And then his hands are on my waist, pulling me in. I slide onto his lap, my legs straddling him easily. He groans when his hands find the hem of my dress, but he just lightly brushes against my skin at the edge.

Beneath me, Chris is hard. My hands rest on his shoulders, more of a steadying grip than an embrace. I could easily melt into a puddle right here.

I don't know how long we kiss, but it's long enough that when Chris finally eases away, my lips are tender, and the cool air of the room is shocking.

Chris looks drugged. There's a hazy quality about him that recedes the more we stare at each other.

I swallow and blink. "I liked it," I say.

His Adam's apple bobs, and Chris licks his lips. "I liked it, too."

The corner of my mouth quirks and draws his eye. "I meant the song, but yes, I liked the kiss too."

He laughs, the sharp movement of his chest jostling my hands down from his shoulders to his pecs. He moves, too, sliding his hands from my thighs to around my waist.

"I'm glad you like it," he says, and I look down at his lips, slightly reddened and plump. I want to kiss him again, but before I move, he parts his lips and says, "You should probably get to bed."

When he sees my hesitation, my slight disappointment, he chuckles. "I'll be here tomorrow. Very excited to see you again. To do that again."

"Okay," I say, and we smile at each other. Chris keeps his eyes on my face while I slide off his lap. His hands curve around the back of my thighs, and in a moment that I know I'll replay a thousand times tonight in my head, he leans in and nuzzles my hip.

"Sleep well," he says, and it takes a colossal amount of strength to pull away from him and leave the room.

When I get upstairs, Jade has left the bedside lamp on for me, and she doesn't stir when I come in. I use the bathroom quietly and change into yoga pants and a T-shirt.

When I try to slide into bed without disturbing her, she lifts her head off the pillow. "Sara?"

"Yeah, it's me."

Her jaw cracks in a yawn, and I click off the light.

"Did you do it?"

I turn toward her in the dark. "Do what?"

"Bang Chris," her voice is slow, and I think she's already falling back asleep.

"No, but we kissed."

"Mmmm," she hums. "Tell me about it in the morning."

"Okay," I say.

"I want all the details."

Now I'm trying not to laugh. I nearly answer, but Jade lets out a little snore next to me.

In the morning, I'll tell her all about it. But first, I'll replay them over and over in my head until I fall asleep.

23

Chris

I HESITATE IN MY ROOM BEFORE LEAVING. I DON'T WANT TO CRASH Sara's weekend with her friends, but I know they will be having breakfast soon and then heading out for their day of sightseeing.

While they were at the baths, I couldn't get the picture of Sara coming down the stairs out of my mind. That short black dress, the long, lean legs. I knew Sara was tall, but some part of my brain hadn't put it together that she's mostly legs. You would think, with her constantly in yoga pants, that I would have noticed. Maybe it was the heels? Or the hemline? Or the extra boost of confidence Sara wore like a cloak?

And while I have certainly fantasized about those legs wrapping around me, now it's those bare legs around my waist, her dress hiking up, and her hands holding on for dear life while her heels dig into my back, and I . . .

After our kiss last night, I wrote furiously. The words quickly became lyrics; a tangle of long legs, black dresses, hot water, and angry words about betrayal and the burden of responsibility.

What's left is a mess—a cathartic mess, sure—but a mess nonetheless. Some threads blended together into angry songs about when a woman's chosen someone else. Some are lusty songs, and I don't have to guess where that train of thought has come from. There's even a ballad, which I hardly ever write, but I decided, after a few hours, that that was my favorite one.

When I couldn't keep my eyes open anymore, I forced myself to bed where I lay, knowing Sara was sleeping somewhere above me, a dull ache in my cock from wanting her so badly and running the kiss over and over again in my mind.

I do set an alarm, though, to make sure I see her and get another kiss before she leaves for the day. The thought of going without one is torture.

It's already eight fifteen and I don't know if this breakfast is a dine-and-dash or a leisurely meal. I can hear the four women in the kitchen when I step out of my room, and I lean against the doorframe before anyone spots me.

Sara stands at the stove, making crepes, while the other three sit at the counter in various stages of eating. Condiments are strewn about, some things I know Sara had bought for her friends to enjoy, like Nutella, jelly, and chocolate sauce. I wonder what she puts in her crepes.

Pan in one hand, Sara takes a step away from the stove and shakes the crepe loose. A count comes up: "Three, two, one . . . ohhhhh!" as Sara flicks her wrist, and the crepe goes airborne and lands neatly back in the pan. She didn't have those theatrics when she made me crepes.

When Sara looks up at her friends, grinning, she catches sight of me, and the smile gets wider.

"Hey," she says, and three heads twist to look at me.

"Oh, dear god," Jade says when my wide grin matches Sara's. "They're going to be insufferable now."

"Eat your damn crepes," Sara says, but the smile belies any heat in her words. When the ladies' attention is off me and back on their breakfast, I stride into the kitchen and come up behind Sara. I put a hand on her waist, and we both lean into each other, her back to my chest.

I want to kiss her so badly, but with a glance to my left, I see all three of her friends have stopped eating again to watch us. Instead of a kiss, I lean in and rest my chin on her shoulder. "Any breakfast for me here?"

Sara's head turns, and our cheeks lightly brush. We stay there for a moment, the soft touch making my breath hitch. I realize wearing my regular lounge pants was a foolish idea this morning because I'm already stiff against Sara's ass.

"Don't let them burn," Tessa whispers, and Sara snaps her attention back to the stove.

"There's plenty to share. And we made coffee already," she tells me while gesturing to the machine.

I turn away from the peanut gallery and busy myself with caffeine, and when my hard-on has gone down, and I've sweetened my coffee, I lean against the counter and watch Sara work.

She's efficient; there's a stack of crepes that the women help themselves to, and soon I have a plate and am slathering Nutella on a crepe. When she pours the last of the batter, Sara makes her own plate, spreading almond butter on the crepe and rolling it up like a cigarette.

"A sweet breakfast taquito," Jade comments. "Nice."

"What are you doing today?" Sara asks me.

I shake my head. "Working. I'm in a groove."

Sara's grin is wide. "I'm glad. We'll be back around five for happy hour. I might light the fire pit since it'll be chilly tonight."

"Come say hi when you get back."

"Really?" she asks, wrinkling her nose. "I don't want to interrupt your work."

She's got a bit of almond butter on her lip; the warm crepe melted it, and it dripped out as she ate it. I want to lick it off, but instead, I use my thumb to wipe it away and then lick my thumb.

"You're not interrupting. You're inspiring."

We hold each other's gaze until Jade lets out a puff of air. She starts fanning herself, and Emma is looking anywhere but at us while Tessa's a little flushed.

"I feel like I should call Luc," she says.

"I could cut the sexual tension with a wet noodle," Jade says. Whatever that means. "Please, Sara, for god's sake, ditch us and bang that man."

Sara's cheeks turn crimson, and Tessa snorts.

"I'm not ditching y'all."

"Wouldn't blame you if you did," Jade says.

"Well, I'm not."

Jade turns more toward me. "Do we need to bring anything back for you? Lube? Condoms?"

Emma chokes on her coffee, and Tessa has to pat her back until she settles down.

"No, I'm fully stocked, thanks," I manage. I would really love to introduce Jade to Alwin.

"And that's enough of that," Sara chastises. "Go upstairs and finish getting ready to go."

"I am ready," Jade says.

"Go brush your teeth," Tessa says, steering the other two out of the room, leaving Sara and me alone.

Sara's eaten her crepe standing up, and I press her back against the counter, crowding her and reveling in her small gasp and the narrowing of her eyes on my mouth. I press into her, harder and hotter than last night, knowing that I'll have to make it quick because I don't want to be that asshole that pulls her away from her friends.

But I was fooling myself, thinking I could make it quick. When Sara's mouth yields underneath mine, and her hands grab onto my shirt, I lose all sense of time. I've never wanted someone as badly as I do Sara, and it's only the sound of laughter and purposefully loud voices coming down the stairs that pull us apart.

"Have fun," I say, stepping back and walking away before the rest of them come around the corner.

I go right to my studio and let the words pour out.

24

Sara

The ladies last about two-point-five seconds after we roll out of the driveway before they break.

"Okay, please, please, please tell me what happened last night," Jade begs.

I sigh, not a sigh of exasperation but a sigh of I can't believe this is my life, and I kissed a rock star last night.

"He wrote a song," I say.

"About you?" Emma asks from the backseat.

"Well, I don't know. I didn't ask. But it was . . . it felt like it was about me. It was so romantic, him singing to me, just the two of us."

Jade screws up her face. "It's hard to picture him singing romantically. His band is all screaming and hoarse voices and, well, loudness."

I explain about the song and how Chris said it was unlike him and unlikely something the band could use.

"He wrote it just for you?" Tessa asks.

"I guess so."

There's a three-in-one swoon inside the car.

Emma, sitting behind me, leans forward and squeezes my shoulder. "I'm happy for you. So, you kissed?"

"Yeah, just kissed."

Jade raises her hand in the passenger seat. "I've got less than two hours after we leave. Anyone else?"

"Till what?" Emma says, and at Jade's glance, she clarifies, her cheeks flushing. "Penetration? Orgasms?"

"Orgasms."

"I'm going with two days," Emma decides.

Tessa taps her chin. "Twelve hours."

"Wow, y'all think I'm going to move pretty quick. Maybe I want to take it slow."

"I think you've been eyeballing each other a lot longer than you realize," Tessa says from the back.

"Maybe," I allow. "But . . ."

My friends patiently wait for me to gather my thoughts.

"Don't you think that this is a bad idea?"

"Why would it be a bad idea?" Jade asks. Orgasms are always a good idea to Jade.

I hold up one finger, ready to tick off the reasons why I shouldn't be with Chris. "He smokes."

Huh. I only needed one finger.

"Okay, that's a pretty good point," Jade allows. "I forgot about that since he hasn't actually smoked in front of us while we've been here."

"Yeah," I say, my brow crinkling. Actually, the kiss last night didn't taste like cigarettes. And when was the last time I saw Chris smoking?

Tessa theatrically shudders. "I bet he tasted like an ashtray."

He didn't. Which makes me wonder if he hasn't been smoking for a while.

"Okay, well, point made, though also, he's a famous rock star, he's my roommate-slash-landlord, and most importantly, *he's a famous rock star.* That's just a whole can of worms I do not want to open."

"I guess so," Jade concedes. "I just think you need a refresher on how good non-solo orgasms are. Stat."

I make a noncommittal noise, though the thought of a non-solo orgasm has me squeezing my thighs together. It has been a while.

"So, what are our plans for the day?" Emma asks, changing the conversation.

Since I slept in this morning and the weather is glorious, our first stop is Lichtentaler Allee, a park that runs along the Oos River. I don't think it's peak fall foliage yet, but some trees are changing colors in the mid-October chill, and there are pops of red and yellow everywhere. The river is calm and lazy, with beautiful viewpoints to see the city's church and cute little bridges that cross the river.

There are several museums nearby, and we take our time in the first one, the Fabergé Museum, until we get hungry and enjoy lunch at a sidewalk café. In the afternoon, we get a little sweaty, hiking up Merkur Mountain to the top, where there are castle ruins overlooking the town.

"You always make us work, Sara," Jade huffs. "And not in the good way."

"No, in the good-for-you way."

Jade grins and catches her breath, looking out at the view. When we all started spending time together, it was at my yoga classes. But then, as schedules changed, we started meeting over food and wine. It feels good to do something other than sit around and drink and eat together.

Jade complains to tease me, and the good news for her is we can take the funicular railway back.

"This is really beautiful," Tessa says, gazing out the window as we ride back down.

"The rest of us picked cities," Emma comments. "But somehow, you picked a place that is so perfect for you, Sara."

I flush, pleased that they like it, though I have to admit that I haven't seen much of the town. Chris's place is too far out into the woods, and I've kept myself too busy.

When we get back to the house, still sweaty from the hike, we're all ready for some wine. The chatter of picking out wine and hors d'oeuvres rouses Chris from whatever he's been doing, and he comes out to say hello, bending me backward into a long and deep kiss that makes my friends heckle us and my stomach flip.

"I'm going to keep working," Chris tells me. "Enjoy the wine. Ladies."

He dips his chin at them.

I'm jolted back to my friends by the pop of a cork. We move outside and sit on the back deck.

"How are things going with your professor?" I ask Emma.

She flushes. "He's not my professor. I mean . . . well, not like that."

I raise my eyebrows. "I didn't say he was."

She looks away. "It's been fine. Very professional."

Tessa, Jade, and I exchange glances. "He's not making you uncomfortable, is he?" Tessa asks.

"No, not at all, I swear. He mostly just ignores me."

I frown, not entirely sure that's a good thing. "Do you like his class?"

"It's one of the easier ones. After doing all the financial stuff for our business, I know the math pretty well. Sometimes the hardest part is figuring out the technology for the class. Everything's done online these days."

"Okay, it's been decades since I graduated college, but do y'all ever have those dreams?" Jade asks. "Where you forgot to print out your schedule, and you can't find the classroom, and when you do, class is almost over, and you look down, and you're naked?"

Tessa tilts her head back and laughs. "Oh god, yeah."

"You joke," Emma says, "but I have gotten lost, like, three times on campus."

"Really?"

"It's not like an ordinary campus." Emma throws her hand up. "It's more like an office building, and all the floors look the same." She shakes her head. "I wandered into the wrong class once."

"Well, to be fair, I've done that in the office too," Jade confesses. "The worst part is that I go in, and everyone's speaking Spanish, and I have to work out if I'm in the wrong room or they're just speaking Spanish before the meeting starts."

When it gets too cold outside, we wander back in, and I start dinner. It's a simple soup, perfect after relaxing in the nippy air outside, and good to eat in front of the TV.

Two by two, we go shower; Jade first and me when the soup simmers. Pajama-clad, we lounge on the couches and chairs while I pull up a movie.

We settle on nostalgia—*The Princess Bride*—and when Wesley reveals himself to Buttercup, Chris emerges from his wing.

"There's soup on the stove," I tell him.

"Thanks," he says with a wink.

A few minutes later, he passes with a bowl heading back to his studio.

"Come join us," Jade calls out, and the rest of them echo the sentiment. Tessa even slides down onto the floor so Chris can sit next to me.

I'm leaning against the armrest of the couch, and Chris sits close to me. I slide my feet over and nudge his legs, burying my toes under his thigh. He leans toward me. "The soup is wonderful."

"Thanks."

I half pay attention to the movie. When Chris finishes eating, he places the empty bowl on the side table and gathers my sock-clad feet into his lap. He rubs my arches, and I sink down lower.

We steal glances at each other, amusement at *to blave* and *perfect breasts* and then, the most romantic of all kisses throughout history.

When the movie's over, I try to get up and clean, but Jade shoves me down. "We'll take care of the kitchen. You," she points at Chris, "keep rubbing. Sara worked hard to plan the perfect day for us. She deserves to put her feet up a bit."

"Yes, ma'am." Chris's thumbs knead the soles of my feet, and I close my eyes and relax. My friends are loud at first, the din of cleaning up and laughter keeping me awake until it fades away, not into sleep because how can I sleep when all I can think about is Chris's hands on me? Instead, they've quietly left us alone, one by one going upstairs.

I open my eyes, and Chris takes it as an invitation. The lights are mostly off, except for a floor lamp in one corner that's been on for the movie night. In the near-dark, Chris slides my feet out of his lap and presses a knee into the cushions between my legs, crawling over my body.

"Have I told you I hate your hoodies?" he whispers, pressing a kiss to my neck, slowly lowering his weight onto me. All the reasons that this shouldn't happen, the ones I listed in the car with my friends, have completely left me, especially because Chris smells like soap and laundry, and the heat of his mouth is overwhelming.

"No," I say on a sigh, and tilt my chin up, giving him more space to put his mouth on me. He sucks lightly, an open mouth kiss that makes me gasp.

His hands slip under the cotton, finding my bare stomach and flattening against my skin. "I miss watching you move. These hoodies cover everything up," he complains, and I giggle.

"So sorry."

Chris presses his body down on mine, shifting his hips,

and I feel how hard he is against me. It makes my hips restless, heat pooling between my legs and my body overheating.

"Take it off," I suggest, tugging at the material, and Chris obliges, pulling the zipper down and pushing the sweatshirt off my shoulders. It stays there, the two of us too lazy—or too involved in our kisses—to pull it all the way off. But then Chris backs off, staring down at me, holding himself above me and devouring every inch with his eyes.

25

Chris

God, Sara is beautiful. Despite the goosebumps on her skin from the cool air, her cheeks and neck are flushed, the spot I sucked on blending into the rest of the redness. A sports bra covers her breasts, but it's not padded, and her nipples strain against the fabric.

I lower myself back down and capture her mouth. Kissing her is so satisfying, like nothing I've ever experienced. I've had plenty of women in my lifetime—there were groupies even before we got famous—and I've never been unsatisfied.

Sara's different. I know her in a way I've never known any other woman, except maybe June. But June is a best friend, someone I've been through so much with. Not once have I thought about her like this.

Our hips grind together, and my cock, hard and solid, pushes against her. I wonder, with a twist of my hips, if I can find just the right spot.

Sara breaks our kiss off with a gasp, and I do the same motion again and again, rocking my hips and watching the flush move up her chest. Her eyes are half-lidded, unfocused, and so fucking sexy.

"Chris," she whispers, and I grind down a little harder. With just her yoga leggings and my cotton lounge pants between us, I find just the right spot and am rewarded by a gasp.

A squeaking noise comes from the doorway, and I pause and look up. One of her friends—Emma, I think, though I only see a flash of a person in the dark room—disappears from the doorway and calls out behind her, "Sorry!"

When I look back down at Sara, she's looking up, and when our eyes meet, she gives me a slow smile.

The moment's broken, though, and when Sara moves to sit up, I get out of the way. She gathers up my bowl and pushes off the couch, walking into the kitchen. I follow her.

"Thank you for being so great with my friends," she says as she rinses my bowl and puts it in the dishwasher.

"They're fun. A lot different from my friends." I pull out one of the stools and take a seat.

"Your bandmates or other friends?"

"The band."

"Tell me about them."

"Ah, well. I met Alwin when I was playing in a ska band, and he kept showing up to my concerts and nagging me to join his band."

"What finally got you to do it?" she asks.

"You've met him. He's got a presence about him. Natural charm. The ska band never got off the ground. Ska bands rarely make it big, and while we were musically sound, we had no idea how to market ourselves."

Sara puts the last dish in the drying rack and dries her hands. "Kind of like teaching yoga. You have to be a skilled teacher, and if you want to make it a business for yourself, you have to do like fifty other things." She comes around the island to stand in front of me, and I spread my knees and pull her in closer.

"Yeah, exactly. June is an amazing bassist but also really smart with numbers and contracts. My eyes glaze over, and I automatically sign anything people tell me to, but June reads that shit and understands it. She played hardball for us before we had professionals to do it. But Alwin, he's the marketer. He's never met someone he couldn't sweet talk into giving the band something."

Sara softly exhales a laugh. "I know some people like that. Back home, we call them FMFs—friendly motherfuckers."

I laugh and squeeze her a little closer. "That's exactly Alwin. Between the two of them, they're a force to be reckoned with."

"And the drummer?"

"Ram. He was the last to join. He's a strong musician and a lot of fun—too much fun."

Sara's hum is thoughtful. "I would imagine that a lot has changed for the music industry in the last decade. It's the same with yoga—more online, less personal. It's hard to reconcile the tenets of yoga with the way the world is changing. I'm not sure how I feel about it sometimes."

"Very true."

"By the way," Sara brings her hand up to my mouth and traces my bottom lip. "did you quit smoking?"

I turn my head, nuzzling into her hand. "Yeah, I did."

"Why?" She cups my jaw.

I look up at her. "You know why."

A smile flits across her face before disappearing. "You should get checked out by a doctor too. Just in case."

Just in case of cancer. Her husband's and my mother's death hang over us.

"I will. I promise."

"Good," she says. She squeezes me tightly and then yawns.

"All right, it's time for bed." I push her gently away. "You've had a long day, and you need to hang with your friends tomorrow."

Sara pouts. "I don't want them to leave."

I kiss her down-turned mouth. "They can come visit any time."

"Good night," she says as she steps away.

"Good night."

———

IN THE MORNING, SARA AND HER FRIENDS TAKE OVER THE kitchen again. It's a mimosa morning, apparently, and there are already two empty bottles of sparkling wine.

"Hey, it's our designated driver!" Jade shouts when she sees me.

Sara glances over her shoulder from the stove, apologetic. "They need to be at the train station in an hour. I can stop drinking, I've only had one, but Jade wanted to ask you to drive us."

"Happy to," I say.

Tessa picks up a half-full bottle of wine and reaches across the kitchen counter to fill Sara's glass.

"What's for breakfast?" I ask, standing behind Sara and planting a kiss on the back of her neck, wisps of hair tickling my face. Most of her hair is up in her usual bun, high at the top of her head. The little wisps of hair are cute, though, more of them gray than in the rest of her chocolate-brown.

"Beans and toast and . . ." she spins around for dramatic effect. "Bacon."

"Real bacon," Jade croons.

I raise my eyebrows at the back of Sara's head. "You're eating bacon?"

"No, of course not," Emma says. "She makes it for us. And maybe you." She eyes me.

There is bacon for me, although it's actually English-style rashers, which Jade complains about when the five of us sit down to a hearty breakfast at the kitchen table.

"Be glad it's not lardons," Tessa says. "That's just chunks of bacon, which is fine, but there's something about the bacon strip and those thin parts that get crispy." She looks lovingly at the bacon. "I can't find the thick-cut peppered and smoked bacon like we get back home."

"Stop, I'm drooling," Jade says, wiping her mouth with the back of her hand.

"We could talk about the amazing food we've found here in Europe," Sara suggests.

"Evil woman," Jade mutters.

"How about the hot chocolate in Madrid? It's unreal," Emma chimes in. "We had some at this cute little café near Jade's apartment where she meets her Spanish tutor. How is Manny doing, by the way?"

Jade presses a hand to her chest. "His boyfriend proposed. They are so cute together."

I'm a little lost in the conversation until it circles back to food again. "Sara," Tessa says. "What about the food around here? What have you found?"

Sara's brow wrinkles as she thinks. "I don't think I've had much local food, to be honest. It's a little hard to eat German food as a vegan."

"That place Friday night was good, but yeah, not really German," Tessa says. "When I think of German food, I think of meaty things. Are we off base, Chris?"

I swallow a bite of the rasher and think. "Traditional German food does have a lot of meat and cream."

"Schnitzel," Jade says.

"Bratwurst," Emma chimes in.

"Spätzle is an egg noodle," Sara says. "But I can eat sauerkraut."

Jade wrinkles her nose. "So, you'll just eat fermented cabbage?" She turns to me. "Prepare to be out-farted."

Sara sticks her tongue out at Jade, and they bicker a bit about German food while an idea forms in my head.

"We need to set our next weekend," Tessa says.

They all look at each other.

"Weekend for what?" I ask.

"We agreed to meet for one weekend a month while we are all living in Europe, and we decide where we will go for the next month while we are all together," Sara explains.

"First, it was Paris." Jade counts on her finger. "Then we went to Rome to see Emma off for the start of school. And now we're here."

"So, it's either Portugal to visit Tessa or Madrid to visit Jade," Emma says.

"Well, you were in Madrid not that long ago with Jade, so maybe we should go to Portugal," Sara suggests.

"Well, actually . . ." Tessa says, and all attention turns toward her.

"I'm moving to Paris," she says.

Surprise wells in the entire group, and I'm an interloper. The room falls silent.

"With Luc?" Sara finally asks.

"Yeah." Tessa's cheeks are pink, and her eyes dart around the group of women.

"I thought your lease in Portugal was for a year?" Emma says.

"And what about the Schengen issues?" Sara asks.

"My apartment manager put up a flier that if anyone wanted to break their lease, they could. With the ex-pat community growing, they are looking to bump up the rent. On my visa, I can stay a little less than two months in Paris, and then Luc and I can figure out what to do next."

The ladies all blink, and then suddenly, the spell snaps, and there's excitement in the air.

"Yay! You're moving in with Luc. That's amazing," Jade says, wrapping Tessa up in a hug.

They all take turns hugging her, and when Tessa finally pulls back, her eyes are wet.

"Well, let's raise a glass," Jade says, sweeping her champagne flute up.

"Yes," Sara says, raising her glass too. "To Tessa and Luc."

"Cheers," everyone echoes, and they drink to her relationship.

———

A half an hour later, the kitchen's still a mess, but Sara's assured her friends that she'll clean up when we get home. They pile into my car, with the three of them in the backseat and Sara up front with me.

When we arrive at the station, I lift their bags out of the back. Tessa and Emma grab their bags from me and walk with Sara to the entrance, leaving me and Jade to walk in together. Just as the three women disappear into the station, Jade puts a hand out to stop me.

"All right, Sara might be the mama bear of our group, but someone has to mama bear her," she says. "If you hurt her, I'll kick your ass."

Jade is petite and about ten centimeters shorter than me, so I swallow my smile and try to be serious. "Understood."

"And," this time she jabs a finger into my chest. "Don't you dare think that you can slack off just because Sara's around all the time. She deserves some proper dating, not some farting on the couch bullshit. Wine and dine her, too, before you try to get her to bed. She never had a grand romance in her life, and while not everyone wants a big spectacle and declarations of love, I know she does."

The thought of declarations of love makes me uncomfortable. Isn't that a little soon? We haven't even had sex yet.

Jade squints like she can read my mind. "Don't commit yourself to more than you are willing to give. Be upfront with her about what this is. Again, I'll kick your ass."

She points two fingers at her eyes, then points them at me, and then back to her eyes, and at me, and so on for an uncomfortably long time.

Fortunately, Sara pops out of the automatic doors to the station. "Jade? Chris? Are you coming?"

26

Sara

The doors slam shut, closing Chris and me inside his car alone now that my friends are gone. Excitement and anticipation replace the flutter of sadness in my chest. Chris is staring at me, eyes hot and heavy in a look that shoots straight down to my core.

I should be content with my vibrator. Chris is the complicated choice, and no matter how much I want him, it would be insane to start something.

And yet, maybe he's actually kind of perfect. We're going our separate ways soon, and sleeping with Chris would be reckless and wild and totally out of the ordinary for me.

Sure, being a heartthrob rock star doesn't automatically mean he'll be good in bed. But in less than a year, I'll be back in Texas, back to my life in the suburbs in my simple house, teaching yoga. I might reflect back on this for the rest of my life as the wildest, hottest thing I've ever done.

Chris sprawls in the driver's seat, his legs spread, and with a passing glance, you'd think he's relaxed. His eyes tell a different story. The heat I feel reflects back at me. His left hand grips the steering wheel, those long fingers tight and white from the pressure. And he's hard, his erection straining at his pants.

I flick my gaze back up to his face, and we stare at each other.

One heartbeat.

Two.

We both rush forward, clashing in the middle. Chris's mouth is hot on mine, his tongue invading and a hand on the back of my head, pulling me to him. He tastes like mint, and when I suck on his tongue, the growl he emits makes my core clench.

"Fuck, Sara," he groans between kisses. "Get over here."

He half-pulls, half-helps me climb over the center console. It's broad daylight, and the cramped space is slowly expanding as Chris reclines the seat with the push of a button. My knees are on his ribs, our groins flush, his erection fitting just perfectly where I need it. I hang onto his neck, and I'm so worked up we're barely kissing. It's more like grinding and breathing together. We could be teenagers in the back seat with this kind of behavior.

Jesus H Christ, I want him so badly.

So badly it's embarrassing.

"It's been a while for me." As if that will excuse the way I'm humping him in public.

"Me too," Chris says. Fully reclined now, the seat still doesn't give us much room, but it does free his hands, and he runs his fingers through my hair and kisses me again. "Like, months."

I pull back too far, and my ass hits the horn on the steering wheel, emitting a loud beep. Out the window, I see a woman loading luggage into her car turn to stare at us. At least the windows are tinted enough, so she probably can't see us.

I think.

But it wakes me up, and I ungracefully roll back over to the passenger seat.

"Excuse me? Months?"

Chris wipes his face with his hands and then reaches for the button to raise the seat again. It slowly starts its motorized ascent.

"Yeah, months. How long has it been for you?"

"Um, years."

Chris stares. Then grips his dick through his pants, squeezing it hard and falling forward, making the car beep again.

He swears in German. "Why is that so hot?" He starts the car. "When we get home, I'm going to make you come. A lot. On my face, on my fingers, on my dick." He swears again. His head hits the steering wheel. Repeatedly.

Beep. Beep. Beep.

"Put your seatbelt on," I tell him. "And stop with the honking. Someone's going to recognize you."

Chris buckles his seatbelt and peels out of the parking space. I grip the door handle and tense as we make the turn onto the street. It's not about Chris's driving, although maybe I should be worried that he's thinking with his dick right now.

But really, all I can think about is sitting on his face.

To his credit, Chris focuses on driving. A few minutes in, Chris reaches over and takes the hand that was clenched on my knee and threads his fingers through mine. It's sweet, even though he's still tense.

Chris's hands are lithe, his fingers long and callused. His thumb rubs the back of my hand, and the combination of the excitement coursing through me and his hand grounding me feels right. I'm even more confident now that it's going to be amazing.

We get back to his house, and as soon as the door closes, we're making out again. Chris presses me against the door, his dick on my hip, his hand turning my head to the side and then sliding down my torso. His fingers trace over my hip, down my thigh as far as he can reach before pressing against my pussy.

He groans, and I thrust my hips forward and against the small circles he makes.

"Fuck, you're wet. I can feel how bad that cunt needs me."

When my body bucks, Chris chuckles and drags his mouth from mine. I'm panting as his lips work their way down the side of my neck, the hollow of my throat, over my pulse.

His fingers leave, and I whimper. The softness of his lips and tongue on my collarbone is replaced by teeth grazing my skin. Chris's cock is like iron between us. My breath catches as he slips his hand inside my pants and cups my pussy. The tips of his fingers stroke through my wetness, and I clutch his head, holding him to me while I strain for more.

He gives me more.

Fingers plunge inside me, and my body curls as Chris presses his palm against my clit.

"More?" he rasps. His breath warms the spot where his mouth was.

"Oh, god, yes."

He adds another finger. His hand and my hips move together, and I press my face into his neck and rise up onto my toes as the pressure builds.

A few more strokes and my orgasm roars through me. I'm crying out into his skin and clutching at him to ride it out.

Chris keeps working me as I shudder and whimper. My body slowly relaxes, and so does he.

I kiss Chris's neck, nudging him with my face until he pulls back and slots his mouth against mine again. The kisses are slower and gentler now.

After a few long kisses, Chris eases away from me. His free hand traces over my temple, my cheek, down to my neck and the opposite shoulder where his mouth was, all while he holds my gaze.

His palm slips down to my breastbone and holds, feeling my pounding heart. Inside me, his fingers twitch, reminding me he's still there. My eyes flutter, and when they reopen, Chris is staring at me.

"Again?"

I pause and think. Chris gives a lazy stroke inside of me.

Sometimes, when using my vibrator, I turn it down and ease off the pressure after coming and relax. If I keep browsing porn, I might feel the urge to come again and turn the vibrator back up.

Same feeling here. I nod.

Chris grins, slow and wicked.

This time is slower. His hand shifts in small circles, fingers slowly pumping in and out.

I watch Chris's face. His gaze darts around, taking in every reaction I have: the sawing breath escaping my lungs as I build up again, the flush I feel on my cheeks, my hooded eyes.

My core starts to tighten, and I grasp his forearm, the one still planted on my chest. He moves, taking the pressure off. "No, I like it." There's a needy edge to my voice.

He presses again, and under my fingers, the cords of his muscles flex and twist. I'm pinned between his hands, squirming.

"More, please, Chris, oh god."

He leans, his face closer, his palms pressing harder, the lower one giving me the immovable force I need to grind against him. Our faces are closer, Chris's pupils blown out by lust. We stare at each other, and I watch that lust shift to carnal satisfaction while I pulse around his hand in another orgasm.

27

Chris

I AM GOING TO WRECK HER.

Sara slumps against me, and I remove my hand from her wet cunt with reluctance. She's breathing hard, chest rising and falling under my palm.

I slide both hands down her to her ass and pick her up. Her arms loop around me, and she snuggles into my neck. Her eyelashes brush the sensitive skin with every blink.

In my room, I lay Sara on the bed and help her strip off her clothes. I kiss the soft skin on her belly, the tight pink nipples, the inside of her thigh.

Her breasts, freed from her sports bra, are perfect. They are soft and fill my hands just right as I cup them and bring her nipples closer together so I can tease them with my lips and tongue. I worship them while Sara sighs and threads her fingers through my hair.

I pull back and strip my own clothes off, gratified when I bring my gaze back to Sara and she's propped up on her elbows, watching my body.

My dick is so hard it aches. It bobs between us as I crawl

up the bed, covering her and returning to her sweet mouth. Her knees press against my hips, squeezing and urging.

There is a strip of condoms in the nightstand, and I rip myself away from her to unwrap and slide one on. I hitch my leg up, nudging her thighs farther apart, and grip the base of my shaft with one hand.

The other tangles with hers, and as I press into her heat, I kiss her. I'm chest-to-chest with her as I flex and press in.

I thread my right hand through her fingers to clasp both sets of hands together above her head. I watch every flutter of her eyes, feel every gasp of air against my lips.

Finally, I'm flush with the cradle of her hips. I sink my weight into her and rock, letting the feeling in the base of my spine build.

My forehead rests against hers. We're both sweating, and I love the noises she makes every time I hit deep.

"Do you like that, babe?"

I kiss her before she can answer, open and loose. When I pull back, she looks drugged.

"Yeah, I like it. I like the way you feel."

"Wrap your legs around me." She does, hooking her ankles together and lifting her ass up.

"Oh god. That feels good." I thrust a little harder and she squeaks at the last syllable.

I squeeze her hands, pressing them into the mattress. "You like that? Are you going to come for me again?"

"I . . . I don't know."

"Tell me how to make you come. Tell me what you fantasize about. Tell me how you touch yourself. Tell me how to make it so fucking good for you."

Sara's eyes focus on me for a moment, and she laughs. "God, you're an overachiever."

I kiss through her smile, and she sighs. "Later, I want to come on your face. Right now, I want to feel you." She pulls at my right hand, and when I relax my grip, she brings our joined hands closer so she can kiss my fingers. Then she grazes a knuckle with her teeth. "Please, Chris."

I bury deeper into her, using the small amount of space I have to piston my hips as much as I can. Her thighs tighten around me, and her eyes close in pleasure.

With every stroke, Sara's body tightens. Even if she's not going to come from this, I am entranced by the flutter of her eyelashes, the press of her breasts against my chest. I'm so engrossed that, embarrassingly, my own orgasm sneaks up on me.

"Oh, fuck, Sara, I'm coming," I grit my teeth against the pleasure shooting up my body and pulse deep inside of her.

Sara arches against me and murmurs, "Oh god, yes."

When my body relaxes, I slump forward, my forehead on the mattress next to her, my mouth by her ear. We're both breathing hard, our fingers still tightly clasped.

Sara stretches her hands, and I let her go, flexing to get the circulation back. I carefully roll my weight off Sara.

She lifts her head, and I wiggle my arm underneath her, lying on my side and pulling her into my body.

We've just proven that, despite our differences, we are very compatible in the bedroom.

28

Sara

WE CLEAN UP SEPARATELY, AND WHEN I EMERGE FROM CHRIS'S bathroom, he's lying on his back on the bed, hands behind his head and soft, uncut cock resting against the juncture of his thigh.

He points at me and then at his mouth, sticking his tongue out. "I made a promise I intend to keep."

I crawl onto the bed and over his body. There are some logistics to figure out, but moments later, I'm kneeling over Chris's face, my back to the headboard, and watching Chris's dick harden just from getting up close and personal with my pussy.

His arms wrap around me, and we both adjust until I'm right where he wants me. Then, his tongue takes a broad swipe between my folds, and I buck forward, catching myself with my palms on his chest.

Chris hums and pulls me down harder. I can feel his breath, the tip of his tongue as it explores, the heat of his mouth as he sucks my clit in.

The noises he makes, the enthusiasm with which his arms tighten around me, and the sight of his cock, hard and with a glistening bead of pre-cum, make me feel sexy as hell.

I trust Chris enough to tell me if my weight is too much or if he needs more room to breathe, and it's freeing. My body is balanced between my hands on his chest, the wolf tattoo peeking from between my splayed fingers, and his face. With gentle squeezes and moans, Chris encourages me to move.

I have no idea what Chris is doing, but my hips rock with him, and the pressure builds inside me. I close my eyes and let my head fall back. His shoulders dig into me as my thighs tighten, and I grind against him harder. Noises fall out of my mouth, wordless moans, and at one point an "Oh fuck that's good," which makes Chris chuckle.

My orgasm is building, and I lean more weight on my palms. I'm not sitting on his face—I'm riding it, and oh god, my skin flushes as my orgasm roars through me and my elbows buckle.

Chris follows me, lifting his head to wring every last bit of it out of me as I collapse on his chest, my legs stretching out and hitting the headboard before I kick my feet up. I clench on nothing so hard my body aches and my thighs clamp around his head.

Soon I'm too sensitive and twitch away. Chris turns his head to kiss my thigh and squeezes my butt with his palms.

I'm limp and satisfied, resting my head on Chris's thigh. His cock is hard against my shoulder, and I wrap my hand around it and squeeze.

Chris just strokes my body everywhere he can reach, from the back of my calves to my back and sides.

"Don't let me fall asleep," I murmur.

"Okay," Chris says, amused.

I give him some incentive and squeeze his cock. "There's something I want to try next."

———

We have dinner plans tonight, the note on the counter says. I've just come out of the yoga studio after a teaching session and am taking a break before I start editing videos. Aside from the note, there's no sign of Chris, and when I check out front, his car is gone.

I woke up next to him this morning. After riding his face last night, we'd taken advantage of the position we were still in and sixty-nined. We'd spent the whole night in bed together, talking and pleasuring each other, staying up later than I have probably since Zoe started sleeping through the night.

Chris was conked out next to me when I woke up, so I slipped out of bed and up to my room to shower and get to work for the day.

Ever since the live session with Chris, my inbox and notifications have been mayhem—and so have my subscriptions. I did a good job working the bare minimum while my friends were here, but now it's an enormous backlog. I answer emails, respond to questions, and post on social media about the second session until the late afternoon when a hand on my shoulder startles me.

"Oh, hi," I say to Chris, taking my headphones off. "Sorry, I didn't hear you come in."

He presses a kiss to the top of my head. I sniff, and he smells like smoke—wood smoke. "It's okay. There's someone I'd like you to meet."

Curious, I get up and follow Chris. When we pass through the great room, I see a blazing fire in the pit on the back patio. We continue into the kitchen, where I can hear someone moving around and muttering. There's a guy with his head buried in the fridge, digging through my produce, and even more food covers the counters—like enough to feed an army.

"Diedrich," Chris says, and the man pulls himself out of

the fridge. Chris says a few more things in German to him. He's young, blonde hair slicked back and a short goatee covering his chin. He washes his hands quickly and offers me a handshake.

"Sara, this is Diedrich, Diedrich, Sara. He'll be cooking dinner for us tonight."

"Hello," Diedrich nods at me.

My eyebrows rise. "Oh?"

"I asked around, and Diedrich is the sous chef at a popular vegan restaurant in Berlin. It's not traditional German food, but he's experimented for himself a lot, and he'll be making dinner tonight and some leftovers that we can freeze and enjoy later."

"What? Really?" My hands go to my mouth, and I wonder how on Earth Chris got this idea. "That sounds amazing."

"Thank you," Diedrich gives me an awkward little bow. His accent is heavy, his speech slower. "Our food is traditionally heavy. With cream and meat. But I make dishes without them for you."

"I can't wait," I say, and Diedrich turns back to his work. Chris guides me out of the kitchen to leave Diedrich to his work.

"He needs about two hours. He's done most of the prep work in advance, but he is cooking a three-course dinner for us tonight that will take some time. I thought we could open a bottle of wine and enjoy the fire pit."

I glance back outside and see that Chris pulled two chairs up by the fire, plaid blankets dropped over the backs. When I turn back to Chris, my heart flutters at the look in his eyes. "That sounds like a date night." It comes out as a whisper.

Chris tilts his head down, capturing my mouth in a kiss. When he breaks away, I get the satisfaction of seeing his eyes lusty.

"Maybe I should change clothes."

Chris's gaze travels down to my yoga pants and hoodie.

"I could wear that black dress again." I'll be cold, but to see that look on his face again? Hell yeah.

Chris reaches out as if to pull me to him but clenches at the air at the last minute. He runs his hands up over his face and into his hair, breathing deeply. The movement pulls his shirt up, and I get a glimpse of tattooed claws and lean muscle. "Go change, temptress."

"Temptress?" I say, stepping toward him. Our fronts brush together, my breasts to his chest and his hardening cock against my stomach.

I feel like a temptress with the way he groans, and in a flash, his hands are gripping me hard, his mouth crushing mine. His kiss is urgent and heated, and I wrap myself up in him until there's a bang from the kitchen that reminds us that we aren't alone.

Chris mutters something under his breath before pulling away. "Go change. I'll change too and meet you outside."

His hands linger, gently keeping me against him as I try to pull away. With a final groan, he gives up and lets his head fall back.

Given the opportunity, I kiss his Adam's apple. He's got a good one, angular and prominent, and I feel his surprise. I'll definitely give it more attention later.

"See you in fifteen," I promise and head upstairs.

———

When I come back downstairs, Chris is outside poking the fire, and I observe him for a few minutes while he is unaware. He dressed up, too, wearing black slacks and a maroon long-sleeved button-up shirt. It hides his tattoos but emphasizes his trim waist, and I enjoy the view.

I'm wearing that black dress, although I didn't want to spend time with as much hair and makeup as before, so my hair is in a low bun at the nape of my neck, and I'm only wearing mascara and lip gloss.

The air is crisp when I step out onto the deck, but he stalks over and kisses me until I'm overheated. We settle on the couch and say "Prost," clinking our glasses of wine together.

We talk about Chris's childhood in Hamburg and mine in Texas. When I try to gloss over my relationship with Kit, Chris stops me, and I end up describing our wedding, and we discuss the effect of a baby on a young marriage. I kick my shoes off and pile them with Chris's next to the couch; a blanket covers our laps, and at one point, Chris runs in and gets me one of his hoodies to wear. My legs are in Chris's lap; his body feels warm against me under the blanket.

"It's definitely hard to feel sexy when you're wiping your daughter's pee off the walls as your husband comes home from work." I shake my head, staring out at the lawn and graying woods around us. "I always wonder what it would have been like if Kit had beat his cancer. Would we be like so many couples who limped along until they divorced, or would we have rediscovered each other when things calmed down?"

"You don't think it was a sure thing? Fate? Soulmates?"

I shake my head. "Don't get me wrong, I loved Kit when we got married. And maybe I thought he was my soulmate at some point. But somewhere along the way, the optimism disappeared."

A throat clears behind us, and when we glance over at the door to the house, Diedrich stands just outside, apron and jacket slightly more mussed than they were before. He says something to Chris, and Chris looks at me. "Dinner is ready."

We untangle and stand. I take the blanket with me, wrapping it around my shoulders as Chris bends to pick up our shoes. When we enter the house, the lights are dimmed, music is playing, and Diedrich has set the kitchen island for two, candles and all.

Once we're perched on the island seats, Diedrich opens the oven door, sets it to low, and removes two plates, protecting his hands with kitchen towels.

"This entrée is a sampling of German street food," Diedrich says as he puts the small plates down on the glass chargers in front of us. He points to the leftmost item. "This is a potato pancake with a sauerkraut and vegan creme fraiche. This here is a currywurst made with seitan. Then a vegetable strudel. Thank you." He punctuates this by walking back to the stove and leaving us to taste the food.

Chris leans into me. "What's seitan?"

"It's a wheat meat replacement. I've eaten it before, and it's got a kind of chewy-meat texture."

Diedrich says something from the stove while stirring, and Chris looks up, and they talk back and forth for a few moments.

"Diedrich made the currywurst with seitan and mushrooms and steamed in a foil packet."

Diedrich glances over his shoulder apologetically. "My English is not good."

"You're doing great," I assured him. "Better than my German, and we've got Chris to translate."

Chris does translate, and I have a thought. "Does he know you are Chris Rächer?"

"Yes, he definitely does," Chris looks at his plate, and I think he's laughing at me.

"What? What's so funny?" I pick up my fork and use it to cut the potato pancake.

"How do you think I got a top chef at the last minute?"

"Okay, good point."

Chris takes a bite of the currywurst and chews thoughtfully. "This is actually pretty good."

I nudge him with my elbow and raise my eyebrows at Diedrich's turned back. Chris clears his throat. "I mean, obviously, it's very good, but I meant that it's similar to a meat-based currywurst."

I take my bite of potato pancake with a bit of sauerkraut and a bit of applesauce. I've had similar things before—latkes with Emma's family—and of course, this one is perfect; just the right level of crispy and tender.

"What exactly is currywurst? How does it differ from bratwurst?" I ask.

"Bratwurst is a type of sausage. Currywurst is really about the sauce, which is a ketchup and curry base. This is a staple German street food." He pops one into his mouth. "Definitely something Zoe had at that festival she went to."

"I doubt they had vegan ones," I say. I spear one of the seitan slices and nibble on it. The sauce is tangy and mildly sweet, with a complexity I wasn't expecting.

We both eat the strudels last, a flaky, savory crust with spinach and mushrooms and spices that disappears way too fast.

"That might have been the best vegan pastry crust I've ever had," I say. "I don't even bother because it's too much of a pain in the ass."

Chris translates for Diedrich, who laughs and says "danke" while assembling our plates.

The next course is schnitzel, also made from seitan, served with spätzle and a glass of Riesling. After my first bite, I moan in pleasure. "I've had seitan parmesan before, and I thought that would be what schnitzel is like, but holy crap, this is way better."

"It's lighter," Chris agrees. "But when you want that cheesy goodness, chicken parmesan is hard to beat."

"Nah," I say. "German food, one; Italian food, zero."

Chris shoots me a look. "You were just in Rome. I hate to tell you this, but chicken parmesan is an American dish that, for some reason, Americans think is Italian. We ate at some Italian chain restaurant in the States when we were there for our first tour, and one of our roadies, who is Italian, thought it was mortally offensive."

Not only is the schnitzel not overwhelmed with marinara and cheese, but it's crispy and a reasonable portion size. I finish mine, and when Diedrich offers Chris seconds, he hesitates. "No, danke," he says.

"In a few minutes, dessert," Diedrich cautions us.

I toast him with my half-full wine glass. "I can't wait."

When Diedrich collects the plates, Chris leans onto the counter with his wine glass.

"You've been to the US for your tour? Where did you play?"

"All over," Chris says. "I think the closest to you would have been Houston. I think we made twelve stops?" He screws up his face in concentration. "To be honest, they all blend together. Touring is exhausting. The concerts are physically draining, and then we party too hard afterward, plus sleeping on the bus is horrible. Ram snores. It's quite different from the past few months." He gestures at the house.

"Are you looking forward to going back?"

Chris spins his wine glass while he thinks. "I do miss it. There's nothing like performing on stage. Having a successful song is thrilling, but trying to write and compose is hard. But performing, that's pure pleasure for me."

"I'd like to see you perform someday," I say.

Chris turns sharply and laughs as if I've said something ridiculous. "Of course, you'll see me perform."

"Your tour isn't for months, right?" That Chris thinks it's such a sure thing that we'll be together that far down the road makes me feel like I might float away.

"Oh, shit. There's a charity concert this weekend. I may have forgotten to mention it with your friends being in town, but I got you a backstage pass so you can come hang out with me and the band. If you want."

"Wow, that'll be different." I don't think I'll fit in backstage at a rock concert. I definitely do not look like I could be back-stage at a concert, and the idea of seeing what it's like is a little overwhelming. I wouldn't know anyone—aside from Chris and Alwin, who will be on stage—so being back there alone sounds weird.

"You don't want to go?" Chris's eyebrows draw together in concern.

"I do, definitely. Where is it?"

"Berlin. It's a daytime concert at one of the stadiums, so it won't be too intense."

"Could Zoe come? She would love it and could keep me company."

"Of course. I'll call Marcus and see about getting another pass."

Diedrich interrupts by putting two plates down in front of us. It's another strudel, this one with a light brown filling and white, lacy drizzle over the top.

The filling is light and spiced, the apples perfectly cooked, and I contemplate licking the icing off the plate—and that leads my thoughts to what else I could drizzle it on, and then that train of thought gets very X-rated.

"My Oma used to make apple strudel when I was very young. It's one of my few memories of her," Chris says wistfully.

We talk about our childhoods while Diedrich cleans up, and we drink the last of the Riesling. Before he leaves, Diedrich shows me the fridge and the stacks of leftovers he's made for us, like meal prep for a week of German vegan food. He gives Chris instructions in rapid-fire German, and I expect we'll have to call Diedrich for a reminder later. Chris gives him a hearty handshake and a back slap, and I offer him a handshake of my own before he wheels a small cart of supplies out the side door and drives away.

"So," Chris says, resting his hands on my hips and

backing me up to the edge of the counter. "What should we do next?"

I rub my hand over my belly. "Excuse me, I just ate a giant three-course meal. I can't possibly be—Ah!"

Laughing, Chris picks me up in a fireman's carry and takes me back to his bedroom.

29

Chris

WHEN I WALK INTO THE YOGA STUDIO THREE DAYS LATER, SARA'S already at her desk at work. She's got her laptop set up, a secondary screen to one side, and a microphone with a pop filter in front of her, huge black headphones on her head.

I have a similar setup back in my studio to record vocals. Maybe I should suggest Sara record in there?

When Sara and I have bothered to leave the bedroom, we've been recording the three yoga sessions for her series. We finished the final one last night, and Sara assures me she just has to edit everything, and my work is done.

In fact, her exact words were, "Get back to your own work, you sex fiend."

I pad over, staying as quiet as possible, and when she catches sight of me, she looks up and gives me a smile, pulling the headphones off.

"Hey," she says. "I'm not recording right now."

I walk normally, coming to a stop behind her chair and wrapping my arms around her shoulders. "What are you working on?"

"This is a voiceover for the third Rock Steady video. I already finished the second one, and it's scheduled to publish today."

I press a kiss to the top of her head. "That's good. You know, you could record in my studio."

Underneath me, she shrugs. "Then I'd have to move everything back and forth."

"Maybe we should set you up with a desk in there."

She nudges me. "I'm not invading your space enough?" she teases.

I look at the software she's using. It's simple, straightforward. I move one hand to the mouse and brush hers away.

"What are you doing?" she asks as I click the record button.

I drop my voice down so it's gravelly. "I have an idea." I kiss the side of her neck, making sure the kiss is wet and noisy, and bring my arm back around her.

"Oh?" she says, and now it comes out breathy.

"Yeah. I thought maybe we could make a recording just for you."

Her breath catches, and her eyes fall shut.

"Would you like that?"

She licks her lips. "Wha—what did you have in mind?"

"You don't have to do anything," I say. "Just sit here and let me tell you exactly what I want to do to you."

Her head tilts back, and I keep talking. Out of the corner of my eye, I can see the sound level meter on the screen following along with my voice. "I love coming out every morning and seeing you dressed like this. All this skin bared just for me." I sweep a hand down her chest, fingers snagging on the edge of her sports bra. "You're a chronic under-dress-er." I chuckle, low and dark. "And I fucking love it. I love how you're always a little cold, and sometimes I just can't stop staring at your nipples."

My finger finds one of them, and they're rock hard, straining against the fabric. I tweak it.

"Of course, now that I know the sweet noises you make when I touch you, the way it sounds when you come, a whole new world has opened for me." I slide my fingers down to her bare stomach. "One where I bury myself in your pussy and make you come on my face."

Sara moans, and the meter spikes.

"You like coming on my face?"

"Yes," she whispers and shifts in her seat.

"If I dipped my fingers in now, would I find you wet?"

Her eyelashes flutter. God, she's so fucking sexy like this, turned on and just a little scandalized. Her lips are parted, bottom lip pink from being chewed on. I swipe my pointer finger under the waistband of her yoga pants, and she gasps, her stomach tensing.

And then she fucking opens her legs.

"Look at you, spreading for me. I didn't even have to ask. You just want it so bad." She whimpers, and I let my other hand wander, diving into her sports bra and pinching one nipple. I cup my palm around the slope of her breast and feel its perfect weight.

"Oh, god."

Finally, I let my fingers brush her clit, slide down and feel how wet she is. "Oh, you need it, don't you? I can feel your body on the edge already."

I circle her slowly, dipping in and spreading her wetness around. I stay quiet for a few minutes, but Sara makes enough noise for the both of us. Her movements grow more erratic, her hips shifting, stomach flexing.

"Are you close, babe?"

"Yes, please, please . . ."

I press harder. "I know exactly what you need. I'm going to reward you for being so good. Are you ready for it, babe? Are you going to come for me?"

Sara gasps, twisting her hips, and I press harder, letting her ride my hand over the edge. She cries out, and I murmur soothing words, easing back and letting her come down with gentle strokes.

Sara's face is flushed, her breathing hard, and her eyelashes fluttering. With my left hand, I reach across her body and stop the recording.

"Holy shit," she says, and I laugh against her hair.

"Don't get too comfortable," I say.

"What do you mean?" she asks, and I click the play button. I reach over and unplug the headphones.

We listen to the recording, and when I slide my hands back into her pants, Sara comes even faster the second time.

30

Sara

Zoe and I arrive at the back door, and when we flash our backstage passes, the security guy lets us in. We weave through the back hallways, and I hold my badge out in front of me.

"Mom," Zoe hisses at me. "Put the badge down. Be cool."

I drop the badge. "I'm at a rock concert for a band I couldn't even name a song of, and I dressed like this." I gesture down at my clothes. "I look anything but cool."

Zoe had called my look "PTA meeting" and begged me to change before we left the hotel. I stood my ground. My top is an aubergine tunic that falls below the hip of my jeans that flare slightly over sensible black boots. Zoe's wearing ripped jean shorts, knee-high stiletto boots Jade bought her while we were in Rome and a black crop top. Chris knows who I am, and there's no point in trying to hide it.

This past week has been amazing. We did another live session on Thursday, and while I haven't had the growth on my Patreon that I had the first week, I'm definitely still gaining supporters, and it's way more than I had before.

I roll my eyes, and we approach the band's room. The security guard here checks us much more thoroughly, inspecting the badge, our faces, the names on the list before finally opening the door for us.

"Chris!" Zoe squeals and launches herself at him like a long-lost friend. It gives me a bit of time to absorb the room, which is full of people, and brace myself when Chris turns his full attention on me.

And holy shit. This is Chris Rächer in all his glory. He's laced up in some complicated black ribbon-and-leather top, the omnipresent leather pants, and his full makeup kit.

He'd mentioned that they have makeup artists do this for the band for concerts and big events, and I can see why. Chris's makeup is flawless and bold, peacock colors flashing at me every time he closes his eyes.

Zoe nudges me, and I stop staring. "Hey," I say.

Lame.

Chris and I agreed that we would keep our relationship a secret. It would be too big of a thing with Zoe and the rest of the band.

At the same time, though, we didn't talk about what was next. I just hit sixty days in the Schengen Zone, and I need to figure out what I am going to do about it. I can only spend thirty more days out of the next one hundred and twenty in the Schengen regions.

I had no idea visas were so complicated.

Chris holds out his arms for a hug, and I come in gingerly. "I don't want to mess up your stage outfit," I say into his chest. He hasn't even performed yet, but he smells like sweat and a little like cigarette smoke, which has me wrinkling my nose, disappointment crashing through me.

"In thirty minutes, I'm going to be sweating and disgusting; there's nothing you can do to ruin this glory," he pulls away and waves a hand down at his body.

I lean back in and frown. "Did you smoke?"

"No." At my eyebrow raise, he crosses his heart with his hand. "A lot of people back here smoked, but I didn't."

"Okay," I say, bracing myself to deal with second-hand smoke all night. "Are you doing okay? Without smoking?"

"I have a nicotine patch on my ass."

Chris glances around at the small group here. Zoe's talking at Alwin, who just looks amused, nodding along to whatever she's saying.

Uncomfortable, I adjust the underwire in my bra. Why do these things always feel like a robot's cupping your boobs? The movement draws Chris's gaze.

Chris plucks at the shoulder of my top. "Holy shit, are you wearing a real bra?"

I bat his hand away. "Shut up. I look like a dorky mom."

"With fantastic tits."

"You're just saying that because I'm wearing a real bra."

"No." He leans in, a wicked gleam in his eyes, and my heart starts to pound. "I've been obsessed with your tits from the start. Sports bras, bathing suits, mashed up against my face, wet and slippery . . ." Chris's voice trails off, and his eyes lose focus. Last night, we'd gotten in the hot tub together, and recalling how Chris cupped and massaged and played with my breasts in the water and knowing that Chris is thinking about it too has my body tightening.

But then Chris seems to remember where we are and that my daughter is here. Distracted, but here.

"Come on," he says instead. "I'll introduce you to the rest of the band. Just don't judge them too hard right now because we all have our pre-performance rituals."

Chris introduces me to the two members I don't know. I barely get a glance from June, but the drummer, Ram, is enthusiastic and happy, whacking his thigh with drumsticks and grinning like a golden retriever puppy.

Zoe wanders over after Alwin makes some excuse and

slips out the door, and then the three of us go to the stage, and Chris shows us where we can stand to watch.

"What about you?" I ask. "What are your pre-performance rituals?"

"It's all taken care of," he says vaguely.

"What is it?" Zoe says, eyes widening with excitement. "Is it illegal?"

"No," Chris says, laughing. "It's not like that."

"So then, why won't you tell us?" I ask, and poke him in the side, right where I know he's ticklish. Zoe almost looks horrified until she raises a finger experimentally.

Chris, bless his heart, lets Zoe poke him.

"Fine, you broke me. I eat a hot dog."

"You eat a hot dog?" I say, mystified. "Why didn't you want to tell us that?"

"Well, you've had me eating vegan for like three weeks. It felt weird to eat one of those cheap shit hot dogs where you wonder what parts of what animals actually went into it. And I used to smoke a cigarette too."

"What do you put on your hot dog?" Zoe asks the important questions.

"Ketchup."

"Huh," she says, clearly disappointed.

On the other side of the black curtain, the general noises of a crowd have been swelling, and our volume increases too. A woman dressed in black taps Chris's shoulder and whispers into his ear.

"It's time," he says. "Stay here, have fun, and enjoy the show."

Zoe grips my arm and squeals while Chris looks at me with longing, like, "I wish I could kiss you right now." But he leaves, and I'm left with my very excited daughter.

She pulls out her phone and holds it up, tugging me closer for a selfie. I smile, and Zoe types away at her phone. Mine buzzes, and it's the photo in a group chat with Jade, Emma, and Tessa.

ZOE

We're backstage!

JADE

Hot damn.

TESSA

Have fun!

I think Emma's studying tonight, so I'm not surprised when she doesn't respond right away.

Zoe and I stay closer together and watch the final adjustments of the gear. Then the band files out, taking their places on the stage. By some signal I miss, the lights in the entire stadium go out and the noise of the crowd swells.

When Zoe grabs my hand, I weave my fingers through hers and am nearly blinded when the lights go on. The curtain's gone, and flames shoot up the stage as Verduistering launches into their first song.

It's loud and rough and entirely in German, so I have no idea what's happening, but Zoe jumps and dances, and before long, I do too.

Chris is on the opposite side of the stage, but it means he's facing me. Watching him is fascinating—of course, I'd watched videos of him playing concerts, but just like all music, it's more magnetic in person.

And he's so in his element, my heart swells. How can it be that this man, the exact opposite of me in nearly every way, can make me feel like this?

At the end of the first song, the band goes silent and the crowd roars.

"Danke, thank you," Alwin says into the mic. "Thank you for coming out to support Regenbogen Zusammen and the rights of the queer youth. It's a project that's been very near and dear to my heart since my parents kicked me out."

The stadium fills with boos, and I'm sure I'm not the only one whose eyes have filled with tears.

"Every child deserves a safe place, and that's what Regenbogen Zusammen is for. Thank you for supporting our community and our band. Now, let's fucking rock!"

They play four more songs before they get to their big hit, the English song that won them Eurovision. Zoe screams next to me, but I only know because I can see her; the crowd drowns out the noise.

When the song ends, I have never seen Chris smile so wide. The crowd continues to cheer and scream as the band walks off the stage, waving and smiling. Alwin blows kisses to the crowd, and I swear the volume goes up another notch.

When Chris's eyes find me, it's a jolt to my system, lighting me up from my toes to the top of my head. His eyes are laser beams, pulling him toward me with single-minded focus until he stops suddenly, close, so close.

31

Sara

Zoe is gone, following the band, and if she said anything to me, I didn't hear it. Everything was too loud, too exciting, and despite myself, all I could focus on was Chris.

Big hands grip my hips, pushing me back through black curtains and around cables and wires. Chris is guiding me, his eyes never leaving mine and a fire in them like I've never seen before.

My back hits a wall, and somehow, we've gotten so far into the curtains backstage that the space around us is dark. One step, and Chris is up against me, his cock hard and pressing into my stomach.

His mouth goes to my ear. "Fuck, knowing you were watching me on stage was so fucking hot."

My fingers clutch at his shirt. Chris feels bigger and broader than ever before. The colors around his eyes are still vivid, almost shimmering, when the heavy velvet moves enough to allow a stream of light in. I stretch on my tippy-toes and bring our mouths together.

I hardly know what's happening when Chris unzips my

jeans, struggling to get a hand into my pants before he yanks the whole thing, underwear and all, down to my thighs, the cold air sending goosebumps across my ass until he grips one cheek with a warm hand. His other hand goes between my legs, plunging in and thrusting deep, making me cry out. I bury my face in his chest to muffle the noise.

Chris's pants are just as tight as mine, and he nearly pops out into my hand when I get his fly down. We're panting and stroking, and his hand is gripping and squeezing my ass with every thrust of his hips.

This isn't delicate and tender; this is urgent and needy. The sounds Chris's fingers make while pumping in and out of me are obscene, and thank god, there's enough surrounding noise to cover it. His dick is hard and tight in my hand, and I swipe my thumb over the slit and spread the pre-come over his foreskin and the ridge of the head.

"Oh, fuck," he says, and his hands disappear, ripping off his shirt and throwing it over my hand before he twitches and pulses into it. His cum splashes onto my fist, hot and wet, while he keeps grinding.

A few shudders and Chris has regained his senses, and his hand is back between my legs. He works me hard, and I curl into him, chasing my own orgasm. A fire licks up my legs, the muscles in my body undulating while I ride his fingers as my orgasm rips through me.

I'm panting hard, coming down quickly while Chris slips his fingers out of me and pulls away from my hand. His fingers—the middle three—go into his mouth, and he cleans the juices off with his tongue, metal bar flashing, before he rolls the shirt around and wipes his hands on a bare spot.

"This shirt is not up to the job," he mutters, and I laugh. The ribbon and leather top he was wearing is ruined.

"Could have used mine," I say, still catching my breath.

Chris presses me back against the wall and gives me a long, slow, lingering kiss. "No one will blink an eye when I walk in shirtless to the band's room. You, on the other hand, might draw some attention."

My hips wriggle while Chris tugs my panties and jeans back up my legs and zips me up. He tucks himself in and reaches into his pocket, pulling out a hair band and sliding it onto his wrist.

He looks me over. "You look pretty well-fucked." Chris holds up the shirt, a filthy bundle of cum and sweat. "Stay right there."

The black drapes flutter as Chris disappears and returns a few minutes later, shirt presumably thrown away. We spend a few minutes tidying up; Chris smooths my hair down in the back where it rubbed against the wall, and then he flips his own head over and twists his hair up into a bun. I'm certain my lipstick is entirely worn off, but it's hard to tell if it's on Chris's lips or if his are just red from kissing.

"Ready?" he says. "I'm sure the rest of Verduistering is back in the room and relaxing."

He leads the way, pushing the heavy curtains aside and making his way through the space. We start to run into a few people coiling power cords and pushing big boxes on carts through.

"Is relaxing a euphemism? Zoe's with them."

"It won't be a punch bowl and passed hors d'oeuvres," Chris says. "But they won't get into too much trouble."

When Chris opens the door to the green room, there are more people than I would have expected. Most of them have drinks, and some are vaping or smoking cigarettes. Despite the weather outside, Chris was right, he's not the only one showing a lot of skin; several people are shirtless, and a woman walks past us with long legs shown off in boy shorts and leather boots. In fact, there are a lot of beautiful, scantily clad women in the room, making my outfit stick out like a sore thumb.

Chris leaves in search of a beer, and I look for Zoe. I make three passes of the room, and worry builds to panic. I'm picturing my daughter having run off somewhere with a band member or a roadie or groupie or something, and will she be safe? I definitely don't want to find her in some corner in a compromising position.

That's exactly what *I* just did. I'm lucky Zoe didn't find me with my pants down and Chris's cock in my hand. Ugh. Having an adult daughter is turning me into a hypocrite.

Then I see Zoe in a spot I'm one hundred percent sure I already looked—next to Ram on the couch.

"Oh, my god," Zoe says. "There you are."

Something about the way she says it is a little weird, and my mama bear senses are tingling. She's leaning forward on the couch, twirling the leather bracelet around her wrist over and over again. She doesn't stop, even when I sit down next to her. Ram is having an animated conversation with two women on his other side, and he doesn't seem to notice when I squeeze between the two of them.

When I touch her arm, Zoe turns to me. "Oh my god, Mom!" She straightens up and blinks rapidly. She takes my hand, threading my fingers through hers, which surprises me because she hasn't done that kind of thing in a while. "We're hanging out with rock stars!"

I laugh and lean back on the couch. She leans with me, and for a while, we just observe the party. While I am glad I didn't find her having sex in a dark corner—yes, despite my hypocritical thoughts, I can't help being relieved—I am surprised that Zoe's not chatting someone up.

And actually, now that I'm paying attention, Zoe's holding her breath and then letting it out, then sniffing hard, and opening her mouth to exhale...

"Zoe, are you okay?"

She turns her face to me with wide eyes. Like, really wide eyes.

"Yeah. Why?"

"You're breathing weird."

A look of relief passes over her face. "Okay, I'm breathing. That's good."

WHAT?

"Zoe." I grab her face and turn it toward me. She doesn't have a drink, but she's still playing with her bracelet, and now she's practically Lamaze breathing in my face. She doesn't smell like alcohol, though, and I wonder if there's anything harder around here. "Did you take something?"

"What? No. I'm totally cool," she says. "Totally cool. Totally, totally cool. Cool." She stares at me. "Cool."

Holy shit, my daughter's been drugged.

Hell hath no fury like a mother protecting her daughter, and I'm on my feet and dragging her with me, pushing people aside until I find Chris talking to Alwin.

The smile that flits over his face when he sees me disappears quickly, and I'm pretty sure I'm broadcasting a murder face.

"My daughter," I seethe at him, "is drugged."

"Mom," Zoe makes an attempt at whining but can't quite manage it. "Don't embarrass me."

Whatever she's on is giving me a flashback to her petulant teenaged days, and it just scares me more. I have to get her out of here and maybe to a police station? A hospital? I don't know.

Next to us, Alwin laughs. "Ah, those bonbons are hitting her hard, hey?"

I wheel on Alwin, stabbing my finger into his chest. I don't know what the fuck bonbons are. "You! You think this is funny? I'm taking my daughter down to the hospital to get tested and treated. Whatever she's on, you better hope to god she doesn't overdose or get addicted or whatever other bad shit happens to the morons who do drugs because I swear to god, I will press charges or sue you or, if all that fails, I will hunt you down and shove a Carolina Reaper so far up your ass you'll be breathing fire, are we clear?"

My pointed finger has crept up Alwin's chest, and he's leaning back, bent over so far to get away from me that his drink is spilling on his chest. Those famous golden eyes are wide and—much to my satisfaction—scared.

My other hand still grips Zoe's, and I whip around, tugging her behind me. The room has gone very quiet, and I storm past Chris, who looks even more shell-shocked than Alwin. He keeps his mouth shut, though, and I make it out the door and wind through backstage until I find a long, well-lit hallway with a proper exit sign that doesn't look like it'll set off the fire alarm. That's when footsteps ring out behind me, and I know it's Chris before I hear him calling me.

"Sara! Sara, wait," he shouts.

I don't stop but grumble under my breath, "Don't make me threaten you, too."

"I know how to take care of Zoe," he says, and yes, that gets me to stop and turn around.

Chris catches up to us, and Zoe tilts her head back to look up at him. "You're so pretty," she says.

"It's just pot," he says, panting slightly. "She can't OD, and it's legal. She doesn't need to go to the hospital, I promise."

I scowl at him. "She didn't think she was breathing."

"Was she breathing? She might be a little paranoid right now, but she just needs time for it to wear off."

We both look at Zoe, who's holding a hand up and trying to flick her wrist to twirl the bracelet one-handed.

"She is breathing," I say slowly. "A bonbon is pot?"

"It's just laced chocolate," he assures me.

"Oh." Oh. Crap. I just freaked out about pot in front of people who I'm pretty sure have done way worse, plus threatened Alwin. My cheeks heat, but I still think the situation is shitty. "So, what, these bonbons were just out, and Zoe ate one?"

Chris shifts uncomfortably. "Yeah, probably." He scratches his cheek, eyes darting from me to Zoe and back. "She might have known, you know," he says quietly.

"Zoe doesn't do drugs," I say firmly.

"Okay," Chris says, holding up his hands in surrender. "I'm sorry, Sara. I'll talk to the band about it."

The band. He'll talk to the band about it, and what the hell are they going to do? They're a rock band, for Pete's sake. My daughter's high, I'm wearing a ridiculous outfit that makes me feel ancient, and I'm dating a guy who's in a band.

Chris is oblivious to my thoughts, though. I hold up my hand. "You've got your meeting with the band tomorrow, and I'm going to spend the day with Zoe. Let's just . . ." I shake my head. "Go back to the hotel, and I'll text you, okay?"

I nod, and for the first time tonight, I don't wish that I could kiss him.

———

IN OUR HOTEL ROOM, ZOE'S STILL LOOPY. WE WASH HER FACE, change her clothes, and I sit on the couch with her with the TV on. She lays her head in my lap and occasionally says in a sleepy voice, "Am I still breathing?"

Until one time, she says, "I'm sorry I ate the bonbon."

I sigh and brush some of her curls out of her face. "You didn't know, sweetheart."

"I did know." Her lips turn down in a pout. "They're just a lot stronger than I'm used to. I thought a half would be okay."

I close my eyes and sink my head back on the couch.

She keeps talking. "I wanted the full experience. And like, Alwin and the rest of the band would think I was cool."

"Sweetie," I say, opening my eyes and looking down at her, stroking her head. "They already thought you were cool."

"No, they didn't," she says, as a tear slips down her nose. She swings her arm around so her hand is in front of her face. "I freaked out when I met Chris. I've got wild, crazy hair. I have no boobs. I took too much pot."

"Why does this sound like a list of things you don't like about yourself?"

"Because that's what everyone sees!"

"No, it's not. We see things about ourselves that no one else does. I promise. Chris has gotten over that first weekend. He's had tons of people freak out when they meet him. And I'm also sure they are no strangers to people who make mistakes with drugs. You know that Ram OD'ed."

"But my boobs!"

"I am very certain that no one is paying attention to your boobs."

"*No one*? Mom! I thought guys are always looking at boobs."

"No one in the band," I correct. I really want to laugh—I mean, it is kind of true about men and boobs, and lord knows I could stop obsessing about how my chest looks, too—but Zoe, with her head in my lap, is getting really upset.

"Honestly, Zoe, it doesn't matter. We're going back to the US soon, and Chris has a whole different life than we do."

A life with drugs and groupies and fame. One that I will never fit into. And one that I will definitely not drag my daughter into with me.

"Are you going back?"

I look down at Zoe, and she's gazing up at me, tear tracks drying on her cheeks and the long, curly hair she inherited from her dad fanning out over my lap.

"Of course, I'm going back."

Zoe looks skeptical. "But you and Chris—"

"Would be ridiculous," I finish. "Come on, could you imagine if this was my life? I would hate it. Sex, drugs, and rock 'n' roll is not my life. My life is back home in our cute little town where I can see you on the weekends and have a studio again."

Zoe is quiet for a few moments, and then she turns onto her side.

"Besides," I say, trying to lighten the mood, "don't you want me back home with you? Where will you go to do your laundry on the weekends or study for finals or have a home-cooked meal?"

She doesn't answer right away, a crease between her eyebrows as she stares unseeing at the TV. "While I appreciate the irony of saying this while my head is in your lap and I'm coming down off a bad high, I think we both need to learn to be better on our own." My heart tightens in my chest. "I love you, Mom, but I also need to be an adult."

Tears spring into my eyes. "I love you, too."

My phone dings on the armrest of the couch, and I lean over to see a message from Chris.

CHRIS

How's our little pothead?

I show Zoe the text and she squeals, covering her face with her hands. "I. Am. Dying. Pothead? Nooooo . . ."

32

Chris

After seeing Sara and Zoe safely out of the stadium, I return to the backstage room where the band is still relaxing. Eventually, we will split up, either headed to clubs or the hotel.

I step into the room and zero in on Alwin. "You. Come with me."

Alwin rolls his eyes and excuses himself from the group he is talking to. Sara is pissed, and I'm pissed at Alwin. The next door I find goes into a supply closet, but it's big enough for the two of us. When Alwin closes the door, I round on him.

"How could you give her pot? You know Sara was nervous enough about this."

Alwin crosses his arms and glares at me. "Seriously? You're going to be pissed at me about this? Zoe is a grown woman, man. She makes her own choices and is responsible for her own actions. She knew exactly what she was doing. She even said something about preferring edibles."

"So, she knew?"

"Look, we've spent enough time around groupies and roadies to get a sense for who's trying too hard and who's partying too hard. Zoe falls into the former. She obviously was in a bit over her head and look how that turned out."

"Still, it's dangerous."

Alwin's eyebrow raises. "More dangerous than Ram's partying? You don't seem to be so upset about the overdoses anymore."

"Ram knows he's walking a dangerous edge," I grind out.

"Or maybe it's that you're trying to be a responsible grown-up around Sara."

"Is that such a bad thing?"

"It is if it's got you wound too tight. This lifestyle comes with its risks and rewards. You're being way too hard on yourself lately. And too hard on us."

"Maybe you deserve it. Marcus told me you stole one of my songs. Where does that fall in the risks and rewards category."

Alwin and I are centimeters apart now, both of us glowering, and I can feel the sweat trickling down my back.

"Did he say that I stole it?"

"He called it your song and read my own lyrics back to me."

"Fuck you, Chris. I rewrote half the damn thing. You know we'll be sharing credit on it if it makes it to the final cut."

"I've been working fucking hard on these songs."

"Why? When did we suddenly become the Chris Rächer band?"

"Because no one else fucking wrote the one hit song we have!"

"Oh, fuck you and your high horse." Alwin pushes me, and I'm so surprised he gets another shove in before I can respond. My back hits the door, and when Alwin's hands grip my shoulders, I try to shove them off, which results in a wrestling match. I hook my foot behind Alwin's knee, and in a flurry of cleaning supplies and expletives, we tangle on the ground.

Neither of us can get an advantage, and after a few minutes, we're gasping for breath. I've somehow got a grip on Alwin's hand, pulling his arm behind his back and wrenching his shoulder while his other arm has me in a headlock.

"You're not the only songwriter in the band. Say it!" he says, tightening the arm around my neck. In response, I pull on his hand, and I hear him grit his teeth.

"I'm a better songwriter than you," I grunt. "That hit is mine."

"God, you're fucking competitive. We'll see about that tomorrow. I'm going to blow your fucking mind."

The absurdity of the situation hits me, mostly because I'm facedown next to a urinal cake. I ease my grip on his arm, and he loosens his choke hold.

"If only the paps could catch us now," he says.

I slump, letting go of his hand and allowing my forehead to hit the floor. I chuckle, and it blows some hair that's come loose from my bun. *"Members of Verduistering Try to Murder Each Other."*

"Lead Singer Found in Compromising Position with Guitarist," he says, and I feel his laughter on my back.

"We Were Right About Rächer All Along," I say. *"Always Knew He Was Gay."*

Alwin rolls off of me. "God, we'd give them such fodder. They are obsessed."

I turn my head to face him, and he looks over at me. A dust bunny by his eyebrow reminds me that we're on the floor of a dirty storeroom.

With a groan, I roll to my feet, offering Alwin a hand. We dust ourselves off.

"Seriously, though. Not every song we come up with is

going to be a hit, but we need an album. Perfection is the enemy of done, right? And we all need to chip into this album, or it's not going to feel like ours."

"The shit Ram has been sending me isn't going to end up on our album."

"Not if you smash it down before it gets a chance to grow." Alwin scowls. "Even Ringo wrote a hit song."

"Did you just compare us to The Beatles?"

Alwin grins at me for a moment.

"I'm John Lennon," we both say at the same time.

"Fuck you," I say. "I do yoga and eat vegan."

"That makes you Harrison. Ono says John was bisexual, ergo . . ." Alwin waves his hand over himself.

"That leaves June as McCartney," I say.

Alwin and I look at each other. "That tracks," we say in unison.

"You should see the stuff she's written lately," he continues. "Might turn us into a cheery pop band."

We both let our mood slip back to seriousness, and Alwin places a hand on my shoulder. "We'll hash it all out together tomorrow."

"Yeah, all right."

"What about you and Sara, then?"

I shrug but can't help smiling, even just at her name.

"Holy shit," Alwin says. "You're in love."

"I'm not—she wouldn't—*fuck*. Totally," I admit.

Alwin groans. "You will be the worst. All happy and in love. Is she going to tour with us?"

My smile slips. "Tour with us? I doubt she'll want to tag along with the band. Besides, she's got her daughter moving back stateside before Christmas."

"Do you think she'll forgive you for the bonbon?"

"Me? It's your fault. You better hope she forgives you."

"She'll forgive me," he preens. "I'm charming."

I shove his shoulder again, but Alwin catches my hand and pulls me into him, wrapping me in his arms.

"Love you," he says, cheek squished against my shoulder.

"Love you too."

Something somewhere crashes, and we pull apart, sighing.

I twist the doorknob and open the door. "Let's go check on Ram."

When I get back to the party, I dig out my phone and send a quick text to Sara.

CHRIS

How's our little pothead?

SARA

She's much better. We're going to bed. See
you tomorrow.

CHRIS

I'm glad she's okay. I'm sorry about the guys.

SARA

It's fine. We'll talk after the band meeting.

We'll talk. That doesn't sound great, and I don't know if it's my guilt projecting onto the messages, but Sara seems short.

Which is fair.

I admire her dedication to her daughter. My mother was like that too, and growing up, I knew how important I was to her. I'm glad Sara and Zoe have that kind of relationship.

What am I going to do when Zoe goes back to the States? Will Sara want to stay, or will she head back home too?

Problems for another day. For now, I rejoin the party and remind myself that I signed up for this life.

———

"Well, fuck me," I say with wonder.

Ram puts the tablet down and looks at the four of us. "What do you think?" he says, without a hint of self-consciousness or pride.

We're in Marcus's hotel suite, going over song choices for our next album, and it's barely organized chaos. I prefer to handwrite, but the rest of the band prefers digital, so we've each got multiple devices plus generous piles of papers around us. Some of them have works in progress, some of them have scratched notes or scribbled-out bars.

We've been at it for hours, and with every hour that passes, the five of us have wound tighter and tighter.

This is good. This is really good. We've revised almost every song I've brought to the table and reworked them with everyone contributing. Well, not Marcus, who says he'd rather piss on an electric fence than try to write lyrics. But the rest of the group is excited and energized and laughing.

And Ram's just blown me away with lyrics he's written.

"Fucking hell," Alwin says, sitting back and running his hands through his hair.

"I think I owe you an apology, Ram," I say.

"What for?"

"I didn't take your song seriously. I'm sorry. I should have paid more attention to it and seen its potential."

Ram's eyebrows draw together. "It was two lines, mate. You don't have to apologize. It was rubbish. But I worked it out."

"Clearly not rubbish," I point out.

"Well, even a diamond comes from shit, right?" he says cheerily.

June, Alwin, and I glance at each other. "Do you mean coal?" June asks.

"But the lines weren't coal," Ram explains. "That doesn't make any sense."

"All right." Marcus moves us on. "We've got twenty-three

songs sketched out enough to have merit. And about two dozen more that have potential. I say we move to London and start playing around."

Holy fucking shit. We have an album. We're going to have another goddamn album.

June throws her head back on the couch. "Thank Christ." With stage makeup and dye, she's the most disguised of all of us. Today, she's without the costume, and her blond ringlets and dimples are refreshing. I've missed her face.

"Can we please, please, celebrate?" Alwin says. Ram sits up, eager as always.

"I wanted to meet up with Sara." I grimace in apology.

"Bring her," Ram says, perking up. "I've got friends in town too."

"She's got Zoe here too."

Ram shrugs. "So? She's nice."

I glance at June and Alwin, who both nod, and I pull out my phone. "Where to?"

CHRIS

Are you two free to come meet up with us?

SARA

You've had a long day and so have we. I think it's best if we catch up later. And I'm going to travel to Munich with Zoe tomorrow. I'll see you back at your house tomorrow night?

CHRIS

If that's what you want to do.

I shake my head. Of course, she wants to spend her time with Zoe. I stare at my phone. I was feeling on top of the world just a moment ago. How is it possible that this woman has made me so mercurial?

Putting my phone away, I tune into the rest of the band

arguing about where to go, and I throw in a few suggestions, mostly to rile Alwin up.

He shoves his hands in his hair. "You know I can't go there. I slept with the maître d, and I know you sure as shit aren't going to change clothes to go there anyway."

Marcus, used to wrangling us, puts his foot down and picks a place—a dive bar.

CHRIS

We're going to a place called Bad Monkey Bar if you change your mind.

It's walking distance, so we exit the hotel and brace ourselves against the chill. On the way, Ram falls back to walk with me. "You're serious about her?"

"Yeah," I say.

"Good. It's about time one of us settles down."

"You made a good attempt," I tell him. Ram's been married twice, neither worked out.

"I made attempts," he corrects. "Not good ones."

After a moment of walking quietly, Ram speaks again. "What about Zoe?"

I groan and throw my head back. "Not you too. And seriously, Sara will kill you. And then me. And possibly Zoe."

"Are you saying you forbid me? Careful," he croons. "Wouldn't want to tempt me with her."

"You're not star-crossed lovers."

"She's a star? An actress? What's her last name?"

"No, she's not. Never mind, man."

All night, I can't stop grinning. It feels good to be back with these idiots.

33

Sara

I'M A COWARD.

From Zoe's dorm room, I text Chris that I'm staying the night in Munich, saying I want to spend more time with Zoe. But in reality, I need time to come up with a plan.

I can't stay with Chris anymore. I like him so much, and living with him, sleeping with him, doing everything domestic and nourishing with him has blinded me to his real life. Drugs and parties are the norm.

I reinforce the need to move out by watching videos of the band—especially Ram—doing their superstar thing. Red carpet events, interviews, and drunken escapades caught on fans' camera phones.

I read articles about Ram's stint in a rehab facility and watch videos of Chris smoking and drunk.

It's painful and sobering.

I do not want that to be my life.

"What do you want to do for dinner, Mom?" Zoe interrupts my thoughts. She's been pretty quiet today. Yesterday we did a few touristy things in Berlin, walking from downtown to the Memorial to the Murdered Jews of Europe and the Brandenburger Tor before having a quiet dinner together. She asked what Chris was up to a few times, I think hoping to see the band again and make a better impression, but I told her they were busy, and she stopped asking.

I hop up from the couch and navigate to her tiny dorm kitchen. "Let's see what you have."

Zoe follows close behind me. "I don't have much, Mom. We could go out. Or order to go. There's a vegan place—"

Zoe cuts herself off when I open the fridge. It's like a flashback: I'm back in Baden-Baden staring at Chris's bachelor fridge.

This is a little better, but not much. There are to-go containers and a sad bunch of kale and an almond milk container, but there's also . . .

Bacon. There's a pack of bacon in one of the drawers and a package of sliced cheese.

"Okay," I say, closing the fridge door. "Let's go out to eat."

Zoe doesn't protest, and I follow her out onto the street.

Munich has a few universities huddled together with museums and shops. Its post-war architecture, rather boring and busy, especially compared to Baden-Baden.

We choose an Indian restaurant and sit down in a booth. I peruse the menu and pick a vegan dish quickly, setting my menu down and looking at Zoe.

She's chewing her lip, contemplating her options.

"It's fine if you don't want to order something vegan."

Zoe sets her menu down and stares at me. "Who are you, and what have you done with my mother?"

"Ha, ha. I'm just saying that I'm not pressuring you to eat plant-based. You're a grown-up, and you can make your own decisions about those kinds of things." I pause. "Even bonbons."

"Thanks," she says quietly. "I still eat mostly plant-based food. And I love it when we cook together. And also, I'm really glad you took care of me last night."

I smile. "Me too. That won't ever stop, so next time you come home, we'll be sure to cook some of your favorites again."

We're interrupted by the server who takes our order. Zoe orders for both of us in German, and my chest swells with pride.

If it weren't for her, I never would have done this trip. She's the one who wanted to leave our little town and try something new, and here she is, flourishing.

"Actually, I was thinking about visiting you in Baden-Baden again. Maybe in two weeks?"

I fold my hands in front of me. "About that. I've decided to fly back home."

Zoe's jaw drops. "What? Why?"

"I came for you, and looking back, I don't think that was the right thing to do. You're doing so well at school, and you don't need me around. I can go back home and get my job back at the yoga studio. I already emailed my old boss and the rental management company. I may not be able to move back into our house right away but—"

"What about Chris?"

"He doesn't actually need a roommate, and his band will be going to the studio soon to work on their next album anyway. And we finished the Rock Steady videos, so I just have to edit and post them."

"Mom! You cannot be this dense! Chris is so into you. You can't just leave him!"

I shake my head. "We're not like that."

Zoe scowls at me. "Did you think I wouldn't notice how you two disappeared at the end of the concert? Or the way you look at each other?"

"Zoe," I say, trying to dredge up patience instead of sadness. I don't want to think about how Chris and I looked at each other or those moments backstage that make my toes curl under the table of this booth. "Can you really see the two of us dating? We have nothing in common."

"He's in love with you."

"He's not," I protest.

"And you're in love with him."

"Zoe," I chide her. "Really?"

"That's not a denial, Mom. And what about the wine club? You promised you'd be visiting them once a month."

"Just like you, they'll be fine."

Zoe stands, rising with her voice. "You always say things will be fine, but maybe that's not good enough. Have you even talked to Chris? Or Aunt Jade or Tessa or Emma? How do they feel about you leaving?"

I keep my voice calm. Zoe and I haven't fought like this in years. "I haven't told them yet, but I will. I booked a flight for Friday, so I'm going to go back to Baden-Baden and get my things. This is done, Zoe."

Her face screws up in anger. "You always play it safe, Mom. You're never willing to risk it when things really matter."

Zoe slumps into her seat, glaring at me, and I try to keep the stab of pain from showing on my face.

———

I'm on the train to Baden-Baden during Jade's lunch break and our usual call time, so I use that opportunity to tell my friends face-to-digital-face that I'm leaving. Tessa and Jade are both at their desks eating, and Emma's in her kitchen making a sandwich.

"Hello, are y'all there?" Everyone's frozen, so I wonder if

I've lost connection, but then Jade snaps into motion on the screen.

"You're going back to Texas? Why?" she asks.

"I need to get back to my real life. It's just not working out here, and I want to give Zoe some space."

"Is this because she got high?" Jade asks.

"Wait, what?" Tessa interrupts.

"How did you know?" I demand.

Zoe had texted Jade and given her a version of the story, which Jade tells, and then I tell mine.

"You can't be leaving just because Zoe had a bad trip," Emma says. "You know she's a good kid, and it's not a bad thing that she did. It was scary, sure, but she's okay."

"It's not just that," I begin. I can tell my friends all the things I couldn't tell Zoe. "Watching Chris with his band is like an alternate universe. It's a different version of him, and I don't fit there. I'm a mom, I'm too uptight, I'm too boring. We've been in a bubble out at his house, and that bubble is going to pop. I can't stand by and watch someone I care about live that kind of life."

"You could come stay with one of us," Emma offers.

"Yeah," Jade chimes in. "I've got my second bedroom. And I'm at work all day."

"I've got a second bedroom too. And I'm visiting Luc a lot anyway," Tessa says.

"Or you could stay with me!" Emma offers.

We all squint at her. "You don't have a spare bedroom," I say.

"No, but I have a queen-sized bed—or whatever the European equivalent is, and I'd share it for you."

"You could take turns staying with each of us," Jade says. "We could pass you around like those traveling pants—Sisterhood of the Broken-Hearted Best Friend."

I gaze out the window of the train. The German countryside is passing by, mountains and beautiful forests and cute little villages.

"I just want to go home."

My friends let it go. There's nothing else they can say. They love me enough to know that I can't be here anymore.

34

Chris

Energized from my time with the band, I work twice as hard when I return to Baden-Baden. Without Sara here, I end up grocery shopping and attempting to cook that curry again, and this time I don't fuck it up too badly.

When I send her a picture of my bowl, she doesn't respond, but by the time I actually get around to eating, it's well past ten p.m., so I'm guessing she's asleep already.

When I move into my studio the next day—at the respectable hour of nine—I leave my door open and my headphones askew so I'll hear her come in.

Despite that, I don't actually hear her until she knocks on my doorframe. I tear the headphones off and launch myself at her. She lets out an "oomph" of surprise when I wrap my arms around her and bury my face in her neck. I've missed her, and it's only been two days since I last saw her.

I guess this is what happens when you fall in love.

And when you spend all your waking time with someone.

"I'm so glad you are back." I trail kisses up her neck to her mouth, occasionally licking and dragging my barbell against her skin while she shivers. My hand slides down to cup her perfect ass. When she gasps, I slide into her mouth with my tongue, tasting and licking until we're both panting.

"We had the most amazing meeting with the band," I tell her, too excited to contain myself. I'm bubbling over with things to talk about, and for fuck's sake, it's only been two days. I want to tell her about every moment of it. "We have an album."

She blinks, her mind catching up to my words. "That's great." Her eyebrows draw together. "Chris, I—"

"Hang on, that's not the best part."

She's seen me through the worst of this year, and she, more than anyone, understands the pressure I've been putting on myself to write.

"It's better than great. It's going to be a really fucking good album." I press myself into her and sip small kisses from her mouth while I tell her about everything that happened after she left the concert. She laughs about my fight with Alwin and listens intently while I describe the four of us coming together and messing with our lyrics, passing lines back and forth, and scratching melodies onto notebooks.

I don't stop my love assault, though. My hands knead until I lift her leg up and wrap it around my hips. Her eyes go a little dazed when our bodies line up just right.

"Remember the song Lebengenießer that I played for you last week?"

"Yeah." Her voice is breathy.

"You should hear the bass lines June's written for it. You could totally do yoga to it."

She smiles, and it's dreamy. "You were thinking of me while working with the band?"

I thrust my hips into her. "I think about you constantly."

"Chris . . ."

I love her like this. I love her. "We're going to get together next week in London," I tell her.

Kiss. I could take her here in my studio. I could bend her over the desk and pull those yoga pants down and fuck her on the broad, polished wood, or . . .

"Come with me. I'll get us a flat in the city with enough room for you to do yoga, and I'll fly you back to Munich whenever you want to see Zoe."

Sara pushes away from me, her palm on my heaving chest. Her breaths match mine, her chest rising and falling and pulling my gaze down. She's still in her clothes from the train ride, so she's got a sweatshirt on which I am dying to help her out of, even if it is just to see which sports bra she has on today.

When my eyes roam back up to meet hers, though, there's a small crease between her brow. Her teeth have caught her bottom lip and are gnawing at it. The arousal haze is gone from her eyes, and she's studying me.

I reach up and pull her lip gently from her mouth and then smooth my thumb over it.

"What's wrong?"

"You want me to move in with you? In London?"

"Yes." I smile, but she doesn't return it.

Her chest presses against mine as she takes a deep breath. And then another, and then she pushes me farther away from her like she can't breathe. "First, I need to apologize." Sara holds my gaze, steady and serious. "I overreacted about the bonbon."

I tilt my head. "You were scared. I understand why you did it. And for what it's worth, I'm sorry too. Even if it was just pot, bad reactions happen, and they shouldn't be taken lightly either."

She nods. "Thank you. The thing is . . . I'm going back to Texas."

I take a step away under my own accord. "Texas?"

"Yes."

"Wait, what? Are you . . ." Of all the ways I thought this

conversation would go, this was not it. I knew—thought—that Sara wouldn't want to go too far from Zoe, that we'd talk it over and figure out logistics, and now she says she's going even farther away? And that she's leaving me? "Hang on, hang on, I'm suggesting that we just—" I gesture with my hands like I'm scooping something up. "—pick up our life here together and move it to London."

"No, you're not."

"How is London different?" I am genuinely confused.

Sara mimics my gesture. "You're picking us up and putting us in Verduistering."

"I'm Verduistering, not you."

Sara huffs out a breath, frustrated. "Come on, Chris, can you seriously imagine that the lines aren't going to bleed over? This weekend was a disaster."

"Your daughter ate some pot. I would hardly call that a disaster."

Sara's eyes narrow. "I know that it doesn't stop at pot, Chris."

"I don't do hard drugs."

"Can you swear to me, with one hundred percent certainty, that there won't be hard drugs around? That the next time my daughter comes to visit in London, she won't see people do coke or get offered ecstasy?"

"She's an adult—"

"And what about me? *I* don't want to be around that kind of lifestyle."

All of the joy and giddiness from before washes out from me, leaving nothing but a hollow pit. Sara's words are final and firm.

"What do you want me to do?" I ask. "How can I make this right?"

Sara's face softens, her voice gentles. "I'm not asking you to do anything. There's nothing to make right." She walks to the door of my studio, stopping and glancing over her shoulder. "I'll pack up today, and then I have a flight tomorrow afternoon unless you need me to be out sooner?"

I swallow, shaking my head. Sara's gaze dips down to my throat and then to the floor. She leaves without a word.

My back hits the wall, and I slide down, letting my head hang between my shoulders and my elbows rest on my knees.

Weeks ago, I told Alwin that we were too dissimilar, Sara and I. Hell, months ago, when she first moved in, I told myself that time and time again. What was I doing falling in love with someone like her?

I sit long enough for my ass to fall asleep. I shift every so often and wince at the discomfort, but I don't care enough to do anything about it.

Eventually, I hear Sara in the kitchen. The clanging of pots and pans, the water turning on and off. The usual humming is absent. A glance at the clock shows that it's too early for dinner, even for her.

This is her last night here. No more of these shared meals or yoga sessions together or watching her love for her friends, for her daughter. No more hot tubs, yoga pants, or sports bras. I'm giving Sara up for a life of groupies and stardom.

It makes me so fucking angry. Not at Sara, but at life in general. For a brief flash, I had everything I could have ever wanted, and it's being taken away. I've struggled for years to get exactly where I am now, and I grasped, for a moment, something I never thought I'd have.

The anger motivates me to get up.

I stalk into the kitchen. Sara stands at the stove, stirring a pot. It smells wonderful because, of course, it does; it's Sara's fucking cooking. She's stripped off the sweatshirt, so she's back to yoga pants and a sports bra in the heat of the kitchen.

It's the pink one.

She catches sight of me and glances up. I glare at her from the other side of the counter, my palms on the cool marble and my body coiled tight.

"Oh, hey. I, uhh . . ." She points back at the fridge. "I thought I'd cook up all this stuff and make you some meals since I won't be taking this food with me. Although, I don't know how long you'll be here . . ."

Her words trail off as I shove off the counter and stalk around to her.

"Chris, what are you . . ." Her eyes widen, her gaze darting down and over my face. She licks her lips and a flush blooms on her chest.

In an echo of our first kiss, I back her into the wall, caging her in. Her pupils are huge, her mouth parted, and I take those delicious lips in a searing kiss, my body aligning with hers.

This time, Sara meets me head-on. Her hands grab at my back, her fingers scrambling for purchase. I grab her wrists and slam them into the wall above her head, using my knuckles to protect her. Sara groans and responds by sucking my tongue into her mouth.

Fuuuuuccccckkkkkk.

I'm hard as nails against her, and she squirms and wriggles, making it worse. I pull back enough to nip her chin and suck on the soft spot right below her chin. She swallows, and I press my lips against the movement.

"You know this doesn't change anything, right? I'm still leaving."

"I know." My voice is coarse, which we both ignore. I keep moving down her body, pressing my mouth against her. It's not soft and tender; it's teeth and torture.

When I get to her nipple, turgid against the thin material, I graze it with my teeth. Sara's wrists shift as she flexes her hands, and her breath catches.

The energy in my body is telling me more, more, more. Sara's body echoes my thoughts with every movement, every needy cry.

I release her hands and slip mine under the band of her

sports bra, pulling it up and over her head with a practiced ease. She tugs at my shirt, and together we strip it off. Our chests are skin-to-skin, and I kiss her again, deep and thrashing, teeth and metal clacking. I wedge a hand between us and pinch her nipple.

"Oh, fuck."

I almost can't believe it at first. Sara says fuck?

But when I look at her, all my laughter dies. She's so fucking flushed and turned on and swollen.

I tweak her nipple again, and her body arcs, torso curving in, and her eyes closing, head falling down.

"Hey," I bite out. "Look at me."

Sara lifts her head, and I grasp her chin with one hand, switching to her other breast with the other.

"Tell me if I go too hard, okay?"

She nods, and I adjust my grip, my palm lightly on her throat, my thumb and forefinger on opposite sides of her jaw firmly holding her.

I keep kissing her, loving the way her body shakes every time I pinch her nipples. I massage, too, a mix of worship and punishment.

And she likes it. I've been so busy loving her I haven't noticed this side before. This flushed, needy, aching woman. A woman who, when I slip my hand into the front of her yoga pants, I find soaking.

"Jesus fucking Christ," I whisper into her open mouth.

She moans in response when I plunge two fingers in. I work my fingers in and out, pumping and coaxing and getting her strung tight enough to snap.

"Chris, please," she begs. "Fuck me."

I swear. "I have to get a condom." I pull my fingers out of her cunt and suck the juices off. She hasn't even come yet, and she's dripping. "Take your pants off."

In my bedroom, I strip off my pants and grab a condom, rolling it on while I power-walk back to the kitchen. It's not graceful; it's more like trying to hit a moving target with every step until I take my cock in one hand and roll the condom on with the other.

In the kitchen, Sara's back against the wall. She's naked, her ponytail askew, and her eyes wide. She's turned off the burner, but there's a cutting board and knife on the counter. I quickly clear everything off, dumping the cutting board and chopped vegetables into the sink.

"I wasn't done," Sara protests.

"Don't care." I shove everything else to the side against the wall, leaving the counter where we've shared so many meals clear.

"Come here," I command, and when she does, I grip the back of her neck. Her breathing, which had calmed down to heavy, shifts to panting. I guide her down, bending her over the counter. I let her lead, let her turn her head to the side, and apply gentle pressure to keep her there. Not that she needs it. Anticipation rolls over her, her ankles spreading apart and a whimper escaping her mouth when I sweep my other hand up her inner thigh.

"God damn, look at this mess." I trace my fingers through the slickness of her inner thighs. All this just from her standing naked in the kitchen, waiting for me? "You want me to fuck you like that? Sloppy and messy right here?"

"Please," she whispers.

I line up and shove in. Her eyes roll back, and she bites her lips to keep from moaning.

"No." I tighten my grip on her neck and shake it. "This is the last fucking time. I want to hear it."

"Oh god, oh god, oh god . . ." Sara chants.

I piston my hips in and out, building momentum. With every thrust, Sara moves forward just a few centimeters. When her hips are flush against the beveled edge of the counter, I go harder, grunting with every thrust while Sara keens beneath me.

Her hands stretch out and grip the far side of the counter, which gives me an idea. I back away, pulling her with me by her hips until we're in the middle of the kitchen.

"Grab your fucking ankles."

I've seen Sara in this pose so many times before. Her legs spread and she bends in half, stretching her hamstrings and wrapping her fingers around her ankles.

Like this, I'm not pounding her into the counter; I'm gripping her hips and slapping us together. It's deep and rough, and the kitchen fills with the sound of Sara's wailing and my grunts. She's begging relentlessly now, and I watch as my cock goes in and out of her. Cream from her pussy glistens, and I grit my teeth, trying to hold on to the giant, looming orgasm.

Sara shatters, crying out and clenching around me. I shout, slamming in a few more times before I unleash my own release, the surge of heat rolling from my toes to my cock.

Sara's legs start to shake, and I grip her harder to keep us both upright. Which works for the thirty seconds it takes for us to slowly slump down onto the floor.

My sweat-slicked skin sticks to the floor. Sara's on her side next to me, breathing hard.

I've never had sex like that before. I've never cared enough about someone to be a complex ball of emotions.

The anger and frustration have slipped away, and as Sara stands up and slips off to the bathroom, I lie on the kitchen floor, realizing that all that's left in my body, the only thing I feel as I come down from my post-orgasm high, is sadness.

35

———————

Sara

"So, let me get this straight: you had rough, hot, banging sex on the kitchen floor, and then you packed your stuff and snuck out?"

Tessa stares at me from her kitchen in Tavira. I got to my house after eighteen hours of travel time, crashed for six hours, and am now up in the middle of the night, which is nine a.m. Tessa's time.

Jade is in a meeting, and Emma's in class, so I tell Tessa everything.

And by telling her everything, I basically berate myself for sleeping with—and getting emotionally attached to—someone with whom I have no future.

"I didn't sneak out," I argue. "It was a mutual avoidance system. He stayed in his studio; I worked in the kitchen and then went to bed early."

"Right, but even though your train wasn't until ten, you got up at six and left."

"I always get up at six."

"But you didn't have to wait around for three hours in the train station."

I rub my forehead with one hand and sip my tea with the other. It's herbal tea, and I'm hoping to go back to sleep.

Memories of my last night with Chris flash through me: the bite of the marble counter on my hips, the sweat breaking out over my whole body, the way my pussy clenched when he said *grab your fucking ankles*.

Tessa had fanned herself when I told her that part.

As terrible as I feel, it is good to be home. The rental management company was very unhappy with me for canceling the vacation rental listing and refunding the people who had booked over the next few weeks, but I did the math, and it was cheaper than renting a place for myself. My house is impersonal, since all of our stuff is in storage, but it still feels like home.

Today, I'll start to get my life back together. Maybe I'll check in with my old boss at the yoga studio or some of the moms I had gotten to know in Zoe's high school class.

But none of them will replace my best friends.

"How is Zoe taking your break up?"

"At first, pretty terribly, but even she can admit that I wouldn't be happy in that lifestyle. I think she's more depressed that she won't be cool by association now. All my life, I avoided dating again, in part because I didn't want either of us to get too attached. As her mom, I just didn't want to bring a guy around that wouldn't be good with her. Go figure that I chose a man who wouldn't be good for me."

At least one place I didn't screw up was with my friends. Tessa, Jade, and Emma have been such an amazing influence on Zoe. Yes, she's closest to Jade, the "cool aunt," but each one of these women has touched her life in a big, impactful way.

"I know I've said this before," Tessa says, "but I can't even imagine what it's like to date for you and Emma. At our age, it feels like the dating pool is so small. You two have an extra challenge and responsibility with your kids. You are such a good mom."

I smile weakly. I don't feel like it. "Despite everything—the drugs, the groupies, the fame, the likelihood that even though Chris has quit smoking cigarettes, his choices will hang over him for the rest of his life—I still want to be with him. I still—" I cut myself off before I say the truth: that I fell in love with him.

Me, the health nut yogi, fell in love with the rockstar. I fell in love with him because he was so humble, he was so driven, and yet he was open to trying new things. Despite a lifetime of bad habits surrounding him, he wanted to explore the things that I loved.

"That sounds like it has more to do with Kit than Zoe."

The pain in my chest is sharp, but it's a fraction of what I went through when Kit died. Even though Chris has quit smoking—whether he continues without me around is a whole other thing—he's going to have a lifetime of looking over his shoulder, a lifetime of screenings. If he gets cancer, he'll have to go through treatments and chemo and surgeries, and just thinking about it makes me want to scream.

I put my head in my hands. "I can't do it again."

"Sara," Tessa says gently. "You know that you could find some nice, vegan, yoga-loving guy—the male version of you, so to speak—and he could get hit by a bus and die?"

"I know."

"And you know that even if something happens, you'll never regret loving someone?"

Tears are welling up now because, as terrifying as it is, Tessa's right. I lost Kit, but don't regret a moment of loving him, even putting aside our daughter.

Even with all its flaws, like our youth and inexperience, I don't regret it. And now I have something that's so deep it makes my heart ache, so passionate that even now, thousands of miles away and emotionally wrung out, my toes still curl thinking about it.

And I gave that up?

"And just to be clear," Tessa continues. "You deserve to fall in love again. And if it's not with Chris because of the drugs and lifestyle, I get that. You deserve a healthy, happy relationship."

I lift my head and sniffle, giving Tessa a small smile. "Thank you."

"What are you going to do?" Tessa asks.

"I don't know," I say. My future may be uncertain, but Chris's future is Verduistering.

36

Chris

I THOUGHT SARA WAS MY MUSE, BUT HEARTBREAK CHANGED THAT idea real fucking quick. I was writing more than ever now.

Was it that she was gone? Was it that the meditation sessions, which I was still doing, had finally kicked in? Or was it that despite everything I'd been through with her, it didn't change the fact that we had a sophomore album to write, and it was going to be a good one?

The day Sara left, I packed up a few basics and flew to London. Marcus had magically arranged for people to box up and transport my stuff over too.

Signs of her were everywhere in that house—she'd boxed up a bunch of meals for me in the fridge, the empty front room echoed now that her yoga studio wasn't in it, and I'd found one of her sports bras mixed in with my laundry.

I cried over laundry.

That's the kind of person I am now.

But over that week, I'd written a hell of a lot. I stuffed all those song ideas—some a few lines, some full songs—into one spiral notebook that I tuck under my arm as I exit the hired car at the recording studio.

It's a nondescript entrance in an alley, nothing to signal that it's a place where magic happens. There's a pub across the street, and it smells like curry and the incoming wet winter.

"Thank you," I tell the driver as I close the door, and he backs the car out.

I stare at the entrance and the small stoop below it. Behind that door are all of my dreams, everything I've built my life toward.

It should feel better than this, I think.

At the entrance of the alleyway, there's a whirring noise, and the driver sticks his head out the window. "You okay, mate?" His car's blocking the sidewalk, and I'm not sure if he's waiting for me to go in or waiting for the traffic to give him room to pull out.

"I'm fine, thanks."

He pauses, squinting at me, and then gives a half-shrug before disappearing into the car again.

I take a deep breath and sit on one of the steps instead of going in. A few minutes later, the car pulls out.

This would be an ideal time to smoke, but I don't have any cigarettes on me. I think I'm over the withdrawal now because Sara leaving would have been the ideal time to fall back into that trap.

I almost bought some at the airport but thought better of it.

Part of me, an arrogant part that's let fame get to my head, thinks that maybe Sara will realize what a mistake she made. If she were to turn up at the end of the alleyway right now to tell me that the band didn't matter to her, that she loved me in spite of the music and not because, I would be ready to pull her to me and . . .

A dark shape enters the alleyway, bundled up with their

head ducked down, and it's a one-two hit of my heart fluttering, wondering if I manifested Sara here, but my head telling me I know that walk.

Ram's here.

He slows when he sees me sitting against the door. "Is it locked?"

"No," I say and start to get up.

With a gentle shove, Ram pushes me back down. Then he sits next to me, letting out a deep sigh.

I get a good look at him. Ram's eyes are bloodshot, worse than at the concert. I had noticed in Berlin that he'd gotten thinner too. He looks like shit, honestly.

A heavy weight sits in my stomach. Looking at Ram now, with Sara's concerns in my head, I think we've fucked up. It's easy to brush Ram's addiction aside when you're in the industry that takes it as due course. I remember the first time I watched someone do ecstasy in the bathroom after a show. The first time I discovered Ram blitzed out of his mind.

When I met Ram, he was practically a kid—he was seven years younger than me, married, bubbly. Now he's hardened, by drugs, by divorce. His whole life is the band—and the parties.

"I've got this idea for a drum solo," Ram tells me. He air drums, mimicking noises as he goes, and I close my eyes and listen to him.

When he's done, I open my eyes, and we're both grinning.

"It's good, right?"

I have no idea how this man's mind works. Sometimes I think he's a savant; sometimes he irritates the fuck out of me. "Yeah, it's good."

He blooms under my praise, and I see that kid again.

We both lean our heads back against the door, and Ram nudges me with his knee. "How's Sara settling into London?"

I sigh. "She's not. She's gone back to the US."

"Oh? And when's she visiting?"

Jesus. Read the room.

"She's not. We're not together anymore."

Ram's face falls, and his eyebrows draw together in concern. I instantly feel bad for being exasperated at him, even if it was in my head.

"Shit," he says, head falling back against the door.

We're quiet for a moment until Ram draws his knees into his chest and shuffles around to face me. His back goes against the wrought-iron rails and his elbows rest on his knees. "I thought you two were in love."

"I was. I am."

"Why'd you break up, then?"

"Because we are in-com-patable," I say, enunciating the word, a bitter taste in my mouth. "Sara doesn't see how her life could fit in with mine. Which . . . I can't blame her for thinking."

Ram lets out a low chuckle. "She stuck out like a sore thumb at the concert. Until you introduced us, I thought she was a reporter or part of the management team. Like, replacing Marcus or something."

Marcus always wears a suit backstage with us.

"Her daughter kind of fits in, though," Ram continues.

"That's part of the problem. Sara doesn't want Zoe to be around bad influences, and when it comes down to it, we're a bad influence."

"You know, Maria said our lives didn't fit together either."

My eyebrows shoot up. Ram rarely ever talks about his first wife, the one he was married to before we took off.

"And she was right. She wanted me to settle down and have babies and buy a house. But I had other priorities."

"Look where it got you." We're exactly where we want to be.

Ram's gaze is unfocused, the past more visible than the future. And whatever he sees isn't pretty. "I'd take it all back."

"What? Really?" Ram has never once seemed to me like he would give this up. I thought he loved the band and our successes.

Ram looks at me. "I loved her, Chris. I really loved her. I see who she is now on social media and stuff, and it breaks my heart because she looks so goddamn happy, and I couldn't give that to her. She's a mom now, you know? Three kids. Last time I saw her was a year or so after the youngest was born when I went to visit my parents. We ran into her in town with all three kids, and one of them had a meltdown on the sidewalk, and she had spit up on her shirt. But I knew she was better off. I knew because I love her, and I'd never seen her so happy before."

I wonder if Ram realizes he used the present tense. "I get that. Sara loves her daughter with her whole heart."

Ram pushes off the ground, climbing to his feet and dusting off the ass of his jeans. "It's too late for me and Maria. But if I had a time machine, I'd say fuck off to the three of you and fix my mistake. I guess my point is, you have to decide what you really want. It sucks to have to choose, but life would be too easy otherwise."

He shrugs, and I just stare at him. Sage words of advice from our drummer was not on my agenda today—or ever, to be honest. Ram offers me his hand.

"That's pretty wise," I say when I am on my feet.

"I like to surprise people with wisdomous things." He opens the door, and I follow him into the studio and my future, shaking my head.

37

Chris

For a very brief period of time, I thought this was going to be difficult. Then I stepped into the vegan bakery in Munich, and the cashier's eyes widened. I had to autograph some things and pose for selfies before I could escape with the giant to-go order of cookies.

I am Chris Rächer today. I did the makeup myself, so it isn't as technically impressive as when the stylist does it, but what I lacked in skill, I made up for in color. My top is lace, long-sleeved and cropped, my jeans black, my boots black. I'd used the dye on my hair and the black locks swing into my eyes often.

Now, as I walk along the street toward Zoe's university, I leave a trail of whispers and camera phone shutter noises behind me.

There's a part of the school near campus housing with a small paved area with benches and bike racks. The buildings on either side of the street look older, the first floor a solid stone wall and the second and third floors painted with bright colors and wood trim. I pass under the shadow of a footbridge made of metal and glass, modernity connecting these two buildings overhead.

There is a cluster of young women who have been following me and laughing for about a block. When I reach the bench, I pop the clear plastic lid off the tray of cookies and offer them. "Cookie?"

"Um, yeah."

They ask for selfies, and I glower at their cameras.

"Why aren't you going on the tour?" One of them asks me, a plump brunette with a Bavarian accent.

"I can't talk about it," I shake my head like it pains me. "But if you know Zoe Wallace, tell her I'm looking for her."

Fingers fly over phone keyboards as they leave, and a small crowd gathers. I shake hands, autograph things, pose for selfies. Some students even run back to their homes and bring back T-shirts or magazines for me to sign.

Finally, a familiar voice pierces the crowd with an American admonishment delivered in German. "Didn't your mother ever tell you not to take candy from strangers?" Zoe's head of dark, curly hair battles its way toward me. She screeches to a halt at the edge of the crowd.

"What," she says—no, seethes—at me, "are you doing here?"

"Okay," I say, snapping the lid back on the cookies. "Show's over. Time to go. Thanks, everyone."

There are groans, but I spin Zoe around and march her away from the crowds.

"Hey! Where are we going?"

"Some place private so we can talk about your mom."

Zoe's mouth slams closed on a retort, and I let her take the lead. We walk quickly, not getting distracted by people trying to stop us for another selfie or ten, and in a few minutes, we enter a residential building and climb a stairwell up to the second floor and enter an apartment.

There's a South Asian woman sitting on a couch in the living room whose eyes widen when she sees me.

Zoe switches to English. "Hey, Rhi. Do you mind giving us some privacy?"

I take the lid off the container. "Cookie?"

"Stop with the cookies," Zoe hisses.

Rhi pauses on her way out and grabs a chocolate chip cookie from the tray. "You're—"

"Yes."

"Can I have your—"

"Not right now, Rhi," Zoe interrupts.

When the door to the bedroom closes behind Rhi, I hold the tray out to Zoe.

"Cook—"

"Chris," Zoe snaps. "I don't like anything about you right now."

"Harsh," I say. "And I bought these cookies for you. They're vegan."

"What am I going to do with three dozen cookies?"

"You're a university student. Aren't you programmed to appreciate free food?"

Zoe eyes me.

I gesture at the couch. "Can we sit? That's what I want to talk to you about."

She huffs. "Fine." Zoe sits on the couch, arms crossed, legs crossed, clearly no longer impressed with me.

"Here's the deal: I need a favor. I want you to fly with me to Austin, give me a makeover, and help me plan a really romantic surprise for your mom."

Zoe's jaw drops.

"But," I say, lifting a finger. "I'm leaving the band."

Zoe jumps to her feet. "WHAT?"

It takes a few minutes of Zoe pacing and muttering, "Holy fuck, holy fuck, holy fuck," for her to calm down.

She stops in front of me. "Is this because of the pot thing?"

"Not really. Or maybe the pot thing is a small part of it. Your mom doesn't want anything to do with that lifestyle, and I understand that."

"Because of me," Zoe says softly.

"Also because of her. Your mom is one of the most wholesome people I've ever met, and it's not for selfish reasons."

Zoe sits back down on the couch and tucks her feet underneath her, leaning her head back on the couch and exhaling deeply. "I know. Mom goes a little overboard."

"I like that about her."

Zoe turns her head to study me. "You're really in? Like, you love her and want to marry her?"

"One hundred percent."

She sags into the couch even more, and her gaze shifts up to the ceiling. She thinks for a few moments, and I wait.

This grown woman is going to be my stepdaughter someday, hopefully. She's got the same eyes as her mother, the same chin. But the nose and her hair, even though it's dark and curly like Sara's, must have come from her father. Zoe's hair is coarser and thicker.

"I know Mom goes too far sometimes," Zoe says. Her voice is quiet and serious. "But I don't want it to stop."

Zoe rolls her head toward me. Her eyes are wide and shining. "I talk to my therapist about this a lot, okay, so don't freak out. But if something were to happen to her, then I'd be all alone. And I know, I'm a grown-up. But still." She blinks quickly, trying to clear the tears from her eyes.

"I get that," I say. "It was tough when my mom died. She worked hard, so I never missed having a dad. And she succeeded—the only time I ever wished for a dad was when she died."

"Oh, shit, Chris." Guilt washes over her face. "I forgot your mom passed. I'm sorry."

"Thank you. I just meant to say that I get it."

She relaxes back. "Okay." But then she sits straight up. "Wait, did you say makeover?"

"Yup."

"Why do you want—oh my god, are we Sandra-Deeing you?"

"Sandra what?"

"You know, in the movie *Grease,* at the end, when Sandra Dee puts on the leather pants and perms her hair to show Danny Zuko she can be bad too? And Danny just gets a letter jacket which is complete bullshit because you're supposed to spend years in extracurriculars earning those things, and how does Danny doing track and getting lettered prove he deserves—"

"Zoe," I interrupt.

She grins. "Yeah, probably good to stop me before I got to the symbolism of the flying car. Now," she taps a finger on her chin. "What exactly do you want to change?"

38

Sara

M_Y BACK DOOR IS UNLOCKED AND HALFWAY OPEN BEFORE I realize there's music coming from inside my house. I freeze and listen.

Is that Jack Johnson?

Six people have the key to my house, me, Zoe, Jade, Emma, Tessa, and the rental agency people. If the rental people came here without letting me know, I'm going to be so pissed.

The other four are still halfway around the world. Zoe texted me this morning telling me she was going away for the weekend with a friend. I talked to Jade, Emma, and Tessa over lunch.

Okay, so it's unlikely to be any of them here. I step forward, wondering why someone would break into my house to put chill vibes music on, but I also pull the emergency button up on my phone.

I live in a good neighborhood—the smallest house in a nice suburb of Austin and I have no idea why some rando would choose to break into my house. But it is nighttime. I just finished the evening yoga class at the studio, and it's well past ten p.m.

It smells like lilies and my favorite candles.

I am so confused. My heart's racing, and my palms are sweating. I leave the door open in case I need to make a quick escape and tiptoe out of the mud room and into the kitchen. It's empty, but the corner of the living room that I can see has a bunch of lit candles casting a soft glow.

When the rest of the room comes into view, there's a strange man standing in the center of the room, surrounded by candles and flowers. His eyes meet mine.

I scream.

His mouth opens and eyes widen in panic, and to my left, footsteps thunder down the stairs to the second floor.

"Mom!" Zoe shouts and slides into the room.

"Sara!" someone else says, and it makes me freeze. I know that voice. "Shit," the man says, dropping the bouquet of roses he's holding.

What the . . .

His hair is close-cropped, and he's wearing a pressed white button-up and khaki pants. And loafers.

It takes my brain a minute to process what I'm seeing.

"Chris?"

"I'm sorry, I'm so sorry, Sara. We thought this would be romantic, but now I see that it's—"

"What did you do to your hair?"

He runs a hand over his head. "I cut it off."

"Mom," Zoe says, turning my attention away from Chris. "He left the band."

"WHAT?" I cover my face with my hands because this is a lot to process. "Holy fuck, holy fuck, holy fuck," I whisper under my breath, the mom in me still trying not to cuss in front of my grown daughter.

Zoe's face, twisted in concern, leans into my view. "Uh, Chris? I think you broke my mom."

"Sorry, Sara. I thought you would recognize me."

"You thought—I would have, but it's dark! And you're supposed to be in London. And have you ever even worn loafers before in your life?"

Chris's lips flutter upward as he tries to contain a smile. "No, in fact, I haven't."

My heart rate is calming down, but I realize I'm sweating under my layers, so I take my jacket off and toe off my shoes. Just wiggling my toes already makes me feel better.

"Okay," I start. "Let's try this again. What's this about you leaving the band?"

"After you left Germany, I realized that I would rather have you than the fame. Your life is different from mine, but it's a good one." Chris's eyes flick to Zoe, who's tiptoeing out of the room. "You care deeply about the people you love, and I want that."

"But you just wrote all these great songs, and you are so excited about the next album."

"My part is mostly done. The album will credit me as a songwriter, and I'll get paid as such, but someone else will play my songs with the band."

"What will you do?"

Chris tosses the roses onto one of my upholstered chairs and gently pulls my hands away from my face. "I reached out to South by Southwest to see if there was an opportunity to work with them here, and I will meet with them this week. I will also continue to write songs. I have connections in the industry and can write for other performers."

"But I thought you kind of hated the writing part?"

Our fingers twine together, and Chris gives a gentle tug, bringing us close enough that our chests touch, and I have to tilt my chin up to look at him. "It's a love-hate relationship with the writing part. Sometimes it's really hard," he acknowledges. His forehead meets mine, and he closes his eyes. "But then you break through and write something amazing, pulling your inspiration from all sorts of places like the beautiful woman who stole your heart."

His lips brush mine. "I love you, Sara Wallace."

My breath hitches in my lungs, and my heart rate picks back up again. Chris loves me. This sex god, heartthrob who has half the world idolizing him, loves me.

And yet I know that there's so much more to him than that. He's funny, creative, passionate, and so, so tender.

"I don't want you to change who you are," I murmur against his lips. "I want you, Chris Müller. I love you. I love your passion and your tattoos and your quiet moments. I was just scared. I was scared that I'd fall in love with you and lose you. And I know that it's still a possibility. But I have to trust you—I do trust you. Don't give up everything for me."

"I'm not," he says. "I'm giving up some of the bad things in my life so I can have better things. Good things. If anything, Ram and Alwin get it. The chance to have love, to have a family. That matters. It's bigger than Verduistering."

Chris kisses me. It's sweet and gentle, and this, right here, with the candlelight flickering around us and the smell of soft, powdery roses in the air, is the romantic moment Chris was going for.

A romantic moment I've never had before.

I pull back before he can kiss me again. "Will you grow your hair back out?"

He chuckles low and drops my hands, running his palms up the outside of my thighs and my hips to my waist, where he dips beneath my top to touch my bare skin. "I'll grow it out again," he promises.

"And ditch the loafers?"

Instead of answering me, he kisses me again. It's open mouth and more forceful, pressing me back as his arms circle my waist.

"And maybe a bit of eye makeup, occasionally."

Chris kisses deeper, his tongue entering my mouth and his

hands sliding down to my ass. I wrap my arms around his neck, and the kissing is slow and tender, but our bodies are flush, his growing erection pressing into me and his tongue stroking my mouth and . . .

I yank back, my eyes wide. "You took out your barbell?"

Chris grins and sticks his tongue out. There's no glint of metal, just a small indent.

"Put it back!"

This time I get a full-on laugh. "You like my tongue ring?" The question is low and sexy, and he doesn't give me time to answer before he's kissing me again.

When we come back up for air, I've almost forgotten what we were talking about, but it's so weird to kiss Chris without the piercing.

"Seriously, how long do you have till it closes up?"

"We've got lots of time, I promise. I'll pop it back in soon so I can do that thing you like—"

A throat clears from the hallway. "I'm still here."

Chris and I reluctantly pull apart. "Okay, it's safe to come back in now," I say.

Zoe twirls around the corner and launches herself at me. I embrace my daughter, tears springing to my eyes. I didn't think I would see her again until the end of her year abroad.

"How did you get here?" I ask when we pull apart.

Zoe offers her hand to Chris, and he high-fives it. "Chris and I flew here together, and I have a flight back in two days. Mom, we flew first class."

I raise an eyebrow at Chris, who wraps his arm around my shoulders. "Are you spoiling my daughter?"

He shrugs. "She was helpful, and I thought you might like to spend some time together, too."

"After all," Zoe says. "You're so far away now. You won't get to see me as often." She looks up at me, giving me sad puppy dog eyes.

When I roll my eyes, she lets her lip tremble.

"I'm trying to give you space," I protest.

"You're missing all your weekends with my aunts."

I narrow my eyes. "Did they put you up to this?"

"Come on, Mom. It makes more sense to live there."

I gaze up at Chris, and the look in his eyes takes my breath away. The love that I see there is heart-stopping.

"Can we really live in London?" I ask.

"Babe," he says, ducking down to press a kiss to my lips. "We can do both. If the South by Southwest thing works out, we could be here. If you want to be closer to Zoe, we can live there. My flat has a room we could clear out for your yoga, a recording studio for me, and best of all . . . no mushrooms in the bathroom. So, what do you say? Will you be my roommate again?"

———

THIRTY-SIX HOURS LATER, I OPEN THE DOOR OF MY HONDA Accord and walk around the front, meeting Zoe and Chris on the curb of the airport.

Chris holds her bag, and Zoe opens her arms and wraps them around me. "Are you sure you're going to be okay without me?" Zoe asks, and I laugh at the teasing tone.

"I'll miss you a lot, but yes, I'll be fine."

When I release her, she turns to Chris and offers him a hug too. When she pulls back, she gazes up at Chris and then gives a dramatic shudder. "For god's sake, grow your hair back out. It's weird."

"You cut it," he says mildly.

"My greatest regret to date."

We only had one full day together before Zoe had to fly back to catch her classes, but it was a good one. We took Zoe shopping for some of her favorite foods she can't get in Munich and went out to eat at the vegan restaurant near her freshman year dorm that's always been our comfort-food place.

Now, Zoe throws her arms around me one last time. "Okay, I'm going before Mom gets all sad. I'll call when I get to Munich, I promise. Love you!" She calls the last over her shoulder as she walks into the terminal, barely giving the single tear that escapes a chance to fall.

Chris turns my face toward him and gently wipes the tear away. "You okay?"

I heave a big sigh and plant my face into his chest. Chris's arms wrap around me.

We hug for about two seconds, and then the honk of a car farther down the drop-off gets us moving before someone honks at us.

While I drive us home, Chris stares out the window. I wonder what he's thinking about. Is he missing the band? Worried about his future? Thinking about song lyrics?

Before I have the chance to ask, Chris speaks. "Texas is really fucking flat."

I laugh, surprised. "Yeah, it is. Especially compared to the mountains we've been living in."

Knowing his thoughts are of the inane variety relaxes me, and by the time we've pulled into my driveway, I've answered about a dozen questions about Austin, and we've bickered over the music choices.

But halfway through our battle for the playlist, Chris put his hand on my thigh and squeezed. The look on his face was enough to cause me to stumble over my words.

No matter where we live, no matter what kind of music we listen to, I'm excited for my future with Chris.

EPILOGUE

Sara

Three months later . . .

THE CAFÉ IN NOTTING HILL IS SMALL AND COZY, LOCAL ART hanging on the walls and the pungent smell of coffee permeating the air, along with Jade's whining.

"Two months and twelve presentations with him! We have to travel together, stay in hotels together, eat meals together. If I end up dead, Carlos is the first suspect."

Jade just found out that her company wants her to go on tour giving presentations about the product she's been working on. And they want Carlos to accompany her to handle the marketing side of it: setting up booths and brochures, organizing private meetings, and translating her presentation.

She points her finger at each of us. "I'll make sure you have his contact information so you can hunt him down and avenge my death."

Emma, Tessa, and I look at each other. "I think out of our

group," Tessa says, "the one most likely to get away with murder is probably you."

Jade gasps in mock outrage. "I would never."

"You're the one who listens to all the murdery podcasts and watches true crime shows," I point out. "Tell me those haven't given you a few ideas."

"I mean, everyone in those shows usually gets caught, and that's the only reason we know how they did it; they get caught."

"Did you talk to Rebecca about it?" Emma asks, getting us back on track.

"Well, she brought it up in front of him, so I couldn't very well say, 'Please don't send me on this tour because I might murder my colleague.' He was right there."

"You've also said he seems to be the most competent person in his department, right? So shouldn't it be a good thing that he's going to do the seminars with you?" I point out.

"Competent, yes. Stick up his ass, also yes. But he's not doing the presentation with me; he's translating it. And I asked Rebecca why we would even need a translator when so many people speak English anyway, and she said that it won't just be contemporaries there, but patients and their families too."

"Speaking of which, how are your Spanish lessons going?" Tessa asks.

Jade brightens. "Wonderfully."

"Could you do the presentation in Spanish yourself?" Emma asks, and Jade's face falls.

"No. I wish. But I'm just not that fluent yet." She props her chin on her hand. "Too bad it's not in Mandarin. I could probably do that. Maybe I should pitch an Asia tour to Rebecca."

The overhead lights flash and interrupt our conversation. In the back of the café is a small stage, and we're at the closest table, all set to enjoy the front-row view of my boyfriend's performance.

Technically it's open mic night here, but there are only two acts tonight. Chris said he and the manager didn't feel right asking anyone to follow his performance, so they booked a small, locally popular musician for the first act, and then Chris will play second.

While Jade outlines her travel schedule for the next few months, I glance around at the crowd. They don't know who's playing, so the energy is low and mellow. Lots of couples, small friend groups, and . . .

My eyes narrow on a guy against the wall. Something about him is familiar, but he's got a hat on low, and I would remember someone with that mustache. It's very thick and groomed and . . .

Fake. That's a fake mustache.

Whoever it is looks right at me, and with a start, I realize it's Alwin.

Two days after I moved—again—to Europe, Chris and I were out shopping for kitchen equipment. It did not surprise me at all that his kitchen, while lovely, was spartan, so I was elbow-deep in copper pans when Chris's phone rang.

It was Marcus, letting Chris know that Verduistering was on hiatus indefinitely. Ram had, for the first time, voluntarily checked himself into rehab, and Alwin and June had decided that without two of their four original members, they didn't want to keep going.

Chris was heartbroken for Alwin and June but hopeful about Ram. Time will tell.

Alwin dips his chin at me, and I flick my eyes to the stage and back.

Does Chris know?

Alwin shakes his head.

The café owner introduces the opening act. She has a keyboard and mic, and does that thing where you record and loop a small bit of music, adding layers on until she can take her hands away from the keyboard and belt out the opening lyrics.

She's good. At the end of every song, the crowd claps, and it's obvious that some of the people are there just to see her. The music's a little funky, but it's got all four of us dancing in our seats.

After five songs, the singer bows to full applause and, blushing, ducks off the stage. There's a restlessness between sets, people getting up to get drinks or use the bathroom, even though it wasn't a very long set.

Nerves are tickling my stomach, and I'm anxiously watching as the stagehand takes the keyboard away and makes room. My gaze flicks to Alwin again, who's staring at the stage, lost in thought.

This time, no one introduces the singer—Chris quietly slips from the back door onto the stage, and at first, there's a blank, hollow quiet while Chris settles the guitar into his lap and perches on the stool.

Then whispers carry, someone behind us saying, "Wait, is that . . ." and the sound of a glass being knocked over and the accompanying surprise.

Chris doesn't say anything, just tunes his guitar quietly. The spotlight is on him, slightly brighter than the café, but lights flash randomly, and when I turn around, there are at least a dozen phones pointed at him.

I catch the start of a familiar chord and turn my attention back to the stage. Chris's fingers strum quickly against the strings, and his voice is low and quiet as he starts singing the song about the dress.

He's been tweaking it over the months we've been here. He still has highs and lows in writing, but writing for other performers has taken some of the pressure off. I'm still shocked when I hear this version of him, though—instead of hoarse screams and furious German, this is so light and gentle and delicate.

I would never admit that it's my favorite, of course, but it is.

The crowd is loud when the first song finishes, and Chris gestures to the previous singer, who comes up to join him on stage for a duet.

After that, Chris plays two more songs, and at the end of every song, the crowd is louder, rowdier. Next to me, Jade turns to look behind us, and her eyes widen. A quick glance over my shoulder shows that the crowd has grown, people coming in from the streets or called in by friends.

That's why we've kept the set list short, and at the end of the fourth song, Chris thanks the crowd, grabs the guitar by the neck, and quickly disappears down the back hallway again.

"Oh, my god!" Emma squeals. "That was amazing!"

"He totally wrote that first song about you," Jade says, and I laugh.

My phone buzzes with a message.

CHRIS

Escaped the crowds, on my way home. You staying out with the ladies?

SARA

We're going to pick up Indian food and bring it home.

See you soon.

Chris sends me a kissy face, his favorite emoji, and I tuck my phone away. Jade, Emma, and Tessa have a hotel room around the corner from our flat.

"All right, ladies, let's get a move on," I say, and we abandon our table and empty mugs, weaving our way through the crowd to the exit.

When we step out, all four of us tighten our coats around ourselves. It's chilly in London in January, and it's early enough that there are people bustling back and forth in the cold and gray. The winter in London was a shock for me after the glorious fall weather in Baden-Baden.

"Can we stop at a wine shop?" Jade asks.

"We've got a few bottles back at the flat," I say.

"Back at the flat," Jade and Emma echo and giggle. I roll my eyes. They've been teasing me about it all week, but that's what everyone—Chris included—calls it, so it's snuck into my vernacular.

"I checked out what you have, but I'd like a bottle of cava."

"Have I had cava?" Emma asks.

"You had some in Madrid when you stayed with me, but it was forever ago. I think it's my favorite now."

"Oh," Tessa says. "Unseating the Moscato?"

"My tastes are maturing," Jade says, affecting a posh air. "Besides, I've grown used to drinking it. When in Rome—or in this case, Madrid—and all that."

I link my arm in Jade's. "Well, then, let's get you some cava post-haste. I know a shop on the way to the Indian place."

Tessa links arms with Emma, and they follow behind us.

"Does Chris have any friends he can hook me up with?" Jade asks.

"Still in a dry spell?" My brows draw together in concern.

"My vibrator has been working overtime. And I think it would be good to focus my attention on someone else instead of worrying about this Carlos thing."

I bite my lip to stifle a laugh. I'm pretty sure this Carlos thing is not just the presentation.

"Well, I hate to say this, but a one-night-stand in London that you're never going to see again probably isn't going to cut it."

"It can't hurt. Orgasms are nice in that way, especially non-self-inflicted ones."

I roll my eyes at her affectionately, and she grins. "Maybe you need to go on an actual date."

"Blasphemy," she says. "Besides, I'd only leave the man behind, brokenhearted, when my time in Madrid is up. We can't all happily settle down like you. And unlike you three, I have a job in Austin to get back to soon."

"Six more months," I say, a musical lilt in my voice. "A lot could change for you in six months."

After all, six months ago, I boarded a plane, my first passport in hand. I'd never even heard of Verduistering, and here I am, in love with a rock-star guitarist and running a yoga course inspired by him.

"Just you wait, Jade. I have a feeling your dry spell will be over soon."

———

Chris

Nine more months later . . .

"Oh, sure. Austin calls itself the live music capital of the world. We can hit a few places tonight that you'll love," Zoe assures Alwin.

Alwin, and the rest of Verduistering, are in our house in Austin. It's still the same house where Sara lived with Kit, where she raised Zoe, where I scared the pants off of her about thirteen months ago trying to be romantic.

It's surreal to have my past life colliding with my new life like this.

Sara and I lived in London for a few months, then moved back to Austin for South by Southwest, then back to London. Sara and I finished the Rock Steady series, and then she launched her first yoga retreat, which was a success, and led to her second retreat in Bali and her third one next month in Sri Lanka.

Zoe's study abroad in Germany ended, as did Jade's year working in Madrid and Emma's MBA program in Rome. Tessa lives in France with Luc now, and Sara hopes to detour to visit her whenever we fly over to London for my work.

Now, Alwin, June, and Ram are in our living room, celebrating Ram's first year of sobriety. Sara is serving flavored sparkling water and her favorite vegan chocolate bonbons—not laced, of course—after a casual dinner.

I haven't seen my former bandmates since Sara's and my wedding five months ago. It was in Crete, a small ceremony attended by the three of them and Sara's friends and their partners, with Zoe as the only member of the wedding party.

Ram looks good. They all look good, actually. Ram's hair has gotten a little longer and has curled out of control, but he's also filled in a little more, bulked up. He's gotten into Crossfit, which has gained traction in Europe now.

June's her natural self today, blonde ringlets and dimples and a four-month baby bump. When the band split, she decided she wanted to have a kid before age became a limiting factor, so she used a sperm donor. She's been talking to Sara about her pregnancy symptoms and happily rubbing her belly.

Alwin looks the same, still smiling and charming and entirely too flirty with my wife.

But Sara just rolls her eyes and swats at him when he tries to convince her to join them out on the town tonight.

"I'll leave it to the young and the young at heart," she says, pointedly looking at Alwin.

He clasps his hands to his chest, wounded. "Are you saying I'm not young?"

Sara smirks and slips deeper into the couch beside me. I kiss the top of her head and let my arm slip from her shoulder to dangle down her chest and tangle my fingers with hers. Sara's dressed up more than usual today in black leggings and a blouse instead of her yoga outfit. Her hair is loose and shows more gray hairs than it did a year ago, but now we compare signs of aging—we both got a good laugh last week when I discovered my first gray pubic hair.

When I glance up, coming back to the party from my thoughts, I find my three former band members staring at me.

"What?"

June and Ram glance at Alwin, whose knee is bouncing. He takes a big breath before speaking. "We want to get Verduistering back together, but do it right this time."

Sara freezes under my arm, and I wish I could see her face. Alwin's eyes dart back and forth between the two of us.

Sara sits up, and I do too. "What does that mean?" I ask.

"We want to go back on tour but hire a consultant," Alwin explains. "Other bands have done something similar, where the consultant works with us to tackle issues like substance abuse, mental health, and interpersonal conflict. Some bands use them virtually, but Marcus and the label are willing to pull someone in full-time if we can get a new album out."

Papers came out, and Alwin explained things like ownership percentages, royalty rates, and song rights for the new version of Verduistering. Sara gets up, enlisting Zoe to help refill glasses and give me some time to process their idea and read the contracts.

My chest is a mix of emotions that I try to get under control. Excitement that perhaps we could still be a success as a band, nervous that the pursuit of fame would cause Ram to backslide, worrying that I'd risk everything—my marriage, my relationship with my stepdaughter, my mental health— for it all to crash and burn.

"You'll stay sober?" I ask Ram. I keep our conversation in English since I'm sure Zoe and Sara are eavesdropping.

He nods. "One hundred percent. I've got a sponsor I can

call anytime, someone who's not committed to the rest of you either." He cracks a knuckle, a sure sign that he's not really one hundred percent confident in himself, but I can't blame him for that. From what I know about addiction, it's going to be a constant, looming fear for the rest of his life.

I turn my gaze to June. "And you'll have a baby on the road?"

June nods and pats her belly again. "We don't have to tour for about another year, depending on how long it takes us to freshen up the songs and get back into a groove again. Then I'll hire a nanny to travel with us."

My gaze turns to Alwin. "And you?"

He stretches out his arms. "This is all I want. The four of us back together, making music. I'm ready. I'll do whatever it takes to make you and Sara happy." He stands, and the rest of us follow. "Hey, Zoe?" Alwin calls.

Zoe's head pops around the wall between the living room and the kitchen. "Yup?"

"Why don't you take us out tonight? Show us your favorite spots?"

Zoe's face lights up, and she flies up the stairs to "get ready."

Five minutes later, we've hugged and said goodbyes while Zoe leads June, Alwin, and Ram out the door. Regardless of what I decide, I'll see the three of them next month when Sara and I go to London for a recording session with a solo artist I'm working with.

Alwin glances back at Sara and me standing in the doorway and winks at us before I shut the door.

Sara leans against the wall. "Wow," she says.

I run my hands through my hair. I grew it out, though not as long as it was before. "Yeah."

I hold out my arms, and she slides into my embrace. I love the way she fits against me even after all this time.

We just stand there for a while, holding each other. After a few minutes, Sara pulls back enough to rest her chin on my chest. "Gut impressions?"

I sigh. "It could be wonderful, and it could be awful."

"Schrödinger's cat."

"Yup."

Sara pulls away, and I follow her into the kitchen, where the mess from dinner awaits. We assume our usual positions, me rinsing and loading the dishwasher while Sara wipes the counters down.

"I have wondered if you could be happy not performing," she says when we're almost done. "You seem to really enjoy the open mic nights."

It's true. I've got a few venues in the area that I enjoy playing. Usually, the manager or owner knows who I am, but the crowd doesn't. Verduistering wasn't big in the States as it was in Europe, and now that we broke up, the media has relegated us to one-hit-wonders.

"I wonder if we're too late," I confess.

Sara squeezes the water out of the sponge she was using and washes her hands in the other basin of the sink while I wash the last glass. When she's done, she crosses her arms on her chest and faces me. "Please, you've become a more versatile, nuanced songwriter since you left the band. You're only getting better with age."

I close the dishwasher and grin at her. "Better with age? I don't think you're talking about my songwriting anymore." I step closer, and her eyelashes flutter. I duck down and put my mouth right against her ear. "Do you remember the night before you left me in Baden-Baden? I remember it very clearly."

Sara shivers and then laughs low. "If you're too old to make another run with the band, maybe I'm too old for that kind of sex," she teases.

"What? You've become a more flexible, sensual woman

since that night," I paraphrase back to her. "You're only getting better with age."

Sara laughs, and I grin down at her.

"I can prove it too." Her brows draw together, but her grin widens. I duck down, sweeping her upper body over my shoulder as she squeals.

"Chris, what are you doing?"

I don't answer and instead carry her through the house to our bedroom, grab the bottle of lube from the nightstand, and then carry her up the stairs. She's gone limp against me, and I smack the seat of her leggings before depositing her on the floor of her yoga studio.

This used to be Zoe's room, but we put her stuff in storage and installed a floor-to-ceiling mirror on the interior wall.

"Show me how flexible you are, babe."

THE END

Curious about what's going to happen with Verduistering?
Sign up for my newsletter for a spicy bonus scene.
Download your copy by scanning here:

Newsletter subscribers also get bonus epilogues and a behind-the-scenes look at the trips that inspired my stories.

Please Review

Reviews are critical to all authors. You can leave a review for *Riesling with My Roommate* at all retailers

Amazon | Apple | Kobo

Barnes & Noble | Google Books

and

Goodreads | BookBub

Also by Liz Alden

<u>The Love and Wanderlust Series</u>

The Night in Lover's Bay (free prequel short story)

The Fling in Panama

The Slow Burn in Polynesia

The Second Chance in the Mediterranean

The Rival in South Africa (novella)

The Player in New Zealand

The Best Friend in Indonesia (free standalone short story)

<u>*Wanderlust Resort Series*</u>

Beach Boss (free standalone short story)

Beach Resolution

Put it in Beach Mode

<u>*Holiday Retellings Series*</u>

Nutcracker with Benefits

Frosty Proximity

<u>*Aged Like Fine Wine Series*</u>

Rosé with My Fake Fiancé

Riesling with My Roommate

Prosecco with My Professor

Cava with My Colleague

ACKNOWLEDGMENTS

While revising this book, I was in therapy for the first time in my adult life and one of the (many) things I talked about was my dad's death in 2009. His passing was one of the most impactful things that ever happened to me, and, as many people who have lost loved ones know, it lingers. Most days it's nearly invisible, but some days it lurks in my heart.

Fortunately, like Zoe, I have a great relationship with my mom. She nourished my love of reading and the outdoors. I am also pretty sure she never saw a writing career in my future . . . not too bad for someone who got a D in freshman English, huh?

Thank you to my early readers, of which there are many: Lillian Lark, Sara Whitney, Karen Grey, Cara Dion, Lisa Lau and Lynn Katzenmeyer.

Thank you to my proofreader, Lisa Matsumura, and to Kate Mahon for the amazing cover.

And as always, a big thank you to my husband, who encouraged me so much from day one, and my parents, all five of them, who supported this book in one way or another.

ABOUT LIZ ALDEN

Liz Alden is a digital nomad. Most of the time, she's on her sailboat, but sometimes she's in Texas. She knows exactly how big the world is—having sailed around it—and exactly how small it is, having bumped into friends worldwide. She's been a dishwasher, an engineer, a CEO, and occasionally gets paid to write or sail.

Follow Liz:
Instagram | Facebook | Twitter | Website